SNOWED IN

With

MURDER

Auralee Wallace

St. Martin's Paperbacks

SNOWED IN WITH MURDER

Copyright © 2017 by Auralee Wallace.

All rights reserved.

For information address St. Martin's Press, 175 Fifth Avenue, New York, NY 10010.

ISBN: 978-1-250-07779-0

Our books may be purchased in bulk for promotional, educational, or business use. Please contact your local bookseller or the Macmillan Corporate and Premium Sales Department at 1-800-221-7945, extension 5442, or by e-mail at MacmillanSpecialMarkets@macmillan.com.

Printed in the United States of America

St. Martin's Paperbacks edition / February 2017

St. Martin's Paperbacks are published by St. Martin's Press, 175 Fifth Avenue, New York, NY 10010.

10 9 8 7 6 5 4 3 2 1

For my mother.
She hates the snow.

SNOWED IN

With

MURDER

Chapter One

"You have arrived."

I wiped a drop of icy rain from my cheek with my gloved fingers. "I'm sorry?"

"My GPS always says that," the voice on the other end of my phone explained happily. "And now I can't stop saying it. It's like finally even technology sees that I'm destined for great things. *You have arrived.* It feels good. Try it."

"No, I will not." I smiled though. If nothing else, my best friend Freddie Ng knew how to make life interesting. I attempted to pull my pea coat even more tightly around my body without letting the strap of my duffel bag slip off my shoulder. I knew I should've worn my parka. Stupid March. Oh sure, spring was just around the corner, but no one could tell you with any certainty where that corner might be, especially not in Otter Lake, New Hampshire.

Most of the year, my small hometown was postcard-perfect. Sparkling lakes in the summer. Rich, colorful trees in the fall. Fluffy snow in the winter. But early spring? Well, there was mud. Lots and lots of cold mud.

Nope, there was nothing really fun about this time of year, other than maybe snuggling under a blanket with a hot, hot sheriff waiting for better weather to come.

Yeah, that might be nice.

Too bad mine had dumped me.

"I can barely hear you. Are you outside?"

"Yup, I just got off the bus. I'm standing on the dock praying my mother remembered to tell Red to come and get me." My eyes darted over the slate-colored lake. Nothing. "So, uh, did you get the—"

"Oh, I got your steaks all right. A bunch of them actually. They're in the freezer of your mom's fridge. I'm tired of you always begging for meat at my door."

"By the sound of your voice, I'm guessing I owe you one?"

"Summer made me pray for the cow's soul, Erica. For ten minutes we prayed for the cow's soul. And then we had to do it all over again because there were a bunch of steaks and she couldn't be sure they were from the same cow." He made a disgusted noise in the back of his throat. "I'm not even sure who we were praying to."

I sucked in some air through my teeth. Yup, that sounded like Summer Bloom. Vegan. Misplaced flower child. Business woman. Mother. Mine to be exact. She ran a retreat called Earth, Moon, and Stars where women, and sometimes men, could heal their souls with nature, yoga, and psychological slash spiritual teachings. It was where I was headed now, but thankfully the retreat was currently closed for the season.

"It totally ruined the hamburger I had for lunch that day," Freddie went on. "I mean I still ate it, but it wasn't the same."

"Sorry," I said blinking away the mist droplets freezing to my eyelashes. "I'm thinking I owe you maybe more than one? Two? Maybe three?"

"You don't owe me anything. Just move home already."

I sighed. "Freddie—"

"Big things are happening with the business. I need you."

I sighed again. Louder. Maybe this time it would make an impression.

Last summer Freddie had come up with the idea of starting a company called Otter Lake Security after the town experienced its first murder in about fifty years. He certainly had the start-up capital. His parents were rich in the way most mere mortals couldn't conceive. But as far as I could tell, all the company really amounted to was Freddie walking Otter Lake's main street in a '70s-style state patrol uniform and harassing teenagers for loitering. Yet, despite all this, he thought it was time to take on a new employee. Me.

"I'll take that noise to mean that you can't wait to hear all about it," he said with enough enthusiasm for the both of us. "So, today I'm interviewing personal trainers. That's why I couldn't pick you up. I have him making me a smoothie as we speak."

"What for?"

"Because I'm hungry."

"Not the shake," I snapped, making a chipmunk squeak. "Why do you need a personal trainer for the business?"

"Don't you mean, why do *we* need a personal trainer for the business? Because we're fat!" he yelled loud enough that I had to pull the phone back from my ear. "Well, you're not fat in the big sense, but you have a remarkable lack of muscle tone. Whereas I need to chisel and sculpt and—Do you not remember how many times last visit we were literally chasing a hot lead, and we had to stop to catch our breath?"

"Um." I screwed up my face as though that might help me remember. "One?"

"God, I hate you sometimes."

I chuckled. He loved me. Our relationship was like that.

"Anyway, this guy specializes in *parkour*!"

My brow furrowed again. "Parkour? The building jumping?"

"Yup. *Parkour!*"

"Why say it like that?"

"Like what?"

"Like you're selling it on an infomercial."

"Because it makes it more exciting," he replied in his most exaggerated *isn't it obvious?* voice. "*Parkour*! You really don't know how to enjoy life do you?"

"I'm pretty sure *parkour!* isn't something—" I cut myself off, questioning whether or not this was a rabbit hole I really wanted to dive into. "You know what? Never mind."

"No. You know what?" Freddie asked. "Forget Grady. I'm about to dump you."

I closed my eyes and shook my head.

"I can only ask you to the dance so many times, Erica. God, this is just like prom." My mouth opened. I almost took the bait. Back in the day, Freddie had wanted us to go to our big dance dressed like we were trying out for *Dancing with the Stars*, but when I told him I wouldn't do it, because, one, we weren't stars, and two, I didn't want to glue my outfit on, well, let's just say our relationship barely survived. Nope, I couldn't let Freddie go down the prom tangent. I might freeze to death before he was through. Our relationship was like that too.

"The business is real," Freddie went on. "You wouldn't believe the phone calls I've been getting after we nabbed Otter Lake's last murderer."

"No. No. You do not say nabbed," I said shaking my head and pointing at my chest . . . all alone in the forest with nobody but the woodland creatures to see. "Not with me. I am not Scooby and you are not Shaggy."

"You're right," Freddie muttered. "Scooby's more fun."

I huffed a laugh.

"Anyway I've been getting a ton of calls now that spring's coming, and I—"

"Freddie, I really don't want to see another dead body in this lifetime. Not one. Every time I come home some-one dies. That's not normal."

"Not murder calls, silly!" he said. "Security calls. For events and such."

"What events?" I asked, tipping a bit of thin ice into the water with the tip of my boot. I was doing my part to help spring along.

"Town dances. Community . . . stuff. Farmer's mar-kets!"

"Farmer's markets?" I asked with all sorts of skepti-cism. "Farmer's markets need security. Really?"

"Hey, I think you overestimate people's ability to control themselves, which is hilarious seeing as you're the one always causing riots at bingo halls," he said with a chuckle.

"One time. And it was not a riot."

"Only because I was there to stop it from becoming one," he said. "But it's not just security. I've been getting all sorts of calls about cheating spouses. That's where the money's at."

I took a deep breath, inhaling air tinged with distant wood smoke. "Freddie you are not a licensed private investigator. *I* am not a licensed private investigator. Weren't you the one who said there were all sorts of reg-ulations about that? We can't just go taking pictures of people doing it in motel rooms. We will go to jail for . . . for being creepy."

"Is that the legal term, Ms. Court Reporter?"

"Hey! I know all the classification codes in Chicago. New Hampshire's weird."

"Whatever. I'm working on the whole legalities thing. We may have to take someone on who is licensed. I'm just not keen about dealing with another employee. Look at the trouble you cause me," he said. "But we can still do security."

"I'm sorry, but every time I think the words, *I'm going to be a private investigator*, or even a . . . what? Security guard?" I asked, eyeing the still empty lake through the fog of my breath, "It feels like a joke. It's ridiculous. It's too like—"

"Your mother," Freddie finished. "Man, why didn't you just become an accountant? That would have shown her how boring you could be."

"Can we just leave off the whole me working for Otter Lake Security for a while? Please? I'm already in crisis mode with Grady. I need to make tonight perfect."

"I thought he already dumped you?"

Yes, Grady—sheriff, die-hard local, love of my life from teenage years to present with just a few blips—had technically dumped me.

Over the phone.

Just when things were getting good!

We had spent an absolutely epic Christmas together. The kind of Christmas that certain cable networks modeled Made for TV movies after . . . and then he went and dumped me! Over the phone! That was a bit of a sticking point for me.

Okay, so fine. I had been kind of dithering on the question of whether or not I was moving home. But in fairness, there were a lot of unanswered questions I still had to figure out. What about my job? I was pretty sure Freddie wasn't offering dental. I wasn't even sure he was offering a salary. And what if Grady and I didn't work out? We had always been a little fiery. What then? Did I still want to live in Otter Lake? And where would I live? With my mother? Could I go back to living in a baconless home? These were real questions that required serious thought.

All that being said, if I were to be completely honest, I think Grady could have hung on while I worked through all these questions . . . but then there had been the *thing* that had happened. At the airport. Just as he was leaving . . .

I shook my head looking at the distant shoreline of hazy trees. "He's coming over isn't he?"

"Are you ever going to tell me what exactly went down with you two? Something must have tipped him over the edge."

"Nope." I meant it too. I didn't even want to think about it.

"Come on . . ."

"No. No way."

"Fine. Don't tell me," Freddie said. "I already know what it all boils down to anyway. I don't care how many times he filled your Christmas stocking. You—"

"Oh my God!"

"Yeah," Freddie said, sounding equally disturbed. "I was trying to use a euphemism there so that I wouldn't have to imagine you two having sex, but it came out way worse. Lesson learned. But my point is that you need to move home like yesterday if you want any chance of keeping Grady in your life."

"Freddie, I can't move my entire life for a man!"

"Are you talking about me or Grady now?"

"Grady! And you!" I shouted, sending a nearby bird shooting for the sky. "If I move home, it won't be because either one of you pressured me into it. It will be because *I* want me to move home. Not because you men want me to move home!"

"Oh, well," he said with an implied harrumph. "Fine then, Ms. Julia Child."

I paused a moment, cocking my head. "Julia Child? You do know Julia Child was a chef, right?"

Freddie paused too. "Are you sure? I thought she was a feminist."

My voice dropped. "I'm pretty sure. I—you know what? I think this conversation has run its course, don't you?

"Meh."

"Thank you for buying me the steaks," I said once again adjusting my bag on my shoulder. "I really do owe you one."

"It's fine. Anytime. And . . . good luck," he said. "I hope it does work out for you two. We all want the same thing after all."

"I'm not sure—" I cut myself off. Again. Rabbit hole. "Sure."

"Call me later; or tomorrow if things go well, and—" I heard another voice talking to Freddie on the other end. "Mmm smoothie. Got to go."

I shoved my phone back into my pocket. Well, this trip was off to a stellar start. Maybe I should just turn around and go back to Chicago before—

"No," I whispered under my breath. "It can't be." Again, I blinked my cold, wet eyelashes. Nope. It wasn't a mirage. There was Red, in the distance, in his pontoon. She hadn't forgotten! My mom hired Red, a retired electrician whose hair hadn't seen red in about thirty years, to ferry guests around. He probably would have done it for free. Red liked keeping busy and puttering around on the lake. He was always among the first to have his boat in the water in the spring. But Otter Lake was the kind of place where the value of work was respected, at least by the older generation, and my mother appreciated what he did for her.

A moment later, he pulled up to the dock.

"Red! Hi!" I yelled with an overly eager wave.

"Yup." He drawled the word, changing it from one syllable into two.

I hurried my way over the slippery wood planks. "I'm so glad to see you!"

"Uh huh."

Red wasn't a big talker.

"I can't believe my mother remembered to tell you to come get me." Granted, I had told her about thirty times and texted her about twenty to do just that, but it was still no guarantee.

"You gonna get in? Or we hunkering down till summer?"

"I'm getting in! I'm getting in." I took Red's hand and climbed into the pontoon.

"Colder than a witch's teat out here."

"Um . . . sure is," I said, not at all sure I knew how cold that was, or if I should really agree with that statement on principle, but given that I was freezing, I didn't care all that much either.

This was a good sign. Maybe the fates were on my side this trip. Maybe—I cut myself off with a mental groan. Freddie had warned me last visit about tempting the universe with . . . optimism, I guess. I had dismissed it at the time as superstitious garbage, but then two people were murdered—and while I'm not saying those murders were all about the universe teaching me a lesson, because that's, well, pretty self-involved, I also couldn't see the harm in being just a little cautious. Then again, as things were pretty crappy already, how much more could the universe do to me?

And I probably shouldn't have had that thought either.

I yanked my hat down over my burning cold ears and just held it there as Red fired up the engine. My eyes trailed over the water to the shoreline as the boat puttered forward. Okay, so even in March, Otter Lake was still a little bit pretty, what with all of its nature. Despite the depressing dark slate sky, the trees did have a faint glow about them, almost like they were thinking about doing something springlike, and the soft browns and grays of everything else were kind of soothing . . . and . . . and that just made everything worse.

I huddled down farther into my seat and wrapped my arms around my chest. Tonight had to be perfect. I needed to fix what had happened. I needed to convince Grady that I was serious about us. Or at least pursuing the possibility of us. Or at least—Gah! This was exactly what he was always talking about.

"Erica," Red said turning back from the motor to look at me. "You're getting to be a regular fixture around here. You moving home?"

"Why is everybody always asking me that?!"

Red's bushy eyebrows jumped up his forehead.

"I am so sorry," I said hurriedly. "I . . . I'm not sure why I said it like that."

"S'all right. Moose are most dangerous during mating season."

I cocked my head slightly and squinted my eyes. "Right."

Oh, I could act like I didn't know what he was talking about, but he knew that I knew that he knew about Grady and me. Or something like that. Everybody knew everything about everybody else in Otter Lake. It was that kind of place.

But there was no time to dwell on all that. I needed to focus. Last time I had been home Grady had prepared a wonderful dinner for me. Fire pit. Wine. Salmon on a plank. Twinkly lights. And I'd messed it up. Now it was my turn to make a grand romantic gesture. My mother was out of the way—doing some downward dogging in the Grand Canyon—and we would have the retreat all to ourselves. Everything was ready to go. I would convince Grady that we were right together. There was no other alternative. It was time to get back some of that magic we had created at Christmas. In fact, it would take an act of God to—

"There's that Nor'easter they were talking about on the news."

I squeezed my eyes shut with my whole face for just a moment.

"They say it could turn into one of those superstorms." Red pointed at some clouds building in the distance just over the tops of the trees.

"I thought . . . I thought they said it would miss us."

"Nah, it's changed paths," he said with a scary amount of certainty.

"Come on. Seriously? No way. It doesn't feel stormy. It's too cold. Cold as a witch's teat!" Nope, still sounded weird. "You can't have a nor'easter when it's that cold. You need a cold air mass," I said, pointing a finger in the air, "and warm air mass," I said, adding another. "And this just feels cold." At least I thought that was how it worked. I hadn't exactly gone to school for meteorology. Meteorology? Was that even right? Sounded right. And sounding right was just as good as science in conversations like these.

"It's coming. You can feel it," he said, looking at the sky. "The air's cold, but every now and then you catch a wisp of something warm. Tropical. You could even get a twister with that."

"Dude."

He shrugged, a small smile forming at the corner of his mouth.

"The news always exaggerates these things," I said. "I doubt it will be that bad."

"I don't know. They seem to really mean it this time. Hurricane winds. Snow. Rain. Ice. The whole lot," he said. "Global warming." He then revved the engine, letting out a big puff of black smoke.

I eyed the monster clouds in the distance. I was pretty sure I saw a face in one of those clouds. A cloud face with fangs. Laughing at me.

Red turned to me again. "You get your mother to check the fuel for the generator. Those underwater cables can go in weather like this. And the electric company won't be able to fix it anytime soon, I'm guessing. Make sure everyone's got what they need."

"It's just me this weekend," I said, but Red had already turned back to the wheel. I doubted he could hear me over the wind. "And Grady."

Suddenly I felt even colder. If this storm was as bad as Red seemed to think it would be, there would be no Christmas re-enactment . . . which sounded very wrong. Grady was sheriff. And a storm probably meant that he had to—

No, no, no. Tonight *was* happening.

Red flipped the boat to neutral as the pontoon drifted toward my mom's dock. Once he had pulled up alongside, he reached for my bag before I could get to it, placing it on the dock.

"Now, I mean it, Erica. You take care." As he said the

words, I thought I felt a small gust of that warm tropical air he had been talking about. "The wind keeps building the way they say it will, the lake will be too dangerous to cross."

"Thanks, Red," I said, climbing out of the boat. "I will."

"And charge your phone just in case."

"Got it."

"And you call if you need any help."

I smiled.

"And stop smiling at me like that." He furrowed his brow, but the little grin came back to the corner of his mouth. He then flipped me a small salute and shifted the boat into reverse.

Otter Lake was a pretty nice town.

I took a few steps down the dock toward the shore before taking one last look at the clouds churning in the sky. As much as I didn't want to admit it, there was that eerie feeling of anticipation in the air. That strange excitement that comes with a big storm . . .

That was totally not going to happen because I had plans!

I clutched my bag to my body and hurried up the steps that led to the lodge.

I had so much to do. Take the steaks out of the freezer. Get some potatoes going. I probably should take Red's advice and check the propane tanks for the generator.

I crested the top of the hill. There it was. Earth, Moon, and Stars. Nature retreat and spiritual healing facility. Huh, my mom had left some lights on for me in the lodge. That was nice . . . and totally unlike her. Not that she wasn't nice. She just hated wasting electricity.

I hurried along the muddy path and up the steps to the wide porch. I reached for the door handle, resuming my list. I also needed to shower, feed my horrible fur-sibling and love of my mother's life, Caesar, then—

I swung the door open and stopped dead in my tracks.

Yup, I had a lot to do.

Number one?

Get rid of all the people standing in my living room.

Chapter Two

"Who's she?"

"Who cares?"

"Julie, when can we start taping?"

"Not until Rayner gets here."

My eyes darted about to each of the speakers who seemed so very comfortable in my childhood home . . . that was supposed to be empty!

"Um, hello?" I said stepping into the lodge, shutting the door behind me.

Nobody answered.

"Hello?"

Despite what felt like one of my most outrageous facial expressions, the group ignored me completely. In fact, they had already gone back to their conversations.

I lowered my bag carefully to the floor and took a breath.

Something was wrong here.

Aside, from the fact that the retreat was supposed to be closed, these people . . . well, they weren't the usual type of visitor Earth, Moon, and Stars attracted.

Three of them sat around the large harvest table where

the guests had most of their meals. The unwieldy piece of furniture had been turned and centered in the middle of the common room, like a conference table. Two women with shiny make-up, maybe a mother and daughter, sat on the side closest to the fireplace. They were having what looked to be an in-depth conversation about nails, judging by the way they were holding up their bejeweled hands to one another. On the other side sat a man, early twenties maybe, dressed in some pretty stylish, urban-type clothes, probably from the kind of label that would sell a white T-shirt for hundreds of dollars. Not that his clothes would have normally stood out to me, but while his style looked like it should be carried by some easy-going pop star on the cover of *Tiger Beat,* this guy . . . well, he was rocking back and forth with his hands pinned between his knees.

Not really sure how I felt about that.

Away from the group, at a table in the kitchen, was another man. Middle-aged. Average-looking. Kind of sweaty. He sat bent over a stack of papers, clutching at his forehead with one hand, yanking at the tie at his throat with the other.

Okay.

Finally, and perhaps most peculiar, was the woman with a hurried ponytail and hip glasses standing by the windows with a camera guy, baseball cap twisted backward, pointing out different spots in the room. For camera angles, I guess?

"Right," I muttered under my breath. "Let's try this again." I cleared my voice loudly. "Um, hello?" I stepped closer to the table. "Have any of you seen my mother? Summer Bloom? She owns this retreat?"

"Could you make me a drink? Martini?"

When my eyes landed on the older of the two women seated at the table, it took everything in me to keep my face completely still. If I had to guess, the woman was in her forties, maybe fifties, but it was really hard to tell given that she had obviously indulged heavily in plastic surgery. The end result was both strangely compelling and repulsive. Like a fish . . . that was kind of hot. Maybe a fish I kind of wanted to look like . . . but not. I opened my mouth to say *something*, but she beat me to the punch.

"Grey Goose?"

I tilted my head.

"Pinot Grigio? Champs? Come on you have to have Champs?"

"We," I said cocking my head even farther, "don't usually keep alcohol on the premises." Even though I hadn't lived at home for years, it was impossible for me not to slip back into the role of employee. I was nearly as invested in my mother's business as she was. *Goddess* only knew, if she lost the retreat, she might turn her attention even more in my direction.

"I'm sorry, did you say no alcohol? Absolutely nothing?"

Well, there was the extra-large bottle of red wine I had in my bag for Grady and me, but she didn't need to know about that. I shook my head.

The woman's eyes widened in shock, but the effect was strange given that her forehead was paralyzed. "Julie, you must have something?"

She was looking at the woman standing by the cameraman, but neither one acknowledged her.

"Julie!"

The cameraman elbowed the woman beside him. She startled and flicked her eyes over. "Sorry, Ronnie. Not today."

The woman flung herself back against the chair, smacking her head a little. "You're telling me, I'm stuck in this backwoods shack with no alcohol? I'm going to be sick."

I squeezed my eyes shut tight, tight, tight, hoping that when I opened them again, all the people would be gone.

Nope.

"Relax, Mom," the girl seated beside the sexy amphibious woman said. She looked like she was in her early twenties, which I suppose meant she was a woman and not a girl, but her cute French braids made it hard to think of her as a grown-up. "I think you still have a Xanax in your purse."

"What were you doing in my purse?"

"Um, looking for Xanax?" The girl laughed loudly at that, making the young man seated across the table jolt and dart a glance behind him . . . at absolutely nothing.

Okay, this was getting weird.

"That's not funny, Ashley," the older woman said, grabbing her purse off the floor. "You need to protect your brand."

The young woman sighed. "The camera's not rolling."

"There are always cameras rolling."

The perky looking girl rolled her eyes. "Don't mind us," she said getting up and walking over. "Do you own this place? I love it! And you're so pretty."

"Oh, well, thank you," I said, avoiding the urge to take a step back. I found girl-bonding awkward, and girls who liked to bond terrifying, but it was something I was working on. "I . . . I . . ." I looked the girl up and down. She was wearing canvas pants with lots of pockets and a thin, long-sleeved T-shirt underneath a faux-fur vest. "I like your outfit?"

"Thanks. I shot this hyena myself," she said holding out the fur. "You want to feel it."

So . . . not faux. Definitely not faux. I felt my eyes

widen as I took a step back without even realizing it. "Maybe later?"

"Sure!" she said with a happy shrug, then walked away revealing a bedazzled cross on the back of her hyena vest.

I backed farther away, whispering under my breath, "What the . . ."

"Brody was here first."

I jumped. I had forgotten about the rumpled looking man sitting at the small table in the kitchen until I had almost backed into him. His eyes quickly shot over to the main room before landing back on his papers. So I guess that meant the twitchy young guy was Brody? I thought about asking him, but the timing didn't seem right. Maybe it was the way he was swatting at his expensive-looking hair like he was being swarmed by . . . something. Hmm, it had been a while since I'd seen frosted tips. And his highlights were really frosted. More blue than blond.

"We've rented this lodge tonight," the suited man added, shuffling frantically through his stack. "I've got the agreement here somewhere. I'm a lawyer."

"Yeah, you just keep saying that, Chuck," the fish woman by the fire shouted over. "Maybe someone will believe you."

"Wait rented?"

The lawyer nodded, still shuffling. "It was all last minute."

I bit my lip and shook my head. So, they had rented the retreat for the night. Well, that was just . . .

"Great," I mumbled. "Fabulous."

"I spoke to your mother on the phone." The man—who apparently went by Chuck—smoothed his quite thin hair down over his head. "I was hoping to meet her."

"So she wasn't here when you arrived?"

"No, not when—"

"I saw her," the younger man, Brody, suddenly said, wide eyes focused on nothing.

I took a step toward him, making sure to maintain a safe distance. I mean, he wasn't very big, but he looked unpredictable. "Do you know where she went?"

"Wait," he said gripping the armrests of his chair. "She's gone?"

"Okay." I reached for my phone, my mind already warring over the priorities of killing my mother and working on a plan B. I swiped my mom's number first. Maybe there had been some sort of mistake. *Unlikely.* Or . . . oh my God! Maybe this was her way of throwing me back into the family business! Maybe—

My thoughts were cut off by the ringing of a cell phone.

The ringing of a cell phone on the kitchen counter.

The ringing of my mother's phone!

"Of course!" I whipped my phone from my face. Of course she would forget her phone. Actually she probably didn't forget it at all. She knew she was in trouble. That's probably why she wasn't here now. She was waiting for me to calm down before she appeared. I mean, there was no way she would have still gone to Arizona. She would never leave a bunch of guests alone at the lodge without *her* spiritual guidance. So where was she? Getting last minute suppl—

"Um, excuse me," a voice suddenly said at my shoulder.

I jumped around.

"Whoa." The woman with the cameraman flung her hands into the air.

I dialed back the intensity of my, well, face a little and took a breath. "I'm sorry," I said carefully. "How can I help you?" I tried to raise my angry furrowed eyebrows in polite question, but I don't think I was very successful given the bemused fear evident in the woman's expression.

"We were just wondering if this place had any more lamps we could use?" she asked, adjusting her catlike glasses. "Maybe from other rooms?"

It took me a moment to understand the question. My brain felt hot.

"Are you okay?"

"No, I—" I shook my head. "What's with the camera?"

She chuckled. "Oh, I should have introduced myself. I'm Julie, and this is Kenny," she said turning to the big man with the camera. "I'm a junior producer with Third Act."

Third Act. Third Act. How did I know that name? Suddenly it hit me. "You're not . . . Third Act. Isn't that the network that produces that show—" I waved my hand in the air, "—about the fighting women?"

She smiled. "*The Real MILF Diaries.* That's us."

I brought a hand up to rub my temple. Okay. Why not? Let's make this moment even more surreal. "Why are you here?"

She studied my face, then said, "You really don't know what's going on do you?"

"No. I don't."

"Well then, you, my friend, are in for a treat."

Chapter Three

"We're taking test footage for a new show," she said nodding. "*Rich Bitches*."

I guess the lack of understanding showed all over my face.

"Ronnie wants in."

"Ronnie?"

She gestured to the glossed creature by the fire. "You don't recognize her? She's like head MILF."

"Oh." I really couldn't think of a single other appropriate thing to say.

"Actually, I'm planning on pitching a new show based on the entire family."

I nodded. I wasn't entirely sure why.

"They're gold. Never see anything like them. They'll do anything to be famous. This could really make my career." She looked to Kenny, the cameraman, for confirmation, but he was too busy squinting suspiciously at something he had just dug out from his teeth with his baby fingernail.

She whacked him on the arm.

"What? Oh, yeah. Go team."

She looked back at me with a wry smile.

"That's, um, very nice. I'm happy for you?" I offered. "But what are they doing here?"

A satisfied smile spread across her face. "Oh, that's the best part," she said before whacking her cameraman again. "Get a shot of that sign over there. It's perfect." She pointed at the small burnt-wood plaque on the wall that had a picture of a dog smiling underneath the words, *I'm the only bitch in this house.* Hearts on the *i*'s. My mother had me get it made on a rare trip to the mall. My adolescence was like that.

As he lumbered away, she turned her focus back on me. "They were summoned," she answered in an unnaturally deep voice.

I blinked. "I'm sorry. Did you say summoned?"

"Crazy, isn't it?" she agreed, nodding. "By the old man. Patriarch of the family. It's an incredible storyline. He's going to—" She cut herself off. "I don't want to ruin it for you. See, right here," she began, pointing at the floor, "right here is where I would put a commercial break."

I briefly looked down at the spot on the floor. There was nothing there. I gave my head a shake and said, "Oh, but it's okay. You can tell me. You see, not to be rude, but I don't really care." Hmm, that didn't sound very customer-service oriented. "I mean, I have plans. Here. Tonight. I need to know—"

"That's what they all say," she said. "But I can tell you are on the edge of your seat."

"No seriously," I replied quickly. "I just need to know how long this thing is going to take. I—"

"Suspense. It's all about the suspense."

"Oh my God!" I suddenly shouted. "Just tell me why they're here!"

"You're funny. And a little on edge," she said looking at me with new interest. "We should talk more. Do you hunt in these here woods?" she asked putting on what I could only assume was a hillbilly accent that I did not appreciate at all. "Ashley hunts," she said gesturing over to the perky girl.

"Yeah. Hyenas. I got that."

"She's all over social media, thanks to her mom. Ronnie's a marketing wiz. Cheerleader taking down rhinos in short shorts with Jesus in her heart. It's a bigger fetish category than you'd probably think."

"I don't think. I mean—" I rubbed my forehead. Why? Why was this happening?

"She's not great for us though. Our viewers don't really want to see Simba take a bullet." She looked me up and down. "But survivalist stuff. Now that's hot."

I shot her a look from under my hand that I now had clutching my temples.

"How do you feel about bikinis?" she went on. "Oh! Or hunting in bikinis?"

I threw my hand away from my face. "You know what? There's a lamp in that room over there," I said pointing to my bedroom. My old bedroom. Whatever. "Knock yourself out. I need to find my mom."

"Great!" she said, shooing Kenny toward the room. "I wouldn't take too long though. *He'll* be here soon. You don't want to miss it. It's going to be great."

I walked toward the front door.

"Oh! And I need you to sign some papers. You don't want us to have to blur your face. You can be the local color. I think I have a spare mic. And don't be late! It will be the most dramatic—"

I slammed the door behind me.

A rough gust of cold air whipped my hair back from my face as I hustled down the steps and veered off the gravel path, heading toward a foot trail in the trees.

It was only mid-afternoon, but the eerie gray light from the storm was making it seem much later. The wind had definitely picked up. In fact, it was almost strong enough to distract me from the anger simmering in my belly. Almost. This could not be happening. It just couldn't. But of course it could . . . and was. This was typical mom behavior. She offered me the retreat! It was her idea! We had gone over the details a hundred times two days ago! But that didn't matter. Nope. This is how it went with us. It was like we were riding a tandem bicycle through life, both of us trying to steer.

The loud crack of a tree branch snatched me from my thoughts. I skidded to a stop on the downward sloping trail, eyes snapping up. Nope. Nothing about to fall on my head. That was good. Huh, maybe an old forest wasn't the best place to be in the beginnings of a storm. But I needed answers. And I needed them fast. Red was right. If this weather got any worse, nobody was getting off this island. I hurried as best I could down the trail, slick with icy mud and wet leaves. In fact, I should probably just call him for an evacuation now. That group back at the retreat didn't seem like the roughing-it types.

This was not how this weekend was supposed to go!

Suddenly my foot slipped out from underneath me, sending my butt crashing to the ground.

I squeezed my eyes shut. Okay, that had hurt.

I took a deep breath as I let my hands flop to my sides.

What was I doing? This was a mess. Maybe I should just—

Another loud crack exploded above me.

Maybe I should just hurry the hell up before a tree landed on my head.

I shot to my feet and hustled the rest of the way to the small cozy cottage glowing in the distance. A moment later I was banging on its thick wooden door, knuckles aching from the cold. "Kit Kat? Tweety?"

Nothing.

I could see a light on inside. I craned my head back to the lake. Yup, their dock was in the water, boat tied to it.

I raised my fist to bang again when the door swung open.

"Oh, thank God," I muttered.

The twins were the only other inhabitants on the island. They had to be in their seventies by now, but their zest for life could rival that of most co-eds on spring break. They drank, smoked, and generally found the daily lives of most people to be somehow hilarious. They definitely weren't the types to, say, back down from a bar fight, but they would certainly be the ones to buy everybody, including those they were fighting with, the first round once it was done. They were also the closest thing my mother and I had to family around Otter Lake.

"Erica? What the heck are you doing out there?" Kit Kat said, brushing down her white permed curls. "Get in here."

I stepped into the warmth of the cluttered but cozy cottage. Well, it would have been *cozier* if it hadn't been for all the dead animals staring at me.

I took a good long look around. It had been awhile since I had been over to their place. Not much had changed. Their father had been a taxidermist, and the twins had held onto all his display animals . . . of which there were quite a few. But the dead animals weren't the only collection in the house. They had an entire wall covered with black leather jingle-bell belts for horses and shelves upon shelves of clay jugs, which were quite possibly filled with moonshine. The place was still tidy enough that they wouldn't quite be considered hoarders, but they were certainly skirting the edge.

Tweety came out from one of the back rooms, suitcase in hand. "Erica, honey, what are you doing here? We were just leaving."

"I'm sorry," I said, pulling off my hat. "Are you . . . where are you going?"

"Everglades. Our cousin is closing down his souvenir shop. We're going to go help him out and warm our bones a little." She dropped her oversized suitcase to the floor with a clunk. "I'll bring you something back from his shop if you'd like?"

"Well, don't go to any trouble."

"It's no trouble. He's got a ton of crap."

"Okay," I said slowly. "Thanks." This was becoming a really, really strange day.

"It's just for a week or two," Kit Kat said. "Until we're sure this winter is over. Maybe you could keep an eye on the place for us?"

I nodded. Spring and fall were tricky times when you lived on a lake. If you wanted to stay the winter, you had to hunker down with supplies until the lake completely froze over—then you could go back and forth by snow-mobile. But it wasn't exactly what I would call comfort living. Even my mom wasn't above renting in town for a couple of weeks here and there or going on yoga vacations. The twins would never admit it, but I couldn't help but wonder if island living was getting a bit rough for them.

"Okay, well, I won't keep you," I said. "I was just wondering if you guys had heard from my mom."

"Wasn't she supposed to be leaving for Arizona this morning?" Kit Kat asked.

"No, no," Tweety said, looking at her sister and tapping the side of her head. "Remember she got that call? Emergency family retreat?"

Her sister squinted back at her.

Tweety looked at me, jerked a thumb at her sister, and said, "I'm going to have to put one of those *If lost please return to* address labels on her, the way her mind's going."

"What are you talking about? You never told me you talked to Summer yesterday."

Tweety's face dropped. "I didn't?"

"No."

"Ha! Better get me one of those labels too." She turned back to me. "Anyway, they were willing to pay big, big bucks to have the retreat for the night, but she, uh . . ." She paused for a moment, grimacing slightly. "She didn't know if she should do it. Said something about promising the retreat to you?"

"Yeah. Well, I guess she made up her mind." I planted my hands on my hips and shook my head. "So, what? I mean, she didn't still go to Arizona, right?"

Tweety squinted, deepening the wrinkles around her eyes. "I don't know, come to think of it. She did say they weren't interested in mediation. They just wanted the lodge. But I can't see her leaving the retreat with strangers. Was her boat there? Maybe she needed supplies?"

"That's what I thought, and, no, the boat's not there," I muttered. "But does she even have it in the water yet?" My mother, like many of Otter Lake residents, stored her boat at the marina for the winter.

Tweety squinted even harder, all of her features nearly disappearing into the folds of her skin. "I . . . don't know. She was going to, but I don't know that she did because of the Arizona thing."

I threw my hands in the air, shaking my head.

"Well, if I had known you were coming over to play twenty questions, I would have prepared."

"I'm sorry," I said quickly. "I'm not mad at you guys. It's just tonight was supposed to be . . ." I shook my head again, letting the thought trail off.

"Oh," Kit Kat said knowingly. "Tonight you were going to bring the Sheriff in."

"Take him *downtown*," Tweety added.

"Put the screws—"

I put up my hand. "Please stop."

"I thought he dumped you?" Kit Kat asked.

I sighed. "He didn't . . . well, he did," I said, looking up directly into the eyes of a weasel sitting on a bookshelf. He was judging me too. I could tell. "But there's a window. I just need to, you know . . . I was thinking maybe if I . . ."

"Just stop, honey," Tweety said with a pat to my shoulder. "You're going to hurt yourself."

"Yeah, you're going all red," her sister added, swirling a finger around my face.

"You can use our place if you like?"

"Thank you," I said, looking around again, startling just a little when I caught a glimpse of the screeching falcon about to descend on me. "Maybe. But I should probably make sure the people at the retreat are okay. And—"

"What, the stuffies don't scream romance to you?" Kit Kat asked dryly.

"Why do you guys keep them?"

"Well, it doesn't seem right just to throw them out," Tweety said, gesturing to the silently hissing fox at her side. "What do we do with them? Do we give them a burial? Put them in the compost? Somebody wanted this fox to last." She poked at one of its fangs.

"Yeah," I said slowly. "Somebody . . . probably not the fox."

She swatted me on the arm.

I smiled. "Okay, well, thanks. You'd better get going before the weather stops you. Actually . . . wait. Do you guys think you could give me a lift into town?"

"Sure," Tweety said. "We could use someone to carry our bags."

After hiking the twin's bags across half the town, we parted ways at their friend Alma's house. She was taking them to the airport. I fended off the invitation to pop in for tea, wished them a good trip, then spent another five, ten minutes making them promise not to bring me a souvenir alligator head home. I left the house still unsure if they really got that I meant it.

I hurried my way into the main part of town, wanting to stop in at every little shop and home I passed along the way. My ear lobes were so cold it felt like they might snap off any minute. One old house in particular caught my eye because of the sign out front. MRG Properties. Huh. So that's where they had set up shop. The brick house had been a flower store when I was a kid, but I guess it was now the temporary home of the real-estate developer that was transforming Otter Lake from a quaint small town to a cottage playground for New Hampshire's rich and famous . . . well, maybe just rich.

Last I heard, the company had put a temporary hold on all developments, given their connection to the murder and attempted murder that had occurred in Otter Lake last year. Well, I guess they weren't really connected per se. In fact, truth was, for a little while there, I may have been responsible for casting a wee bit of suspicion on their in-town representative, Candace. Which may have been a teensy bit motivated by the fact that I thought she was dating Grady. But it turned out Grady totally thought she had done it too—which, really, you know, shows how much we think alike.

I hurried past the house just in case Candace had decided to come back to town. We had left things on kind of an awkward note. I had apologized to her a couple of times on social media because she had blocked my number from her phone, but I gave up after a while. Really you can only be declined as a friend so many times before you have to accept that a person just doesn't like you.

I hustled on, blowing some air over my thinly gloved hands before shoving them deeper into my pockets. Man at this rate, by the time I got to the sheriff's department, my nose would be running uncontrollably and my lips would be too numb to talk.

This day sucked.

And, of course, the instant I had that thought, the engine of what sounded like a monster truck roared behind me.

My eyes jumped over to the camouflage-painted beast rolling up to my side. Hmm, this didn't seem promising. Nope, especially not with that flag depicting the naked silhouette of a girl holding a shotgun hanging on the back window. Maybe if I just kept walking—

"Yo, Erica."

Nope.

Chapter Four

What now?

The passenger-side window of the truck rolled all the way down, releasing a tangy combination of nicotine and some other smoke, most likely of the *make your own* variety.

I blinked past the cloud, waving my hand in front of my face.

"Weasel?" I shouted before snapping my mouth shut. I mean, it was one thing to call a guy Weasel in high school because, well, he looked a lot like a weasel—actually, nope, it probably wasn't okay then either. "I mean, Dave! How are you?"

"I'm good. I'm good," he said scratching the sparse stubble on his chin. You're looking—" He was cut off by the hand of the driver pushing him against the seat, so he could lean around, and . . .

Nuts.

Well, this was going to be awkward.

"Jake," I said weakly. "Hi." I tried to pop some fingers up in greeting, but they were having none of it.

Jake Day. Cousin of Laurie Day. The woman I had helped put away for murder last summer.

He tossed me a casual nod, but his eyes felt very heavy on my face. "I've been hoping to see you around town, Boobsie."

I clicked my tongue. "Yeah, I don't go by Boobsie anymore." I probably could have made that sound more indignant if I hadn't just called a grown man Weasel.

"Really?" Oh boy, there was no hiding the nasty undertone in his voice. "I still like it. Fits."

I sighed as my eyes darted up the sidewalk. I should just keep walking. I mean, Weasel—*again!*—Dave, was a harmless enough guy. I didn't want to be rude to him, but then again, I had never been fond of the company he chose to keep. See, he had always been a little like one of those feeder fish that follow sharks around, and Jake was definitely a shark. Actually, no. That was insulting to sharks. Jake was a jerk. Through and through. He was the kind of guy back in high school who would hit on another guy's girlfriend right in front of him just to try to start a fight. He was missing a couple of his front teeth as a result—probably had taken a lot more though. Somehow, I was getting the impression that not much had changed.

I took a step back from the truck. "Well, it's been nice seeing you guys. But I have to get g—"

"My mom just visited Laurie a week or two ago up in state."

I slowed my walk but didn't quite stop. "Uh-huh." That really didn't feel like a comment that wanted my input.

The truck rolled beside me.

"Not really having a good time there."

"I wouldn't think so," I muttered, stepping over an icy puddle.

"Especially tough considering she's innocent."

Okay, that stopped me in my tracks. "You know she confessed, right? And held a bunch of us at gunpoint?"

"Yeah," he said, before biting his lip roughly. "I heard your story."

"No, she's right," Dave, the feeder fish—*nope, still bad*—said. "I heard it from Freddie too. He—"

Jake pushed him back against the seat again.

"Easy, Jake! I didn't mean anything by i—" This time Dave was cut off by the flag hanging against the back windshield, falling on his head.

"Again?" he muttered, pushing it up off his head. "It's always doing that." He swiveled in his seat, trying to re-attach it, but Jake snatched it away. "Leave it."

"You know what?" I said, jerking a thumb down the sidewalk. "I gotta go, and you guys really seem like you have enough going on here."

"Yeah, sure," Jake said revving the engine. "But you might want to watch your back, Boobsie. Not everybody in town is happy with you and Freddie sticking your noses into other people's business."

I stopped to look him in the eye again. I guess my expression had the effect I was going for because Dave shrank back into his seat. "What exactly do you mean by that, Jake? Is that like some sort of threat?"

He didn't flinch. "Threat? I would never threaten the sheriff's girlfriend, but . . . oh, that's right." He snapped his fingers. "He dumped you, didn't he?"

He threw me one last nasty smile before speeding away, leaving me standing in a cloud of exhaust.

I puffed some air out in a full-body scoff—which nobody was really around to appreciate—then shook my head. *Some things never change*, I thought, stomping my way back down the street. I mean, I guess I should have been . . . what? Intimidated? But really, Jake was just a bully. I didn't think he meant to accomplish anything by this little conversation other than to have a story of how he shook up Erica Bloom to tell his family. And who did he think he was driving around in that ridiculous truck?

I fumed my way all the way to the sheriff's department. Amazing how a little anger will put some pep in your step. I wasn't even cold anymore.

As I climbed the steps to the building, my heart sank. It was packed.

And by packed, I mean not one, but two extra officers were talking with Rhonda at the front desk. That was two more than usual, and that had to mean that they were preparing for the storm—which also meant that the odds of my evening going as planned were even slimmer than they were an hour ago when I discovered my mom's lodge full of people.

And that was pretty slim.

Any other day, under any other circumstance, it wouldn't have been a big deal. We could have just postponed to another night. But the amount of convincing it took for me to get Grady to agree to this night, well, it made me think he'd use this delay as a reason to call the whole thing off, and that was not happening.

I hustled up the stairs of the building, the glowing yellow lights welcoming me inside, but before I could even reach for the glass door, I saw deputy at large Rhonda Cooke's head whip around. The look on her face was enough to make me second guess putting my hand on the handle.

I stared at her a moment, trying to figure out exactly what her expression meant. Surely it didn't mean what I thought it did . . . and if it did, surely it couldn't be meant for me? I took a quick glance behind me to see if anyone else was standing there.

Nope, no one there.

This was weird.

Rhonda and I were friends.

I put my hand back on the handle and swung open the door. She was probably just on high alert because of the storm, and—

"Don't you even think about it!"

Chapter Five

"Not one more step!"

I threw my hands in the air as Rhonda stalked over, her finger pointed at a pretty severe *Bad dog!* angle.

"What did I do?"

"Oh, you know exactly what you did."

I gaped at her. This was crazy. Rhonda was my biggest supporter when it came to Grady. She thought we would be great together. She even thought we'd make cute children! She had given us both all sorts of advice last time I was in town. In fact, you could say she was probably *overly* invested in our relationship . . .

Oh . . . right . . . *crap*.

I took a half-step forward. "Okay, I get it. But can we just talk about this ins—"

"No, you cannot come in."

"Rhonda, come on," I said, looking briefly at my hands that were still in the air before dropping them. "I just want to talk to him."

"I am very upset with you," she said shaking her head, making her curly red hair shudder.

I scratched absently at the back of my head, mentally calculating my odds of making a dash through the tiny little space between Rhonda and the door. Unfortunately, all the scenarios ended with me getting slammed up against the aluminum threshold. I'd seen Rhonda wrestle back in high school. "Okay, what exactly is it that you think I did?"

"What did you do? What did you do? Look at him!" she said pointing back into the department. "He is a broken, broken man."

I inched forward to see Grady walk out of his office. He was talking to one of the other officers and hadn't noticed us yet. My heart clenched at the sight of him. And for the record, he didn't look broken at all. He was wearing a black turtleneck sweater with a leather sheriff's jacket. I had never seen that look before, but I certainly should have. It forced you to imagine all the muscles that jacket was hiding. Then there were his fitted black pants with the stripe down the side, which seemed to accentuate—

"Stop it!" Rhonda snapped. "You don't get to look at him like that! That view is for paying customers only."

"Okay," I said before pausing to roll my jaw. "I don't know what you think you know, but I'm pretty sure you haven't heard the whole story."

She raised an eyebrow.

"Grady dumped me."

"Only because you forced him to."

Suddenly my cheeks felt hot. "Just let me in, Rhonda," I said, inching forward again, pulling the door open wider.

Rhonda held her ground. "You've been stringing him along for months now."

"What?!" I cried. On some level, obviously, I could see her point, but we were rapidly approaching the part of the argument that was beyond all reasonableness. "That is completely untrue!"

"Really," she said, folding her arms across her chest. "The way I hear it, you've been telling Grady you want a relationship but haven't made one concrete step to move home, or—"

"Moving my entire life is a big deal!"

"I wasn't finished," she said looking dangerous. "*Or* listened to any option that involved him moving to Chicago. Which you know would really suck because he's an awesome boss, but does Erica Bloom care about that? Noooo."

I rubbed the side of my face with my gloved hand as I very calmly said, "Grady wouldn't want to move to Chicago. He loves Otter Lake. He belongs in Otter Lake."

"Then you move home!"

My hand flew into the air. "It's not that easy!"

"You got issues, Bloom."

"Oh my God! I never said that I didn't! But Grady . . . we're just at the beginning . . . and it's a big deal . . . I have a lot of questions, and . . ."

She folded her arms over her chest. "You can't even commit to one sentence."

"Oh ho, ho, ho! Good one," I said, chuckling unpleasantly and wagging a finger at her. I was about to say something else when Rhonda's face dropped into something serious.

"Grady's ready, Erica. He's ready for the whole shebang. Marriage. Kids. A dog named Butch. Maybe a—"

"I want a dog named Butch. Who said I didn't want a dog named Butch?" I asked in a harsh whisper. The officer who wasn't talking to Grady was giving us a quizzical look. Why? Why was I having this conversation in the threshold of a sheriff's office? I wrapped my coat more tightly around my body. "I just need to be sure."

"But you can't just expect Grady to wait around for something that might never come."

"I'm not—"

"Listen to me. I consider both of you to be friends, but Grady took a big chance in asking you to stay last time you were home. Which, was totally my idea by the way," she said, planting the tips of her fingers on her chest. "One that I now completely regret. It was supposed to be all romantic. Like one of those movies where the man chases the woman through the airport and catches her just before she gets on the plane." She shot a faraway look out the doors before turning her disgusted eyes back on me. "I mean, what do you want?"

I had no idea how to answer that. Good thing she didn't know about what had happened at the actual airport. "Rhonda, that was all wonderful, but—"

"Grady deserves someone who is all in."

My mouth snapped shut. In fact, it took me a few moments before I could even mutter, "I so hate you right now."

"Good," she said adjusting her belt before quickly adding, "but not really though, right? We're still going to go out for beers sometime?"

I huffed a breath. "Not if you're just going to lecture me from relationship books all night."

She shrugged. "Might help."

I let out a breath that sounded a bit like a growl. "Look, I hear you, okay? I see your point. In fact, I see everybody's point!" I threw my hand in the air. "You all win. So can I talk to Grady now?"

"No."

"Rhonda!"

"We're really busy preparing for the storm. I don't want him all distracted."

I inched my way closer again even though there weren't

that many inches left to cross. "Okay, now you are over-stepping."

She planted her feet a little wider than hip-width apart and re-crossed her arms over her chest.

"This building is public property. I have a right to go in."

"Are you moving home?"

"I don't need to justify—"

"That wasn't a yes. So sorry, but you can't come in," she said. "It's for both of your goods really."

"Rhonda!"

"Erica!"

"Everything all right over there?" a new voice asked.

I sighed. "Hi, Grady."

Chapter Six

"It's okay," Grady said, patting Rhonda on the shoulder. "I can spare a few minutes for Erica."

They locked eyes, warring a bit, before Rhonda stepped aside. "I hope you know what you're doing, boss."

"Oh, come on," I said with a scoff, not giving Grady time to answer. "What do you think I'm going to do to him? I'm not some praying mantis who eats her mate's head after—"

"Black widow spider," Rhonda corrected.

"Oh, I'm, uh, pretty sure it's a praying mantis."

"Are you now?" Rhonda said walking backward toward her desk. "Why don't we just see what the Internet has to say about—"

"It's fine," Grady said again, before corralling me into his office. He flashed the other officers an awkward smile on the way. I threw them an awkward half-wave. I was starting to see Freddie's point about farmer's markets needing security. I couldn't even behave myself in a sheriff's department. And for the most part, I was a pretty normal person. Well, most of the time, when I was back in Chicago.

Once inside, Grady closed the door and faced me. Neither one of us said anything for a moment.

"Go ahead," he said, giving me an *out with it* roll of his hand.

I planted my hands on my hips. "I'm sorry? Out with what?"

"You look—" he squinted, "—mad."

I bit my lower lip and pulled it roughly between my teeth before saying, "So what? You and Rhonda just sit around all day talking about your feelings?"

He chuckled quietly and nodded. "Not all day. And Rhonda does most of the talking."

I blew some air out. "And just so I know, have you turned the entire town against me? Or just your second-in-command out there?" I didn't want to say that. Especially not in that ugly way. I didn't want to fight at all. I wasn't even angry at him! And yet, while I could hear the words coming out of my mouth, I just couldn't seem to stop them. That seemed to be happening a lot when Grady and I talked these days.

"That's not fair," he said quietly. "You should know, better than anybody, that I can't control what this town thinks. Nobody can." He took a breath, then added, "Look. I know you're hurt. I am too. This is not how I wanted things to turn out."

"No," I said with a sharp finger point. "We are not doing this here. There's been a small hitch to our plans. My mother rented out the retreat for the night. But—"

"I was going to cancel anyway."

I tried to meet his eye, but he looked away. "Grady, no. At least hear me out. I—"

"It's not that. Well, it is that. But this storm," he said looking to the window. Just then the wind gave the pane a good rattle. I could see whose side it was on. "It's supposed to be a bad one. Rain. Freezing rain. Snow.

Maybe lots of snow. Everyone's going to be working overtime."

"Oh." I looked down to the floor trying to blink away the stinging sensation suddenly going on in my eyes.

When I looked back up, he was studying my face. He almost looked like he was about to say something more, but then he clenched his jaw and the look was gone. "Besides, I'm not really sure what there is left to say."

"You don't mean that."

He sighed then muttered something that sounded an awful lot like "I can't have this conversation again."

From outside the room a voice shouted, "You stay strong, Grady!"

He looked down again at the floor, one hand resting at his hip, the other sending Rhonda a half-hearted thumbs up.

My eyes snapped over to the office window as I near yelled, "You and I are about to throw down real soon!"

Grady sighed again. "Please. Don't rile her up. As it is, she's probably going to make me listen to her playlist again."

"Her playlist?"

"She made a playlist to help me get over y—" he cut himself off. "I can't listen to Beyoncé's 'Single Ladies' again. I just can't. And she's already trying to set me up with her cousin."

I felt my eyes widen to dangerous levels before I whipped them back to Rhonda. She startled just a little.

"Got a cousin do you?"

Her face dropped before she had the good sense to slink back to her desk.

Grady took another noisy breath. "Really, Erica, I think maybe it's better if we don't—"

"No," I said, hating the pleading in my voice. "There are things I want to say. Things I need to say."

Again with the sigh.

"I'm ready. I think. I just need to be sure. I'm so close to just packing up and—"

"Right," he said with a slow nod. "But I can't wait anymore."

"If this is about what happened at the airport. I want you to know—"

He waved a hand. "It's not about what happened at the airport."

"Please let's just talk this through." I took a step toward him. "Alone."

His turned away to stare at nothing on his desk. "I don't know about alone."

There was something about the way he said that—nervous, kind of—that made me smile. "What? You afraid of my seductive powers?"

He licked his lips and nodded. "Little bit. Always have been."

"Well, you should be afraid," I said stepping all the way forward and putting my finger on his chest. "Very afraid."

He huffed a small laugh. "I love it when you do awkward sexy, but . . ."

I smiled up at him. "But what?"

He gently gripped my finger and moved it away. "But I can't keep doing this."

"No. Let's talk about it," I said. "Really talk about it. Please."

He shook his head then suddenly his face changed. "Wait, did you say your mother rented out the retreat? Tonight? How many people?"

I stepped back. "I don't know. Half dozen or so."

He rocked back on his feet. "Do they know about the storm?"

"I don't know, but—"

"You should really tell them if they don't come mainland soon, there's a good chance they'll be stuck there at least for the night." He walked over to his desk and made a note on a piece of paper. "How are your supplies?"

"I don't know that either. I thought the retreat was going to be empty. I mean, I bought steaks for us and that wine we had at Christmas." My voice dropped off at the end.

Grady froze, pen midair, but didn't look up from his desk. A moment later, he cleared his throat and said, "You should really let them know. The roads are getting dicey if they want to make it to a hotel. And if you're going to stay on the island tonight, make sure you have everything you need."

I took a breath. "Right."

Another heavy moment passed.

He squeezed his eyes shut, then added, "And . . . I will come check on you when I can."

"Really?" I clapped my hands together. I may have even hopped a little.

He put a hand in the air. "I don't want to get your hopes up. I meant everything I said, but I should probably tell you . . ." He stopped and took a breath. "There are some things I need to say too."

I pressed my lips together and nodded. "It's true. You should check on me. I might perish all alone in the elements, Caesar gnawing on my frozen corpse."

Grady rolled his eyes. "I'm pretty sure you know how to start a fire."

"Body heat's better. Scientific fact."

He shook his head and mumbled, "Get out of my station."

I smiled and reached for the door.

"And for everybody's sake, try to get those people to the mainland."

* * *

I wandered my way back through town looking for my mother and trying to figure out how I was going to get over to the island while trying even harder not to think about how I felt after seeing Grady. I mean, I was really happy that he was going to try to make it over, but there had been all that other stuff he had said, like . . .

I can't wait anymore.

Still, he was going to check on me. That was the important thing.

A few people bustled around main street, but the weather was making it pretty unpleasant to be outside. The twins were leaving their boat with Alma. I could probably go back and ask her if I could borrow it, but then I would definitely have to stay for tea, most likely a game of euchre with her husband and his brother who always licked his thumb before he dealt the cards. At least he used to do that when I was a kid visiting with the twins. That kind of memory doesn't leave a person. And the card game would probably then turn into a dinner invitation, and if I told them I couldn't do any of that because of the weather, they'd want me to stay the night. Probably invite the guests too. And that was just all too . . . no. I knew I could call Red again—and I would if I had to— but it felt like too much of an imposition. Freddie couldn't help out either. His last boat, *Lightning,* was in the shop after some local kids had taken it for a joyride, and his spare wasn't in the water yet. Besides, who knew how many more personal trainers he was interviewing today?

I needed to do something though. I had to get all those people off the island. Soon. They needed to hit the road. I doubted the family could get a flight out today, if they were flying, but they would have a better chance of finding a place to stay near the city than they would in Otter Lake.

This was ridiculous. I flipped up my collar and buried my chin into my chest. Imposition or not, I needed to call Red. Maybe he knew where my mother was and—

Suddenly a hand landed on my shoulder. "Erica?"

I had my nose buried so deeply into my chest I hadn't realized I was about to walk into someone.

"Matthew?"

Chapter Seven

"Hi," he said, taking back his hand. "Sorry. I didn't mean to startle you."

Matthew Masterson.

Of course, I'd run into him. I mean, why not? I'd nearly run the gamut of emotions today. The only one missing was guilty lust. Thanks, universe!

Matthew was the only son of the oldest family on Otter Lake, owners of the beautiful Hemlock Estate. Matthew and I had gone to school together before his parents sent him off to a private men's college. We had reconnected, so to speak, on his last visit home. His father had been murdered, and Kit Kat had been accused of the crime. In solving the case, Freddie and I had nearly gotten his mother killed, but we had also kind of saved her at the last minute and exposed the real killer, so . . . so nothing, we didn't know what we were doing. But Matthew was kind enough to forgive us anyway.

"You okay?"

"Fine. I just wasn't watching where I was going." I caught a smile spreading its way across my face—a smile that I quickly put a stop to. I mean, I was really happy to see Matthew, and that was just . . . bad. You see, last time I was home, Matthew had kind of let me know that if Grady and I didn't work out, he would be interested in us getting to know each other better—which was really kind of annoying because if I were to be super honest, a part of me wanted to get to know Matthew better too—in a purely hypothetical fantasy type of way. Not, you know, in a real-life Grady way. And to be super, super honest, I was also kind of irrationally mad at Matthew because he was probably hoping that Grady and I *would* break up and, of course, I didn't want Grady and I to break up, *but* I also probably kind of liked it, just a little bit, that Matthew felt that way . . . and really, these were all ridiculously complicated feelings to be having when I just needed to find a damn boat!

"Are you sure you're okay?"

"Fine. Fine," I muttered, trying not to look into his aggravatingly electric green eyes. Why did I have to do all my thinking on my face?

"I heard you and Grady broke up. I'm sorry."

"We didn't break up," I scoffed. "Who told you that?"

"Grady."

"Oh. Right."

"You look cold. Do you want to go get a hot chocolate or something?" He jerked a thumb behind him. "I was just going to—"

"Are you kidding me? I can't do that!"

Matthew's eyes widened. "No, no, I didn't mean for it to be anything other than hot chocolate," he said quickly. "But I can see how maybe it's too soon for . . . uh . . . hot chocolate."

"No, I'm sorry," I said, shaking my head. "I'm just . . . I don't know what I am."

A small smile touched Matthew's lips. "It's okay. I get it." One of the things I liked best about Matthew was that he was smart. He knew exactly what I was thinking and going through. We had talked about his first love last time he was in town. He seemed to be of the belief that relationships that were always having problems were problematic relationships. I tried to explain to him that Grady and I weren't like that, but I don't think he believed me. "Things are still complicated."

I squeezed my eyes shut and said, "What do you say we talk about you?"

"Okay."

"How is it going?" I asked. "Are you living here full time? You said you had plans to fix up the estate? How's your mother?"

"Um, it's going pretty well," he said raising a finger. "I spend about sixty percent of my time here." He raised another. "The renovations are going well. I'm in town actually to pick up a permit." Another finger. "And my mother is doing well too, all things considered." He looked at his hand. "Did I get them all?"

I smiled. "I think so." A moment later I added, "I'm sorry I'm acting so crazy. It's been an interesting day."

He nodded.

We stood there in silence another moment before I suddenly surprised myself by asking, "While I'm at it, though, can I ask you one more question?"

"Go for it."

"Are you happy here?"

He crinkled his eyebrows together. "What do you mean?"

"I mean, I know it's only been a couple of months, but you've been living in New York," I said, pointing in what I hoped was the direction of New York. "Coming back to Otter Lake is a big change of pace."

He scratched absently at his temple. "I still love New York, but the longer I'm back here—without all the problems that came with living with my parents—the more I'm kind of liking it."

I made a noncommittal noise.

"This lake has a way of sinking its hooks in you. The clean air. The natural beauty. The people. Especially the people."

"Freddie thinks Otter Lake is a black hole." I waved some half-hearted warning hands in the air. "That nobody can escape its clutches."

Matthew chuckled. "He may be onto something. I don't know what I expected would happen when I started renovating the estate. I thought maybe I would just use it as a summer home. Maybe even sell it. But then I go to one historical society meeting, and all of the sudden I'm hosting all these events, and—"

"Events?" I asked screwing up my face.

"Yeah, like maybe a picnic on the lawn in the summer, and a big Christmas party next year. I blame Mrs. Watson and her homemade fruit cordials." Suddenly Matthew was studying my face. "What happened? What did I say?"

I sighed. "Nothing. It's just Christmas."

"Isn't Christmastime supposed to be a happy time of year?"

"It was . . . is! I mean, it is."

"Oh," Matthew said with a nod. "That's right. Grady went to visit you in Chicago this past Christmas, didn't he?"

"How did you even know—" I shook my head. "This freaking town."

He smiled. "Sorry."

I tried to say *it's okay*, but it came out all garbled, so I just waved my hand.

"So, I take it you're asking me these questions because you can't decide whether or not to make the big move?"

"I want to move home," I said, subtly trying to wipe my nose with my gloved hand. It was really cold. "At least I think I do, but everything always seems so crazy here."

"Otter Lake is a special kind of place," he said, looking around the street. "I think you kind of just have to roll with it."

"So you're telling me you weren't even the slightest bit scared moving back home, knowing full well everything that comes with Otter Lake?"

"Well," he said with a faraway expression, "the town is a lot quieter when you're not around." He peeked down at my face and smiled. "I'm kidding. Kind of." He then shoved his hands deep in his pockets and rocked on his heels. "But seriously? No, not really."

I sighed.

"That being said, I think I've felt what you're describing before though."

"You have?"

"Well, when I fell in love for the first time." He tilted his head side to side as though considering his answer. "And the second."

"Really? Love?" I rolled my eyes. "You just *had* to go there didn't you?"

He chuckled. "At some point, you just have to have a little faith."

"In love?" I asked dryly.

"No," he said, smile widening. "In the belief that you can handle it if the love thing doesn't work out."

My jaw dropped. "You . . . that sounded a lot like . . . have you been talking to Rhonda?"

His features froze, and I could have sworn his cheeks flushed.

"You have!" I shouted, pointing at his chest.

"We go out for beers every now and then," he said

with a nod. "But it's not like we talk about you and Grady all the time. She's actually trying to set me up with her cousin." He closed his eyes and shook his head. "It's a long story."

I felt my eyes widen then whip back around in the direction of the sheriff's department. "I'm going to kill this freaking cousin of hers," I muttered under my breath.

"What was that?"

"Nothing," I said, turning my face back around with the most pleasantly neutral expression I could muster. "I didn't know Rhonda had a cousin."

"Yes, yes, she does."

"So are you going?" I wasn't sure if I was asking because I didn't want this so-called cousin of Rhonda's cozying up to Grady . . . or, and much worse, I didn't want her cozying up to Matthew—because even though I wasn't about to claim him as my toy, I didn't want others playing with him either. And that would just make me selfish.

"I don't know," he said slowly, capturing my eye with his. "Maybe? Rhonda's giving me the hard sell, and it's not like I'm doing so well getting dates on my own."

Suddenly I realized that we were holding eye contact way too long. And the way he was looking at me . . . well, I was finding it hard to breathe.

"But the point is, as crazy as this town can be, people do care," he said looking away, which was good, because my lungs started working again. I had been getting dizzy there for a moment.

"So, you headed back to the retreat? The weather's getting pretty nasty. Do you need a ride?"

"I don't want to put you out," I said, mentally running through my options again, "but I kind of do."

"It's no problem. Really." He took a step. "We just

have to stop at the Dawg and pick up the hot chocolate I ordered." He froze and shot me a pretty flirty look. "None for you though. I know how you feel about hot chocolate."

"That it's warm and delicious?" I asked with a hard swallow.

He smiled just as he moved to jog across the street. "Feelings we definitely don't want you associating with me."

Too late.

The boat ride across the lake with Matthew had been just a wee bit menacing. The water wasn't too rough yet, but the clouds, with all their churning and building, well, they were carrying a pretty heavy message of doom. There also wasn't any rain or snow yet, but you could tell the wind was driving something in. I considered it a personal victory that I only thought about wrapping my arms around Matthew's torso for warmth one time as he steered the boat.

Stupid Grady.

I wouldn't have even thought it the one time if he would stop dumping me already. Probably. I was only human.

As we approached the island, I noticed another boat tied to the dock.

"I thought the retreat was closed?" Matthew shouted over the wind.

"So did I," I said, quickly realizing he couldn't hear me. I raised my voice a notch. "Apparently the lodge is now the location for a reality TV show."

Matthew shot me a look.

"Oh yeah. New series. *Rich Bitches.* I'm getting a sneak peek." Huh, that sounded weird. I was getting a sneak peek into the *real* life that I was experiencing right now. Then again it would probably look entirely different on TV.

Matthew cut the engine, almost at the dock, the water pushing the boat forward the last couple feet. "I take it you didn't know about this."

I smiled, popped two little fists in the air and cheered, "Surprise!"

He huffed a laugh. "Wow, being home for you is a little crazy, isn't it?" he asked gripping the wheel as the water slapped roughly against the side of the boat. "Do you want me to come in?"

"It's fine," I said. "You have done more than enough. Thank you." I stepped onto the dock being careful not to lose my footing on the slippery planks.

"You sure?"

"I'm sure."

"Okay," he said, starting up the engine again. "But just remember if things start to get hairy, an alliance is the only thing that can save you."

I raised my eyebrows.

"What? I like TV," he shouted, putting the boat in reverse. "I can't just draw buildings all day."

I waved as Matthew pulled away, then turned my attention to the boat tied off on the other side of our dock. It had the Otter Lake Marina logo—a waving beaver—airbrushed on the side. Yes, *Otter* Lake's mascot was a *beaver* named Betsy. Oh, how people could laugh and laugh about that. Not me though. Betsy and I had gone way back. She was dead now. Not because of me, of course. Despite what some people may think. It was a long story.

The family's so-called patriarch must have rented the boat from Ken. He owned the marina and had a couple of nice loaners. This one was a decent-sized cruiser. Solid looking. Nice and roomy. Could fit a lot of passengers.

And that was the first bit of good news all day . . .

. . . because it was time to get these people off my island.

Chapter Eight

"Disappointment! Disappointment! Disappointment!"

I froze two steps through the door of the lodge. I was just about to announce that the island needed to be evacuated due to the storm, but the *disappointment* in the air kind of threw me. It had come from an older gentleman with angry eyes at the head of the harvest table, his family sitting all round. I couldn't really focus on any of them, though, because right in front of me was a man in a black business suit. A very, very big man.

"I'm going to need to pat you down."

My eyes trailed from the man's torso, up, up, up to an intimidating face. He had pale blue eyes, a military-style haircut, and a jagged, crescent-shaped scar that ran down from the side of his forehead to his jaw. Overall his look could probably best be described as . . . scary Bond villain, maybe? I almost told him he could be an actor, but, then, you know, didn't.

"Spread your feet. Hold out your arms."

I took a step back, struggling to find just the right thing to say, but all that came out of my mouth was "No." I also tagged on a slow finger point.

"Then you will have to wait outside."

"Um, no?"

"Leave her," the man shouted from the head of the table. "She's not important. Watch the family."

The bodyguard didn't move. Just held me in his gaze. I peeked up at him from under my eyebrows, throwing him a weak smile. After a pretty uncomfortable moment, he stepped to the side.

I kept my eye on him as I side-shuffled my way over to the producer, Julie, seated on one of the sofas that had been pushed against the wall to accommodate the new placement of the table. She had her hands pyramided at her mouth, eyes intent on the action. Kenny, her cameraman was gliding around the room with a seamless grace that I guess came with the job.

As I got closer, Julie patted the cushion beside her, and I sat down even though there really wasn't time to get comfortable. I needed to announce we were all leaving. Unfortunately, the man at the head of the table was still shouting—he had moved on to lecturing the group about the importance of legacy or some such thing—and I couldn't quite figure out how to interrupt. I whispered to Julie, "I take it my mother hasn't shown up?"

She shook her head no.

I sighed. Where was she? This was getting ridiculous. "So, what exactly is going on here?"

"I thought you didn't care?" she replied, raising a self-satisfied eyebrow. I guess I could I throw a pretty loud disappointed look too, because she added in a hurried whisper, "Well, you missed the beginning, but that's Rayner Boatright. He—"

"You made that name up," I said.

Julie placed her hand on her heart. "Swear to God, I didn't." She smiled, then said, "Rayner is the one who gathered the family here today. He just sat down." She squeezed her shoulders together in excitement. "Things are getting real."

I shook my head. Okay, well, that explanation told me nothing. But it didn't matter. Forget finding the right moment. I needed to nip this thing in the bud. "I hate to break it to you, Julie, but whatever this is," I said, gesturing at the table, "it's going to have to move to another location. I was just at the sheriff's department, and there's a storm on the way. We need to evacuate." I planted my hands on my knees to push myself back up again.

"What!" Julie hissed, grabbing my arm, yanking me back down. "No. No way. Not now. He's just about to tell them that—" She snapped her mouth shut. "I don't want to ruin it."

"Okay," I said, looking at the hand gripping my arm. "You're going to need to not do that."

Julie smiled. "You've got a temper. I like that." Then the smile disappeared. "But you need to sit down now and be quiet. I moved mountains to make this happen. Getting Rayner on board? That was not easy. He only agreed to do the show because—" She stopped again, pinching her lips together.

"Let me guess. You don't want to ruin it."

"Exactly. Now buckle up, Hillbilly Girl. This is a'happening."

I blinked a few times while mentally reciting, *Don't slap the producer, Erica. Slapping is assault. Slappers go to jail.* A moment later, I took a breath and said, "I'm not sure if you are aware, but there is a superstorm coming." I gestured to the window. "Do you really want to be trapped here all night with these people?" I was thinking in particular of the hyena vest girl. Ashley, I think it was. She kind of had the look of one of those creepy horror movie dolls that comes alive at night and stabs you while you're sleeping.

Julie's eyes darted side to side. "Oh my God, that's even better. Nobody's going to make it out alive!"

"What?"

She patted my leg. "That's how we'll sell it." She held her hands out like she was envisioning a far-off marquee sign. "We're trapped. In the storm of the century. It's terrifying. I couldn't script that."

"Okay, I think you might be missing the point here. I get that this is all building up to some kind of family drama, but—"

"Oh, this is much more than just your average family drama. Do you think Third Act would send me out here for just anybody?" Julie's eyes darted around my face like she thought I might be crazy. I wasn't offended this time. I felt kind of crazy. "Rayner is worth over five hundred million dollars. And that's just what's in his bank account."

I felt my eyebrows shoot up as my jaw dropped. "Five hundred million dollars?" I shot a look back over to the guy still yelling at the head of the table. "Wait, is that in real-life money or in reality-TV money?"

"Sometimes they are the same thing."

Five hundred million? I couldn't quite conceive of that much money. I had barely wrapped my head around the fact that my mother had inherited a couple million back in the day. She had bought the island, then donated the rest to some charity. I was probably better off not knowing which one. For all I knew, it could have been, *Save the Beavers!* Not that beavers shouldn't be saved from whatever it was threatening them. It was just—I cut the thought off by pressing some fingers into my forehead. "Why? Why is this my life," I muttered to no one in particular.

"Thank you! Finally you understand," Julie hissed. "Now hush."

I blinked a few times, trying to figure out what had just happened, but was soon distracted by the older man at the table snapping his fingers. I watched the behemoth of a bodyguard produce a case from behind a chair. He opened it on the table, pulled out a glass, and then a bottle of what I assumed was Scotch, and poured the man a pretty sturdy helping. I guess you can afford on-the-go booze service when you're that rich.

Once the glass had been poured, Rayner picked it up and gave it a good swirl. "All right, now," he said, taking a big gulp, "you all want to know why you're here? I'll tell you."

"Finally," Ronnie, the head MILF said, before she jolted up and added, "I mean, tell us, baby. Please." She placed a hand on Rayner's arm but turned her head to the camera, pouching out her swollen lips.

Julie's face twisted into something pretty vicious as she swirled her finger in the air. Ronnie's head whipped back around. "How many times do I have to tell her not to look at the camera?" she muttered.

Rayner glanced down at Ronnie's hand placed on his arm then up to her face. This time he jumped. "Who the hell are you?"

"Ha. Ha. Rayner," she said, adjusting the neckline of her white catsuit around her boobs.

"Ronnie? Good God woman. What the hell happened to your face? You pick a fight with some bees?"

She rolled her eyes and reached for the bottle of Scotch. He yanked it away, shooting her an unpleasant look.

"They're married," Julie whispered in my ear, "if you couldn't tell. She's his second wife. They hate each other. But they're both pre-nupped into submission."

"Of course they are," I said dropping my hands between my knees.

"He may not like her plastic surgery, but it's gold for us. Viewers love it. I mean, once you start looking at her face, you just can't look away. She's like the child of the swamp thing and Pamela Anderson. Hot and scary."

Suddenly I was feeling a little bad about thinking she was a hot fish earlier. I mean, it was one thing to think it, but hearing it out loud made it sound kind of mean.

Julie rolled a hand in the air, which Rayner seemed to take note of.

"Okay, let's get to it," he said, banging the table.

The twitchy young man with the highlighted hair at Rayner's side skidded back in his chair.

We all stared at him. His eyes moved side to side for an uncomfortable moment before he scooted himself back up to the table.

"Boy," the old man said, the side of his nose lifted in disgust, "we need to get you fixed."

I kept my eyes on the group, but asked Julie out the corner of my mouth, "What's with that guy? Why is he so jumpy?"

"That's Brody. Rayner's grandson. He's messed up. It's a long and twisted story," Julie whispered quickly. "But also kind of funny. I'll tell you later if there's time."

I buried my face in my hands. There wasn't enough time in the world for me to want to listen to any more of this. I really needed to—

"Just tell us what's wrong, Daddy."

Ew. I peeked up from my fingers. Hyena girl. There was something just a little bit creepy about a grown woman using the word, Daddy. Apparently Rayner thought so too because he shot a look at Ronnie.

"I'm sorry," she said. "What do you want me to do? You're the only father she's ever known. I think it's sweet."

He grabbed his glass and took another sip of Scotch

as though to wash away the bad taste in his mouth. "We've been married a year. Granted it's been the longest year of my life. But just a year. I'm not her d—"

"Whatever. Can we talk about this later?" Ashley whined. "I really need to go, you guys. I have my convention in Atlanta."

Rayner gave a fullbody shudder as the girl went on talking.

"Mom says they want to promote my Hunting with Jesus clothing line. Brody, you can come with if you want." She pinched her lips and looked over at him, but he didn't look back. I think his terror of unseen things had him frozen.

"She's talking about this televangelist super church thing she's been invited to," Julie said quietly, leaning once again toward me. "She's trying to add religion to her persona. And I know, I know. You're thinking, do televangelists even exist anymore? Didn't they die out like vampires when their maker Tammy Faye passed? But you'd be surprised. They still pull in big cash."

I pressed my fingers into my temples. This must be what an aneurysm feels like. "You . . . you talk fast."

"It's the job. Got to size up people like that," she snapped her fingers in my face.

"Okay, but—"

Julie suddenly grabbed my arm again as Rayner cleared his throat. I guess the real show was about to begin.

"So," he said furrowing his eyebrows together into something so bushy, it almost looked alive and . . . mean. "Let me start by saying, this family hasn't had an easy run." He looked around the table making eye contact with each person. It was then I realized, the lawyer, Chuck, was sitting by himself in a chair by the fire . . . nibbling his lip . . . nervously.

"I know you all have your reasons for hating me."

Ronnie yelled something in protest, but I couldn't focus on what she was saying because I was too busy staring at the light fixture hanging above the table. It had flickered a little. Shoot. I knew I should have checked to make sure the generator was on standby.

"Oh, save it!" Rayner shouted. "I don't want to hear it. Truth is, I have my reasons for hating all of you too. That's just how it goes sometimes with family. But I never thought . . ." He shook his head. "Now's the time we put everything on the table."

"That's right. Let's get it *all* on the table," Julie whispered more to herself than me.

Oh no, I thought. *Here we go.* I had seen enough of this type of show to know what was going to happen next. This was going to be a rehashing of every bit of family drama that had ever happened. They would scream and argue and probably throw some drinks. And it would all be about ridiculous stuff, like *The color of the car you bought hurt my feelings!* Or *There were three pictures of so and so on the mantel and only one picture of me!* And they would probably take about five hours of footage, just to get twenty minutes of the real juicy stuff, and . . . and I couldn't take it anymore. There was a Nor'easter coming.

"Truth is," Rayner began.

I jumped to my feet. "I'm sorry but—"

"One of you is trying to kill me, and nobody is leaving here until I find out who."

Chapter Nine

"Booyah," Julie whispered as I dropped back down onto the couch.

"Rayner," Ronnie said. "You can't be serious. You know that—"

Suddenly she stopped talking.

In fact, they had all stopped talking.

It was probably because someone was laughing.

Huh. Would you look at that? It was me.

"I don't see the humor in this situation, young lady." Rayner said, staring me down from his place at the head of my mother's table.

"You're right. I'm sorry," I said, nodding. "Really. It's just that I thought . . ." I shook my head holding back more laughter. "But now I realize . . ." I swallowed hard and held up a hand. "You're right, this is very serious."

His eyes widened.

"Deadly serious." I pushed myself up to my feet and waved my hands in the air. I couldn't believe I had been so gullible. Happy, happy relief rushed over me. I mean, it had been staring me in the face! The timing? My mother going missing? *Rich Bitches?* I continued my list out loud. "Five hundred million dollars? A storm? A murderer?" I said, making my voice all scary. I suddenly turned to Julie. "Okay, you can tell me the truth now. Freddie put you up to this, didn't he?"

"Freddie?" she asked, voice still in a whisper. "Who's Freddie?"

"Oh, you're good," I said with a point. "So what? This is some kind of practical joke show?"

"What? Where?" The young twitchy man shouted.

I gave him a careful look before turning back to Julie. "Or . . . oh my God! Don't tell me Freddie set this whole thing up just to get me to solve a crime?"

She threw me a squinted sideways look.

"Boost up my detective self-esteem," I said, shimmying my shoulders side to side, "so I'd get on board?"

She deepened her squint.

"Julie," Rayner snapped looking to the producer. She jumped to her feet, holding up some placating hands. "This is not what you promised me. Who is this chirpy squirrel?"

"Chirpy squirrel!" I shouted with a laugh. "Fantastic. I love it."

Chuck, the lawyer, cleared his throat and said, "Her name is . . ." He shuffled wildly through his sheets of paper before thrusting one into the air. "Erica Bloom! She is the daughter of the proprietor of this lodge."

"Well, tell her to put a sock in it already. This is family business," he grumbled before adding, "and she's stealing my moment."

"Hilarious," I said, noticing Kenny had turned the camera on me. I ducked, before I realized there was no getting away. "You guys are fabulous actors. Really."

Rayner snapped his fingers at the bodyguard. "I was wrong. Pat her down."

I smiled and raised my hands in the air as the guard slash actor made his way back over to me. Might as well be a good sport. I couldn't help it. I was happy. One, I had figured out what all this was, so I wouldn't look like an idiot on TV—if it really was a show, and not just all Freddie's idea to get me to sign onto Otter Lake Security. My mother would have been completely on board if it meant pushing me in the direction of moving home. Two, because this was all a hoax, I also knew it wouldn't go on all night—which meant there was still a chance I could salvage my evening with Grady. Although I was kind of ticked at Freddie. He knew I had a bad history with practical jokes—"Hey," I snapped, yanked from my thoughts. "Getting a little handsy down there."

"She's clean," the bodyguard said in a voice so deep I could have sworn the floorboards quivered.

"Julie," Ronnie said, trying, I think, to look shocked, but failing horribly given the forehead paralysis from all the Botox. "Is she telling the truth? Are you doing another show?"

"No!"

"Young lady," Rayner said, turning his angry eyebrows on me, "given the amount of money I've paid to rent out this place, do you think you could sit down now and control yourself?"

"Oh sure," I said with a big wink. "Let's do this thing. I bet I can find the would-be murderer before you can."

I was really proud of myself.

Julie grabbed my arm and pulled me toward the sofa, whispering, "What are you doing?"

"Come on, you can tell me the truth now. It's okay."

"What truth? What are you talking about?"

"Oh, you really are good," I shot her a thumbs up. I meant it too. "Way to hold character."

"Now, where was I . . . ?" Rayner said looking around the table.

"You were . . ." Ronnie shot me a comically concerned look before finishing. "You were saying that one of us was trying to kill you, baby? But you can't mean that. Ashley and I are your family."

"You are not our family!" Rayner's grandson, Brody, suddenly shouted.

"Not family! I have done more to your grandfather—I mean for, *for* your grandfather, than you could ever imagine. I am part of this family," she said, cringing a little. "I've earned it."

I snorted a laugh and shot a smile at Julie.

She was still holding character.

"Rayner, darling, you're just confused—"

"I'm not confused!" He pounded the table again.

"Okay," she said with a sigh. "Let's say you're right. Someone's trying to kill you. How exactly do you propose we find out who?"

"One of you is going to confess."

The group exchanged unsure glances. A moment later, Ronnie said, "This is crazy. Crazy." She flashed a look at the camera that really drove her feelings about the craziness home. I heard Julie sigh.

"Well," Ashley said getting to her feet. "I'm not staying, you guys. I need to get to Atlanta. Besides, I have nothing to confess."

"Me neither," Ronnie said. She then got up and pointed at me. "Fire up that boat, squirrel. We're leaving."

I planted my hands on the sofa, to push myself to my feet. I mean, if they wanted to cut this thing short, that was fine by me.

"Sit down all of you," Rayner said.

I dropped back down.

"You will do as I say."

"Or what?" Ronnie snapped.

Rayner looked to the security guard and said, "Bring him in."

He nodded and headed for the front door.

"Where's he going?" Ronnie asked.

I whirled my head around. This was quite the production.

Julie snapped again at Kenny and shooed him and his camera over to the door.

"Mom?" Ashley asked.

Ronnie shook her head. "Rayner, what's going on? Who's outside? We're all h—No!" she gasped. "Please tell me *he*'s not coming."

"Who?" Ashley asked. "Mom, who?"

"You know who."

"I . . . don't know who," I said to nobody in particular. But nobody answered.

"Julie, did you know about this?" Ronnie asked.

The producer pinched her lips together.

"You did!" Ronnie threw her head back against the chair. "Oh my God! I can't believe this! What else haven't you told us?"

"He's a freaking monster," Brody murmured, before jerking to look behind his chair at the nothing that had been bothering him earlier.

Just then the lights flickered again and the front door swung open.

Everyone jumped as our heads flew around to see a silhouette illuminated in the threshold.

"Hello?"

Then the lights snapped out.

Chapter Ten

Angry shouts and yells exploded in the near dark.

Okay, suddenly this wasn't so amusing anymore. This whole scenario might be a hoax, but the storm outside wasn't.

"Everybody relax," I yelled, getting to my feet. "If the power doesn't come back on, the generator will kick in."

Hopefully.

Everyone quieted down. Thankfully, the sun hadn't completely set, so we had a little light. Good thing too. The dark is a completely different animal when you're away from the city, especially during a storm. Thankfully the lodge was well stocked with flashlights, lanterns, and candles—I just needed to get to them without smacking a shin. Really, who told these people they could move the furniture all around? Just as I moved to get one of the lanterns, the lights snapped back on, and I turned to the door to see who had everyone so freaked out.

"Seriously?"

Again, nobody answered me.

"You have got to be kidding me," I mumbled, hurrying to the door. "Come in. How long have you been out

there? You look like you're freezing to death." I ushered
the teenage boy inside. The security guard followed in
behind. The kid was maybe fourteen, fifteen. He was
wearing an oversized navy blue hoodie and a knit hat,
pulled down over his black hair, a flop of bangs sticking
out from underneath the brim. He also had really pale
skin, big nervous-looking eyes, and braces that glinted
in the light.

"Kyle, my boy!" a voice shouted from behind me.
Rayner had his arms flung wide in welcome. "Come here!
Come here!"

"Gross," Ronnie said, rolling her eyes. "He's going to
touch *it*."

The boy made his way over to the head of the table,
while I shot a look out the window toward the lake. I
couldn't see Red's boat, but he must have dropped him
off. When I turned back around, Rayner had the boy
locked in a very awkward hug.

Okay, I couldn't do this anymore. Having a minor on
the premises changed everything. I was too tired from
traveling and too hungry from, well, not eating, to deal
with any of this anymore.

The lights flickered again.

My cue.

"Everyone," I called out. "Everyone?"

Nothing. The group had gone back to complaining
among themselves.

"Everybody, listen to me right now!"

That got their attention.

"Obviously you all have your reasons for wanting to
do whatever this is," I said, smoothing my hair back. "But
we have a real-life situation on our hands. So, I'm going
to go outside now to check on the back-up generator
because unlike the rest of you, I am staying the night, and
I need electricity." I grabbed a small flashlight from the

basket on the top shelf in the hall closet. It was getting pretty gloomy outside. "I suggest you all use this opportunity to collect your things. It's time to go."

A moment later I was standing on my porch letting the cold wind whip my too warm cheeks.

It was a good, good feeling.

Cold. Sharp. Real.

I took a long deep breath then pulled out my phone and texted Freddie.

Tell me right now if you signed me up for a prank TV show. If you tell me the truth, I won't kill you.

I waited a moment for the reply.

Um . . . are you having a stroke? Should I have someone come get you?

Well, I guess that answered that question. Fabulous. In my attempts not to look like an idiot on TV, I had pretty much guaranteed I'd look like an idiot on TV. At least I hadn't signed a contract. Then again, knowing my mother, she'd probably already done it for me. Where was she? I sighed and shoved my phone back into my pocket.

Okay. Time to change tactics. Worrying and getting angry would not help me here. And really this was just a part of being home. It was like that serenity prayer my mother was always quoting. The one where you're supposed to let go of the things you can't control. I could not control the fact that the lodge was full of crazy people. I could not control the fact that it was looking less and less likely that I would be seeing Grady any time soon. I certainly couldn't control the weath—a blast of icy rain hit my face, cutting me off from my thoughts. It might have even been wet snow.

"Yeah, I get it," I muttered, wiping the moisture from my cheeks.

No, I couldn't control any of those things. But what

I could do was ensure that I had electricity for when all of this was over. Then I would get these people on the boat, take them to the mainland, and get back here before the storm really picked up. My mother was sure to be home by then. After that I would make myself a steak—two steaks! Grady would understand if I ate his—and bring my blood sugar up to a less murderous level.

I walked the porch all the way around to the back of the lodge, clutching myself against the wind. For those who have never had one, generators are a pain in the butt although kind of essential when you're living on an island. Thankfully, my mother had invested in an expensive propane model—she had to for insurance purposes—that could keep the retreat in power for days if need be. She was pretty good at making sure the propane tanks were filled. Believe me, it's not the kind of mistake you make twice. You also make sure the generator is on standby mode when you're in the middle of a storm. Red was right. The underwater power cables could go at any time in a storm like this.

I eased my way down the slick back steps. I could already see through the slats of the cooling vents that the power was on. That was good. I lifted the lid of the enclosure. Now I just needed to check the—

I froze.

No.

I stepped closer.

No. That couldn't be right!

I stared down at the tiny little computerized screen that was supposed to say *Ready to Power*, but instead blinked—

Error.

The wind gusted, sending my hair flying around my face.

I pulled my hat out of my pocket and shoved it over

my head. Okay, I just needed to stay calm here. I had obviously read it wrong. My eyes *were* a little watery. I blinked them a few times, then looked back down.

Frick!

I tapped the screen with my finger and waited a moment.

Nope, tapping didn't help.

I angrily hopped up and down on the spot a few times . . . but that didn't seem to help either.

I mean, I knew how to fix our old portable gas generator . . . but this thing . . . this thing was complicated. And it had lots of tubes . . . and shiny bits . . . and wires. But none of that should have mattered because the machine was supposed to be completely reliable.

I took another breath. It was time to handle this the way I would any other malfunctioning piece of computerized equipment.

I would turn it off. Wait a moment. Then turn it back on.

I reached out to flip the power switch when the wind gusted again, freezing my hand mid-air.

Come on . . .

I took a long breath in through my nose. I didn't smell it before, what with the wind, but that last gust had sent an unmistakable stench right up into my face.

Rotten eggs.

Propane.

Chapter Eleven

I whipped my flashlight out and darted it around the inside of the generator. I couldn't see anything, but . . .

I leaned down, edging my head closer inside.

I could definitely hear something.

Hissing.

No. No. NO!

I clicked on my flashlight and aimed the beam of my torch on the spot where I thought I heard the leak. Given that it was probably a valve, I didn't really expect to see anything.

Except I did.

My light caught a good-size nick in a thick piece of tubing.

I took a step back from the generator and raised my flashlight in a defensive position as though it might attack. Then I realized that probably wouldn't help me if the sucker blew up. I turned my body sideways and reached one finger out to quickly flip the power switch. Then I reached in even farther to turn the little knob that I thought led to the propane tank.

I then jumped back again, and threw my hands into the air.

I waited a moment, fully expecting to be blown apart, but when that didn't happen, I stepped forward and cocked my head, bringing my ear slowly back toward the generator.

No hissing.

I let go of the breath I hadn't realized I had been holding and slapped my hands down my body a few times. Not exactly sure why I did that. They weren't dirty. But that had somehow felt like a dirty job.

I stood in front of the machine a few seconds, doing nothing, but blinking.

Way down deep in my conscious, there was something stirring, something a little like panic, but I was putting a lot of effort into ignoring that something, because I really didn't like what it was trying to say.

Eventually, I gave into it a little bit and flicked my beam back on the tubing where I had seen the nick.

Now, how the heck had that happened?

I mean, I obviously didn't know a lot about these machines, but it almost looked like . . .

A deliberate cut.

No, I thought, stepping away. Why would someone vandalize my mother's generator? Nobody hated my mother. She was a beloved oddity in this town . . .

. . . but maybe she wasn't the target.

I wiped some more wet snow from my face.

Watch your back, Boobsie.

No . . . couldn't be.

Jake? No.

I had known him my entire life.

Like I had known his cousin. The murderer.

I gave my head a shake. This was crazy. Maybe I had

inhaled too much propane. But suddenly I was feeling very unsure about everything. My eyes flicked back to the retreat. No. No way. Unh-uh. This was . . . it was just the storm getting to me. Everything was fine. I was just stressed and tired . . . and getting really, really hungry.

Still . . .

All the more reason for us to get out of here.

The wind gusted again, strong enough to nearly make me lose my footing on the slippery ground.

Well, no sense staying out here staring at a broken generator. I turned slowly away from the machine back toward the lodge, every muscle in my back tight. I rolled my shoulders a few times and took a careful step onto the slick stairs of the back porch.

Bad tubing. That's all.

Maybe I could duct tape it? Didn't duct tape fix everything?

No. Better not. It was fine. The lodge had the fireplace and lots of lanterns. I'd be fine.

I shuffled back around to the front door. I mean, I would for sure get Grady to have a look at it the next time he was over—if he ever came over again—but in the meantime, I needed to focus on the real threat. The sun was going down fast, and the last bit of daylight was almost gone. If we were going to leave, it had to be now.

Hopefully, that little power-outage scare and my yelling had been enough to motivate the group to get ready. Julie wouldn't be able to film in the dark anyway. I reached for the door. If they still didn't want to leave, maybe I could scare them with the whole propane-leak thing. I mean, I didn't think it was a danger now, but they didn't need to know that. Whatever it would take. Playtime was over. We needed to go before something really went wrong.

I stepped inside, pulled off my hat and gave it a shake.

"So is—" I cut myself off before I even knew the reason why.

It was quiet.

This was not a quiet group.

I looked around, trying to meet someone's gaze, but they were all on their feet staring at the harvest table.

I took a few careful steps toward them. All my senses on alert. "What's going on?"

Julie looked at me, face sick.

"He's dead. Rayner's dead."

Chapter Twelve

Julie stepped aside, just far enough for me to see Rayner collapsed over the table. Chuck stood over him, hand at his neck.

"Are you sure?" Ronnie asked.

"I think so. There's no pulse," the lawyer said, snatching his fingers away. "And I took this course one time, and they said if there's no pulse it means, you know, he's probably dead."

"No way," Brody said, stepping back, pulling a chair in front of him. "No way, man. This has gotta be some kind of . . . Wait! She did it! For the show!"

All eyes snapped to Julie who was shaking her head so quickly it almost looked like a shudder. "It's not. It wasn't. I swear."

"Then he's faking," Brody yelled, looking back to the man slumped over the table. "To make us talk." Suddenly, he leaned around the chair and struck out his foot, heel connecting with his grandfather's seat.

The body tipped over ever so slowly then thumped onto the floor.

A bunch of us screamed as Ronnie jumped back into

her daughter, sending them both tumbling into a heap. Brody threw himself back against the wall, looking horrified by what he had done.

"Wait!" I yelled. "Has anyone tried CPR?"

That killed some of the noise. The question got me a lot of looks but no answers.

I pushed my way around the end of the table through the scattered chairs toward the fireplace, but Chuck side-shuffled into my path. "I'm sorry, but I can't let you do that," he said, pinning his lips together.

"Why not?"

"My uncle, I mean, client, had a Do Not Resuscitate order. Heart condition."

"But—"

"Besides," he said, tapping his wristwatch frantically, "it's been over six minutes. Brain death has already occurred. They said that too. In my course."

I looked around for confirmation. Julie was the only one to say anything. "Yeah, he's right. It's been at least six minutes."

"You're going to need to move now," I said looking back at Chuck. "I want to check for myself."

"Sure. Sure. Good idea." He skittered around me to stand back beside the wall, his hands in the air.

I kept my eye on him as I moved past. For some strange reason, I wasn't quite ready to look down yet.

Come on, Erica. You can do this.

I stopped walking after a few more steps. I had arrived at the body. Ha! *You have arrived.* Just like Freddie's GPS. Funny the things you think about when you're totally freaked o—*Focus, Erica.* I took a breath and clenched my fists. This was silly. I couldn't exactly check for a pulse without looking. Right, so, time to just woman up and do this thi—

My eyes dropped down to the body lying on the

floor, still in a seated position . . . just a tipped-over one.

Oh boy.

Despite all of my experience with murder as of late, I had never actually touched a dead body.

My eyes shot up to the ceiling. Why had I thought this was a good idea? Chuck knew what he was doing. He had taken a course. I looked around to the others. They were all looking back at me. Waiting. Okay, time was a wasting. Brain death time. I pulled my hair back and twisted it behind my neck. It was fine. All I had to do was put my fingers on his neck and—

"He's not getting any deader," Ronnie snapped.

I jolted. Right.

I quickly dropped to my knees, and I carefully put my fingers on the man's still warm neck. Nothing in that spot. I tilted my head to look at the ceiling and slid my fingers a little more toward his throat. Nope. Nothing there either. I slid them a little higher—

"What are you doing down there?" Ronnie asked.

"I just want to be sure."

But I already was.

"Is he dead or not?"

He was dead. Like really, really, dead.

I shook my head and leaned back on my heels. "Pass me that blanket," I said, pointing back at the afghan draped over the top one of the sofas. Chuck hurried to retrieve it, stumbling over the corner of the hearth. I laid it gently over Rayner's body before rising to my feet. This . . . this couldn't be happening. I brought a hand to my cheek. This night . . . these people . . . I couldn't remember the last time everything felt normal. At the sheriff's department? Talking with Matthew? This was just—

"We all need to calm down."

Who said that?

Oh. Me, again.

Good thing somebody knew what to do.

But funny thing was, I really didn't need to tell everyone to calm down because everybody was already pretty calm. Nobody was upset. Nobody was crying. Everybody was just quiet. Shock, I guess. Either that or nobody really liked Rayner. My eyes moved to the teenage boy, Kyle, standing at the end of the table. It was hard to say what he was feeling. His face was still. Good thing this family had money for therapy.

"What happened?" I asked, looking round the room again.

"He just clutched his chest," Ashley said, putting a hand to her furry vest. "He was . . . he couldn't breathe. Then he just collapsed. Oh my God, I can't believe this is happening to me."

"Okay," I said slowly, throwing her a look that was completely wasted. "Here's what's going to happen. You are all going to sit back down and—"

"By the body?" Ronnie shrieked.

"What? No! I don't know. Find another seat," I said, waving to the couch. "Or, actually, don't sit! Get your stuff. Who has the keys to the boat docked outside?"

The security guard raised his massive hand.

"Get her fired up." I gave myself a pat down trying to find my phone. "I'll call the police. Then we go."

Nobody moved.

"Do it!"

I gave my fingers a shake in the air then pulled my phone out of my jacket pocket and took a step backward toward the gloom of the kitchen. I needed privacy. It seemed rude to have the group overhear me tell the authorities how crazy I thought they all were.

I tried calling Grady first, but there was no answer, so

I tried the station next. As the phone rang, the lights flickered once again in the living room. Great. That's what this situation needed. Darkness. I blew out a shaky breath. I really should have pulled the lanterns out already.

"Come on. Come on," I muttered into the still-ringing phone.

"Otter Lake Sherriff's Dep—"

"Rhonda! Thank God!"

"Well, well, well, look's who's ready to apolog—"

"No. Rhonda, listen to me. There's no time for that. I'm at the retreat and—"

"Oh! That's right. I forgot. Erica Bloom apologizes to no man."

I hustled over to the back corner of the kitchen, where the others wouldn't be able to see me. "Rhonda, seriously. I've got a situation here. I—"

"Regular old heartbreaker, aren't you? I bet—"

"Dead body, Rhonda! Dead body at the retreat!"

A half-second of silence passed before she said, "Say what now?"

I shook my head frantically . . . at nobody. "Dead body at the retreat."

"Really?" she asked, her voice rising in pitch. "Again? Man, they don't call you Erica Doom for nothing."

I blinked. "What?"

She paused a moment. "You've never heard that before? Forget I said anything. What do we got?"

I hurriedly filled Rhonda in on Rayner's keeling over, but before I could get to any of the other details, she cut in with, "Okay, well, it sounds like a heart attack. We'll get out there as soon as we can, but I gotta be honest with you, Erica. Everybody's already out on calls. Grady's over at Honey Harbor. There's some missing kids on the water. So it may be a while before we can get anyone out to you."

"That's fine," I said quickly. "We're leaving now. I won't lock the door."

"Whoa. Whoa. Whoa."

An icy-cold sensation rushed down my body. "What? What's the problem?"

"That's not going to happen."

I knew. I already knew what she was going to say, but—

"Sorry, Doom, it's too dangerous. You're stuck on the island until the storm passes over."

Chapter Thirteen

"Rhonda, this is so not what I want to be hearing from you right now," I said giving my phone an angry stare.

"Look, I get that it's not"—she paused for a moment—"pleasant, but, come on, it's not like it's your first body. Why are you so freaked out?"

"It's just that it's been a really weird day. There was a lot of stuff that led up to the death. Like family drama stuff." I pinched my lips together and looked up at the darkened ceiling. I didn't know where to start. I peeked back into the living room, then darted right back. Yup, they were all looking at me again. I dropped my voice. "I don't even know how much of it was real. Then there's the whole thing with the generator and—"

"What thing with the generator?"

The kitchen window suddenly shook in the wind. "It's probably nothing." I launched into what I had found out back—the propane leak, the nicked tubing—and what Jake Day had said about watching my back. I then finished where I started, with, "So, I mean, like I said, it's probably nothing."

A moment of silence passed before Rhonda hissed, "Holy crap, Erica!"

"What?"

"That's really freaking creepy," she said almost in a whisper. "A dead body and a sabotaged generator! I just saw this movie last week where there was this killer who cut the power to a cabin before creeping inside with his big hunting knife and—"

"Rhonda!"

"Okay, okay, sorry. Calm down," she said almost more to herself than me. She then found her normal volume of voice and said, "You're right. It's probably nothing, *although* it does kind of seem like—"

"Still not helping."

"Right. Right. You're right," she said. "I mean, it's creepy, but probably nothing. And the old guy who died probably did just have a heart attack. Family drama is pretty upsetting. I mean it's not like there was anything else suspicious about—"

"Well . . ."

"Doom?"

"It's just that before he died, he did kind of accuse his family of trying to kill him, but—Rhonda?" I thought I heard the phone drop on the other end. "Rhonda?"

A moment later, after some fumbling noises, she said, "I'm going to need to ask you a few questions."

"No, Rhonda, listen—"

"Okay," she snapped in her most authoritative voice. "Is anybody else at the lodge currently being murdered?"

"What? No! Nobody is *currently* being murdered." I peeked back into the living room just to be sure, *and* they were all still looking at me. "No."

"Good. Good," she said. "And for the record, next time we have one of these calls, why don't you lead with the victim suspecting he's about to be murdered?!"

I gripped my forehead with my hand. "I don't know if he really thought he was going to be murdered, or if it was just like for the show."

"What show?"

Oh boy. I shook my head and told her everything I could in the shortest amount of time.

"Wow" was all she said when I was through.

"I know."

"I love *The Real MILF Diaries*. Cassandra's always throwing fits about—"

"Rhonda!" I snapped, chopping the air with my hand. "I can't . . . can we please just focus?"

"Right. Of course."

"So as I was saying, because they're all working on this new show, I don't know how much of this drama is— was—scripted." I wrapped my free arm around myself. I was suddenly feeling a little cold.

"Well, this is all very weird."

"You're telling me."

"Okay, listen to me," she said. "Let's take a breath." I had to pull the phone from my ear to protect it from the sound rushing through the other end. A moment later, she said, "We're getting carried away. I mean people don't just go around murdering each other all the time. Well, they do around you, but—"

"Rhonda," I warned again through my teeth.

"Right. As I was saying, here's what you're going to do. Stay calm. Keep everybody in the same room. And wait for help."

"Okay," I said nodding to myself. "I can do that."

"And I mean it, Erica. Don't let anyone out of your sight. Because in that movie I watched last week, the minute the group split up, that's when somebody would get their throat slit. One by one. They all—"

"Rhonda!"

"Sorry. Sorry," she said. "I'll get someone out there to you as soon as I can."

"Okay. Good," I said chewing on the side of my thumbnail. "Anything else I should do?"

"Don't touch the body."

I chuckled unpleasantly. "Yeah, I wasn't planning on it, but . . ."

"What now?"

"One of the other guests kind of *kicked* the deceased out of his chair," I said, peeking out again into the threshold. "So it might be a little late for that."

"What the hell is going on over there?"

"I don't know, okay?" I near shouted, hurrying to stand back by the fridge. "This whole night has been really strange! And these people are not normal people!"

"Okay, okay, stay calm."

"Do you think I should tell them about the generator?"

"Are you crazy? No! The people on these shows are always excitable, dramatic types. Your job is to keep them calm."

"Right."

"Besides, on the off chance there is a murderer, you don't want to let them know you're on to them, or you'll be the first to get it. Play dumb. That's how you live."

"Play dumb. Right. Got it. Thanks. That's great advice," I said, staring absently at my mother's broken cuckoo clock. "Really."

"I am a professional."

I took a heavy breath.

"It's going to be fine. Just . . . distract them. Keep them happy. These kinds of situations, especially with the storm, they can play with people's heads."

"Okay." I heard voices rising again in the other room. I probably needed to get back out there.

"And listen, you keep your phone on, and call me if

anything goes sideways. If you don't get an answer, text me. I won't be able to hear you if I'm outside."

"Got it." I was just about to end the call when I surprised myself by saying, "Rhonda, one other thing."

"Yeah?"

"You haven't seen my mother, have you? Around town?"

"She's not at the retreat?

"No. Her boat's not either. She was planning to go to Arizona." I suddenly looked around the kitchen floor, realizing that I still hadn't seen Caesar. He normally liked being out with the guests. But maybe these people were even too much for him. "But I don't think she would have left the guests."

"Huh. I'll make some calls. I'm sure she just got delayed somehow with the storm."

"You're probably right," I said. "And thanks, Rhonda. I'm sure this will all be fine. I'm just . . ."

"Erica Doom."

"Would you stop saying that?"

"Sorry," she said quickly. "Just trying to lighten the mood. You've really got me freaked out."

I ended the call and slid my phone back into my pocket, taking a breath. This would all be fine. I just needed to keep everyone in the same room, keep the fire going, maybe find us all something to eat, and stay calm.

I walked back into the main room. All the guests were standing, dressed, ready to go.

"What did the police say?" Julie asked, zipping up her jacket.

I was about to answer when I remembered that the security guard had gone out to get the boat started. "One sec," I said, rushing for the door. "There's been a small delay." I knew that I would have to tell the group eventually that we were stuck on the island for the near future, but we needed some time between crises.

As soon as I stepped outside, I knew Rhonda was right. Nobody was going anywhere. The wind whipped my hair back from my face. I could barely see. I clicked on my flashlight and eased my way down the slippery steps of the porch.

It was slow going making my way down to the lake. Big chunks of wet snow pelted my face as I squinted after the small beam my flashlight was casting. I was actually kind of surprised the security guard had made it to the boat—I mean, I was having trouble getting to the dock, and I lived here. Correction, used to live here.

But he had made it to the boat.

He had made it to the boat, and he had left.

"Son of . . ." I muttered, peering out toward the dark lake. I couldn't see a thing. I shook my head. Maybe he had a lot of boating experience, but given that he was willing to risk the storm in the first place, I was betting that wasn't the case.

I trudged my way back up the steps to the lodge. Once I was on the porch, I took out my phone again. I texted Rhonda a quick message about the security guard being out on the water. She needed to let Lake Patrol know. I waited outside for the reply. The frigid air was helping once again to clear my head.

A moment later, my phone buzzed.

Ack!

I screwed up my face and typed.

Huh?

It only took a second before I got a message back.

Ack-nowledged Doom.

"Oh," I whispered to no one, sliding my phone back in my pocket when it buzzed again.

Is anyone now currently being murdered?

I shook my head.

No. Nobody is currently being murdered.

Good. Keep everyone calm.

"Yeah, easier said than done," I muttered, pushing the door to the retreat open. Unfortunately, just at that moment, a gust of wind barreled into it, sending it smashing against the wall with a *Bang!*

A few of the guests screamed.

Well, that was a great start.

I took a long, deep breath.

"So," I said pushing the door shut behind me. "Who here likes steak?"

Chapter Fourteen

Turned out everybody liked the idea of steak. A lot.

It also turned out that Freddie had bought about fifteen steaks and put them in my mother's freezer. I guess he really was tired of me begging for meat at his door.

I was surprised by how well the group took the news of the bodyguard's desertion. Apparently, they were used to losing help. In fact, they seemed to be taking everything that had happened in stride. In mere moments, Julie had Ronnie crying—in that delicate way women do when they are wearing lots of mascara—in a chair by the fire, recapping all that had happened. How we were trapped . . . *trapped!* with her beloved deceased husband in a superstorm with people who, you know, maybe had cousins for parents. I was assuming she was referring to me on that last bit. I bet Julie was already planning the banjo music to play in the background. I quickly excused myself to the kitchen, before I truly went hillbilly on anybody's ass. Again, some things were really not worth going to jail over.

Thankfully, my mom had a lot of supplies on hand, even though it was low season. I pulled out some potatoes to go with the steaks and grabbed a batch of twelve-vegetable soup from the freezer. After everything that had happened, it felt good to be busy and productive—almost mundane. This day needed more mundane. Well, as mundane as it could be with a corpse in the living room. And as an added bonus, it also meant I didn't have to make small talk with the Boatright family.

After some peeling and chopping, everything did feel a lot less crazy. What had happened to Rayner? Him dying like that? Well, it had been shocking and sad—although nobody seemed that sad, at least not when the cameras weren't on them—but these things did happen. I mean, I'd heard that every established hotel has had at least one person die in a room, so it wasn't all that surprising that it had happened at the retreat. In fact, we were probably due. And the whole generator thing? Who was I kidding? I wouldn't know what a deliberate cut in tubing looked like. As far as I knew, this kind of thing happened all the time. Or it could have been a defect. Really, wherever my overwrought, food-starved mind was going with all that, well, it was just silly. Jake couldn't hang a flag in the rear window of his truck, so I really doubted he had plans to blow me up with my mother's generator. Yeah, it had just been one, long crazy day, and the storm was messing with my head. All I needed to do was keep everyone calm for the next couple of hours—these storms were never as bad as they made them out to be—and help would arrive.

I opened the cupboard to pull out some spices when I spotted the round tins of cat food. Okay, where the heck was Caesar? I rubbed at the tension in my neck and shoulders. It was possible my mother took him to stay with somebody in town before she changed plans. It wouldn't be the first time. But I had offered to take care of him despite the fact that his favorite place to yak up a fur ball was on my bedroom pillow. I should probably go peek under some beds or someth—

"Can we help?" Julie asked, popping her head into the kitchen. Kenny peeked in behind her.

"You're all through with the confessionals?"

"Yup. Ronnie's spent," she said, waving a dismissive hand. "And she wants to change outfits. She's got a black catsuit that she thought might be more suitable for mourning."

"Okay, well, I guess." I couldn't hide from the group forever, and maybe I could use this opportunity to find out more about the people I had been marooned with.

I got Kenny started on peeling more potatoes— because starchy foods are pretty much essential in a crisis, and I got Julie defrosting steaks under the tap. Once I had everyone settled, I said, "So, given everything that's happened, I gotta ask, the Boatright family, all the drama, how much of all this is . . ."

"Real?" Julie asked, shooting me a knowing smile.

"Yup, that's the word I'm looking for. I mean, you're probably used to all this . . . whatever this is," I said swirling my knife in the air. "But from an outsider's perspective . . ."

She laughed. "It's crazy."

Just then I heard what sounded like a splash and then an outraged scream come from the living room.

I jerked my head around as Julie said, "Don't worry. Ronnie and Ashley are just practicing their beverage throwing."

I made a noncommittal noise and turned back to the steak I was preparing.

"To be honest," Julie said. "I feel I should apologize. I can see how walking in on all of this drama could be a little much. And I was playing it up earlier. I couldn't help myself. This was supposed to be a big night for me. And you're our target demographic. Female. Youngish. Binge watching TV shows is the closest thing you have to a relationship?"

I blinked at her.

"I just got carried away. This wasn't exactly how I planned the taping to go. As for the family, well, even Ronnie hasn't quite found her groove with the camera yet. They're performing. Amplifying. I see it all the time. Well, maybe not Brody," she said leaning back to look out to the living room. "That's not an act."

"What's his deal?" I asked trimming a bit of fat off a steak. "You said something earlier about it being a long story? Is it drugs?"

Kenny let out a loud, "Ha!"

"Nope, not drugs," Julie said. "Well, at least not entirely. I mean, I doubt he'd pass a drug test."

"Then . . . ?"

"Hmm, where to begin?" She pushed her glasses up her nose. "Let me start off by saying, that not unlike a lot of rich kids, Brody has always wanted to be famous. For a while, he tried to be a rapper. Even got Rayner to hire a team of people to help him cut a demo and make a video, but it flopped."

"Okay," I said wondering where this all could be headed.

"Then, you know those viral videos of people doing idiotic things that could potentially get them killed?"

"Like the cinnamon challenge?" I asked. "Or weren't people lighting themselves on fire in the shower at one point? Just so they could . . . actually I don't know why they were doing that."

"For the glory!" Kenny shouted, raising a fist in the air.

"Anyway," Julie drawled, while shooting him a smile.

"Yes, those kind of videos. Well, Brody has tried all of those. Sent himself to the emergency room twice. And that somehow led him to magic." Julie swirled her fingers in the air.

"I'm sorry?"

"You know, like those street magicians with the hour-long TV specials?" she asked.

"I guess."

"Unfortunately for Brody, that kind of production takes real money."

"Rayner," I said, pointing to the living room with the knife. Then I realized I should probably be pointing up . . . or down . . . or maybe just not at all. "Cut him off?"

"Yup. After the rap-star fiasco, he decided not to back any more of Brody's ventures. Cut off his allowance too."

I raised an eyebrow.

"He was worried Brody was going to spend all his money on hookers and blow."

"And wasting all the rest!" Kenny said, jumping in. He then threw a potato in the air and caught it with a level of gusto that Freddie would have appreciated.

Julie closed her eyes. "Every time he says that. Every time." She was trying to sound annoyed, but the smile at the corner of her mouth spoke to something different. "So, anyway, to make a long story short, he was planning out a trick, and it went pretty wrong."

I waited.

"Well, he was scouting out locations for some great Houdini escape and—"

"He got trapped somewhere?" I guessed.

She nodded. "A port-a-potty. At some park."

"What? He locked himself in a port-a-potty!"

"No. No," she said with a chuckle. "He dropped his

phone in the port-a-potty when he was taking a break," she said, shaking her head, "and when he tried to reach for it . . ."

"Oh my God." I briefly flashbacked to when I had first seen Brody sitting at the table. It suddenly occurred to me that those weren't blue highlights!

"Yeah. He was trapped in there for nearly two days."

"Are you serious?"

"Happens more than you think."

I shot her a look.

"Seriously, look it up."

I thought about it, but decided it wasn't a good idea. Knowing the Internet, there would probably be pictures.

"You should see the little bit of footage he got before his phone—"

"Wait for it," Kenny interjected.

"—crapped out."

They both laughed.

"See?" Kenny said. "I'm not the only one who makes bad jokes."

I blinked at them both a few times.

"Anyway," Julie continued. "It was very *Apocalypse Now*. Some people just can't be alone."

"Especially without food and water," Kenny said, "and surrounded by poop."

I suddenly felt a headache coming on. "But didn't anyone realize he was missing?"

"You have to understand, Brody is a bit of a . . ." Julie frowned in question.

"A poser douche-bag?" Kenny suggested.

The producer snapped her fingers. "Yeah, that works. So no. Well, Ashley did, but that's another story," Julie said with an expression I couldn't quite read. "Anyway this all just happened a couple of weeks ago. Not long enough to be officially diagnosed as PTSD, but I think that's where it's headed. He somehow thinks death is coming back for him to finish the job."

"Wow," I said under my breath. "But what about his parents? Where were they in all of this?"

"I don't think Brody's mom was ever in the picture, really, and Rayner put a lot of pressure on Brody's dad to go into politics. He couldn't take it, so he changed his name to Kurt and ran off to join a grunge band."

I blinked again at her.

"Seriously. Died of a staph infection." When she caught my expression, she laughed, then added, "I was just messing with you about that last part." She looked away. "I think maybe he was beaten to death."

"I . . . I have seen a lot of people pass through this retreat, but never a group that was so—"

"Terrible?" Kenny said jumping in. "They are terrible, terrible human beings."

"And yet they have more stuff than any of us could ever dream of," Julie said, waving her hands out like a game-show model. "A reality show is born."

"Yay!" Kenny cheered, trying to juggling some more potatoes and dropping two of them.

"I wasn't sure I was going to say terrible," I went on. "I'm not sure what the right word is."

"Okay, well, fine," Julie said. "Ronnie's not exactly terrible. She's actually pretty funny, and she married her first rich husband really young—" She cut herself off by throwing a hand up at Kenny who had his mouth open like he was just about to say something. "So help me if you start singing 'Lyin' Eyes,' I will gut you."

Kenny snapped his mouth shut and shot her a pretty disappointed look.

She sighed. "Every time. Anyway, he divorced her and

left her and Ashley with nothing. Good lawyers. And at that point in her life, Ronnie really didn't have any life skills other than marrying rich."

I slid another steak over to my cutting board. "Wow." Funny, how I couldn't stop saying that.

"She genuinely wants a better life for her daughter. Ashley's lucky in that," Julie said, for a second almost looking sad. "Ronnie's just got some weird ideas of what that life might look like."

And I thought I had it tough with my mother.

"As for Chuck . . . Rayner's nephew?" she went on. "He may be a totally incompetent lawyer, but not a bad guy either."

"I'm sorry. Say what you want about Ronnie, but Ashley's terrible," Kenny said, jumping in. "Don't let the cute French braids fool you. I have nightmares about her mounting my head on a wall. I mean, don't get me wrong, the dreams are kind of hot, but scary too. No joke."

"No. No," Julie said, whacking him on the arm. "She's just . . . in the process of finding herself."

"But what about the kid?" I asked. "How does he fit into all this?"

"You mean Kyle? Rayner's love child?" Julie asked, making a disgusted sound in the back of her throat. "Good question. In fact, this could really mess things up for Ronnie, for all of us, especially if—" She cut herself off.

"If what?"

"I don't think I should say."

I shot her a look.

"No, I'm not being dramatic," she said putting an *I swear to God* hand in the air. "It's just that given everything that's happened, there might be some legalities involved."

Huh. I turned back to the steak I was working on.

Regardless of whatever Julie was hinting at, I really needed to talk to the kid. See if he was okay. It wasn't looking like anyone else would.

Yup, I would do that next. Just as soon as I figured out the best way to talk to a teenager. As a general rule, adolescents made me nervous. They had that uncanny ability to make everything and everyone seem uncool. Me in particular. But regardless of that, he had just witnessed his father's death. That was a lot.

"Look, you don't have to worry about Kyle," Julie said as though reading my mind. "I know he's acting all poor lost lamb right now, but believe me, he's an a-hole."

I let the knife fall to a clatter as my jaw dropped. "You can't call a kid an a-hole!"

"Can. Did. Will probably do it again," she said with a shrug. "Kenny?"

"He's an a-hole."

Just under an hour later we had all the food on the table—on the far end, away from the body still lying under the afghan on the floor. We were all pretending like it wasn't weird, but it was definitely weird. Unfortunately, we didn't really have a better option. My wine had made it out too. Ronnie had *stumbled* across it on her way to the bathroom apparently. Not quite sure how that had happened, seeing as I'd moved my bag into my room earlier, but whatever. At one point, I did try to suggest that maybe bringing alcohol into the mix wasn't the greatest idea, given everything that had happened, but I was overruled by a heavy majority.

Watching Ronnie pour herself the first big glass—before any of us had even sat down—was a sad moment. That wine was meant for other people . . . doing other things . . . snuggled under a blanket by the fire. But I needed to stop kidding myself. Grady wasn't coming tonight. The storm was really rocking now. We were lucky we still had power. Nope, now was the time to make the best of it.

Just before I found a spot at the table, I noticed the kid, Kyle, sitting by himself on a couch with his phone in his hands.

"Hey," I said walking up to him. I think for a moment there I was going to tag on a *Champ*, but I caught myself. "Whatcha doing?"

He rolled his eyes up to mine. "Farming."

"Oh, I love that game! I just upgraded my barn and bought a goat and—" The look on his face cut me off. "You're probably not that interested in my farming progress right now." I took a breath and tried again, "So, *how* are you doing?"

"My dad just died."

"Right," I said with a slow sympathetic nod. "That's . . . not good."

His eyes moved side to side in a *Can you believe this person?* motion before settling back down on his phone. Yup, this was going well. I rocked a little on my heels. "You know if you need someone to talk to, I'm a good listener." I flashed him an awkward smile. "At least I think I am."

This time he just stared at me. Waiting for me to be relevant, I guess.

"Well," I said, the force of his gaze pushing me back a step, "I just wanted to make sure you were okay."

All of the sudden he seemed less defensive and much more sad. "Okay? My long-lost father just died in front of me, and I'm trapped on an island full of people who hate me."

"I'm sure no one hates y—"

"I do!" Ronnie called out from across the room.

I shot her a warning look as Kyle said, "See?"

I sighed. "Just hang in there, okay? Help is going to be here soon, and . . . and I know at least one person who doesn't hate you." I flashed him yet another awkward smile.

He huffed a breath that almost sounded like a laugh as he wiped a bit of sweat from his cheeks. He looked sort of clammy. "Great. Thanks."

"Right." I clapped hands together. "There's dinner if you want it. If you don't, that's cool too. I'll just be over here." I jabbed a thumb back toward the table.

He nodded.

"Good."

And yup, that was a pretty big chunk of my high school experience in a nutshell.

Most of the group came to the table for dinner.

Chuck, the lawyer, was among those who decided not to partake in the thrown-together feast. He had mumbled something about not being hungry, while once again shuffling through his many documents. I guess there was a lot of paperwork involved with a multi-millionaire's death. He had moved all of his stuff—files, briefcase, phone—away from the kitchen table to the armchair by the fire. Probably didn't want to be alone in the other room. I could hardly blame him. What with the storm howling outside and the dead man lying on the floor inside, the atmosphere was a little tense. But the way he kept pulling at the neck of his shirt and rubbing his shoulder, I couldn't help but wonder if something more was going on with him. Maybe he had lost something? I should probably offer him a glass of wine before Ronnie drank it all. Brody decided not to eat either. Well, *decided* probably wasn't exactly the best word to describe it. I wasn't even sure if he could see the food Ashley had put in front of him. He was too busy watching for the grim reaper. So, you know, that was reassuring.

But the rest of us, well, we got down to eating pretty quickly and pretty quietly. Even Kyle managed to find his way over.

The food was gone in about twenty minutes, maybe half an hour. We had all needed the comfort apparently. I was actually feeling kind of proud of myself. It's not like I was the best cook in the world, but everything had turned out pretty well judging by the empty plates being pushed aside. And, just like Rhonda had ordered, my hosting efforts were keeping everyone calm. Yeah, it was starting to look like I could maybe pull this thing off after all. Hey! Maybe next, I could get out some games. Parcheesi! Actually, that was probably too exciting. Best to stick with Scrabble.

"Everyone," I began. "What do you say we—"

"Have a toast!" Ronnie shouted, jumping in. She then grabbed the oversized wine bottle off the table. She had been doing a lot of that. I watched as she poured, no, dumped the wine into her glass. I held out a hand for her to stop, but somehow she managed to whip the bottle back up just as the liquid reached the very, very top. She then leaned forward and sucked back a good inch, inch and half, before raising the glass over to the afghan. "To Rayner. Rest in Peace, you old son of a bitch."

Well, Scrabble had been a nice thought.

Kyle didn't look up from his phone, but I heard him mutter, "Nice," under his breath.

"Hey! Hey! Nobody asked for any comments from the children's table," Ronnie snapped. "Besides, I'm just being honest. It's healthy. Ask her," she said waving a sloppy hand in my direction.

I froze. "Um . . ."

"You work at this spiritual vagina mono-lodge. You know what I'm talking about."

I pinched my lips together to stop the first thing I

wanted to say from coming out of my mouth. "I don't work here. This is my mother's place."

"Right. Whatever. But some of it must have rubbed off on you. Honesty's good, right? What would your mother say?"

I tried to come up with something wise and therapeutic-like, but for some reason *Denial isn't just a river in Egypt* kept popping into my head—and that didn't seem right. "You're only as sick as your secrets?"

"Hey!" Kenny shouted. "My fortune cookie said that last week . . . then again, the other one I got said my inattention to hygiene would keep me from finding true happiness." He shrugged, enthusiasm all gone. "So there's that."

We all stared at him a moment.

"Fortune tellers are dicks."

"Right, and there you have it," Ronnie said, raising her glass to him. "Honesty's the way to go. Ashley and I don't have any secrets, and we have the best mother-daughter relationship on TV."

Kenny choked on his wine just then, causing Julie to slap him on the arm. They exchanged looks, and I saw him shrug and mouth, *What? I couldn't help it.*

"Jesus," Kyle muttered, nose still buried in his phone.

"What?" Ronnie asked, looking over.

"Nothing," Julie said quickly. "Go on."

She frowned at them best she could. Again, Botox. "As I was saying, I'm not going to pretend that I'm all crazy-devastated by Rayner's passing. We all know that he too could be a dick." She nodded at Kenny. He shot her a thumbs up in return. "And now, without his interference, I can finally launch Ashley's career properly." She turned to her daughter. "Next week, I already have you doing a Diana Virgin Huntress photo shoot. We'll—"

Kenny barked out another laugh. Julie whacked him even harder this time, muttering, "Not the plan."

"I'm sorry," he said, still snickering through the hand over his mouth.

Ronnie's eyes swiveled to her daughter. "Ashley? Why is the cameraman laughing?"

Her shoulders jumped up and down. "I don't know." But the fear in her eyes told a different story.

Just then Brody began mumbling something. Too low to hear clearly, but definitely something. He was also rocking back and forth in his seat a little more violently. Ashley's eyes darted over to him.

What was going on here?

"Why is he doing that?" Ronnie asked, pointing a jeweled finger at Brody. "And why are you looking at him like that?"

"Like what?" Ashley asked, straightening her vest. "I'm not looking at him like anything."

"Wait . . . and why did you get that plate of food for him? Since when do you care if—"

Suddenly Brody's fists hit the table, making all the dishes rattle. "Leave her alone!"

Whoa.

Everyone froze.

Julie then leaned toward Kenny and whispered, "Get the camera."

He jumped to his feet.

"Brody, don't . . ." Ashley said.

"You're always telling her what to do!"

"I knew it!" Kenny hissed, hiking the camera up to his shoulder. "They *are* doing it! It's just like this movie I saw the other week, *Step-Sibling Love*—"

My face dropped into my hands. Oh God, not another movie.

"And by movie, I mean porn on my laptop."

Oh, well, okay then.

"What did you just say about my daughter?" Ronnie said, rotating her head back to Kenny in an *Exorcist* kind of motion.

He threw his hands up. "Nothing. Nothing."

Ronnie's demented eyes turned back on her daughter. "Ashley?"

"Mom, I was going to tell y—"

"Ash?" Brody suddenly mumbled in a frightened voice.

She almost reached for his hand, but one look from her mother stopped her.

Nope, I did not like the direction this was taking at all. Forget games. We needed something else . . . like more food! They were quiet when they were eating. "How about some dessert, everyone?" I jerked a thumb back to the kitchen. "I think I might have some vegan carob brownies?"

Kenny shuddered all over. "Vegan carob brownies? Way to sell it."

Ronnie ignored me completely and said to her daughter, "What are they talking about? Tell me . . . *tell me*, you are not sleeping with the poop boy."

A whole bunch of emotion warred over Ashley's face. For the first time, I actually felt kind of sorry for her. She looked so young all of the sudden, and it wasn't because of the French braids or the pink lip gloss. Nope, it was all the fear and vulnerability in her eyes—kind of like a hunted animal. A hunted animal who just might be in—

"We're in love!"

"What?" Ronnie shrieked. Wow, she looked like an angry, angry fish now. It was like her lips were growing in size. Soon she'd swallow us whole.

Ashley straightened up in her chair, trying to look

defiant, but the way her face was quivering, she wasn't quite able pull it off.

"I don't believe this," Ronnie said.

"I know, right?" Kenny whispered at her. "I always pictured your daughter going for like some muscled dude that smacked bears in the head with a two-by-four while off-roading."

"I don't expect any of you to understand. Especially you, mom," Ashley said, tilting her chin in the air. "You've never been in love."

"Hey! Watch it!" Ronnie snapped, little veins popping out of the tissue-thin skin around her eyes. "You don't know what I felt for Rayner."

"You just called him a son of a bitch!"

"Yeah, but he wasn't always like that," Ronnie snapped. "Not at first. He was fun then. He was always taking me to Vegas and . . . and he could spend money like a boss." She looked almost comically sad for a moment as her eyes drifted over to the afghan on the floor. "Plus, he always made me feel like I was . . ." She shook her head. "Really hot." Then something in her snapped. Her eyes jerked back around and landed on Kyle. "But that was all before he came along." Kyle looked up at her, but didn't say a thing. After a moment, she straightened her bodysuit and turned back to her daughter. "And let me tell you, Little Miss, there are more important things in this life than the *love* you're feeling right now."

Ashley threw her hands in the air. "Like what?"

"Survival!"

Whoa. This was really getting out of hand. Ronnie had shouted the word with so much force, I kind of wanted to duck for cover—and I didn't even do anything!

Suddenly I could hear Rhonda's words in my mind.

Keep everyone calm, Doom.

Right.

"Um, everyone?" I said, pushing my chair back. "Maybe we should take a breath here. Who feels like playing a game of Scr—"

"I will not let you screw up all that we've worked towards!" Ronnie said, knocking a chair over. "That's not happening!"

Well, at least I could tell Rhonda I had tried.

Ronnie flung her hand in Brody's direction. "Especially not for that *thing*!"

Suddenly Ashley's eyes lit up with a little fire of her own. "When are you going to get it? It's my life! It's not up to you!"

I could see Ronnie struggling to get ahold of her emotions. She was making it worse, and she knew it. Brody was becoming more attractive to Ashley by the second, and that was an impressive feat. Ronnie took a long breath before saying, "Ashley, I just want a better life for you than I had." She reached for her daughter's hand, but Ashley folded her arms over her chest. "You have limitless potential. The Internet loves you. Well, portions of it anyway. And the hunting mixed with religion? Baby, you could be president."

Ashley stayed mum.

"But none of it will happen with him by your side. He's a national joke! The stink will never leave him."

I frowned. Interesting choice of words.

"What about what I want?" Ashley couldn't stop herself from looking over at Brody. "Maybe I don't want to go around killing hyenas for the rest of my life. I mean, I do. Because it's awesome. But maybe I want to do it *with* somebody."

Ronnie brought her hands to the sides of her head. I

guess to stop all the violent shaking it was doing. "You don't know what you're saying."

Ashley shifted in her chair. "And maybe I want to live a quiet life, you know, get married, have kids with somebody I care about." She shot Brody another look, but he didn't catch it. In fact, just then he bounced up out of his chair and hurried over to one of the front windows. As he rushed by, I thought I heard him mutter, "Something's out there."

"Really?" Ronnie said, throwing her hand after her step-grandson. "That's what you want for your future?"

My eyes snapped back to Ashley. I felt a little like I was watching a tennis match that I suddenly was deeply, deeply invested in. This was honest to goodness Romeo and Juliet stuff. I mean, if Juliet was a little bit of a psychopath and Romeo had both visual and auditory hallucinations. I was starting to see why people got addicted to these shows. They were even more engrossing when you watched them in real life.

"Exactly! You just said it!" Ashley shouted, putting her hand to her chest. "What *I* want. Let's talk about what *I* want for a change."

Ronnie slapped the table. "What you want? What you want! You are such a child. You have no idea what you really want." She jumped up and paced the floor in front of the fireplace in her spike-heeled boots. "Do you have any idea what it's like to live life like a so-called normal person? If you're not careful, you . . . you could end up like her!" she shouted, tossing a hand in my direction.

"Hey!" I looked around to the rest of the group, expecting to see my outrage mirrored in their faces. But only Julie met my gaze, and she just shrugged.

"Is that really what you want?" Ronnie asked.

"Well, I know what I don't want," Ashley snapped, refolding her arms across her chest.

"Oh, well, don't leave us in suspense. Tell us. What *don't* you want, Princess Ashley?"

"To end up like you."

Chapter Fifteen

"Oh no she didn't," Kenny whispered.

"Julie?" I said in a low voice while keeping my eye on Ronnie. Man, she looked like she had been slapped. No, worse than slapped. She looked like her entire world had been blown up. "Julie?"

She didn't turn, which was weird, because she was definitely in earshot.

"Julie!" I tried with a little more oomph.

Nothing.

I almost said her name again, but she suddenly jerked around. "What?"

She looked flustered. Almost guilty. Kind of like she had earlier when Ronnie had to call her name a few times to get her attention. My brow furrowed again. Soon I'd need to ask Ronnie about Baby Botox. "Do you really think this is the best time for filming?" I whispered harshly. "Especially, given the "—I gestured to the afghan—"you know."

"Sorry, but this is good stuff." She shook her head. "Dirty job."

"Okay then," Ronnie said, snatching all of our attention back. "You want to go off and live your white-picket life? Be my guest, baby girl."

Ashley kept her eyes on her mother, waiting for the rest. We all knew there was more coming. I couldn't help but feel sorry for her again. She was sitting there still as a statue. Well, except for her chin, which was quivering.

"But have you thought about how you're going to pay for this "—Ronnie looked around the table as though she might find the word she was looking for there— "*insignificant* existence of yours?"

Ashley's face fell as two little spots of color rose on her cheeks.

"Oh my God. You haven't even thought about it, have you?" Ronnie chuckled unpleasantly. "After all I've done . . . I guess, you thought the money just fell out of the sky." She twirled her manicured fingers in the air. "Well, don't expect me to pay for this happy ever after with Prince Paranoia over there."

We all looked over to the prince in question. The way he was darting from window to window, like a jumpy dog, well, you'd think he was playing for Team Ronnie.

"It's only been a few weeks. He's getting better." Ashley shot another look over to Brody, maybe for support, but he was beyond hearing us again. "And *we* don't need your money."

"Oh, really," Ronnie said, pouting out her lips. "Aren't you forgetting that Rayner cut him off?"

Ashley froze a moment, but then leaned back in her chair into a surprisingly confident pose before meeting her mother's glare. "He cut off his allowance," she said, twisting one of her braids around her finger. "But he didn't cut him out of the will."

Ronnie stepped back from the table. You could tell by her face that she had forgotten about the will.

Chuck hadn't though.

The lawyer had been strikingly quiet this entire time, sitting still as a mouse in his chair by the fire. But he'd jolted at the mention of the will, and I wasn't the only one who noticed it.

"No . . . no, no," Ronnie said, looking down at Chuck. He rolled his eyes up to hers, nibbling on his lip. "Is that true? I thought Rayner cut him out completely. Tough love and all that."

Tiny beads of sweat winked on the lawyer's forehead in the firelight.

"Chuck?"

He swallowed hard, his Adam's apple bouncing up and down. "I don't think I should really say anything at this point in time."

My stomach dropped. This could not be good. Where was that Scrabble? "Okay. Everyone? Now's really not the time to be reading any w—"

"Chuck," Ronnie said again in a scary, scary voice. "Answer the question."

He wiped a handkerchief over his gleaming face. "I . . . I don't want to."

"Why not?" Ronnie planted a hand on the back of a chair and leaned toward him. "Do you think Brody's going to hurt you? Because—"

Chuck's eyes widened, and he shook his head. "It's not really Brody that I'm worried about."

"Then who?"

His shook his head again.

Uh-oh.

Ronnie's face hardened into something almost unrecognizable.

"Monopoly!" I blurted out. "Who wants to play Monopoly?"

"Nobody wants to play any games!" Ronnie shouted

at me before whipping back around. "Spill it, Chuck. Everything."

"You don't have to," I tried, my voice sounding almost like a plea. "You really don't."

"Oh, but he does," Ronnie said, her voice dropping into something even more terrifying. Eerie almost. "Remember, Hillbilly Girl? You're the one who said you're only as sick as your secrets. Doesn't he look sick?"

I peeked one eye over to the pale, sweaty man who looked like he might throw up at any minute. "You look great, Chuck," I said with a weak smile. "Really . . . awesome."

"No, Ronnie's right," he said, nodding and looking down at his hands. "You're all going to find out anyway."

"Find out what?"

"I'm so sorry, Ronnie," the lawyer said, once again rolling his pathetic eyes up to hers. "But Rayner changed his will. And he didn't just cut Brody out. He cut you out too."

Chapter Sixteen

"What did you just say?"

Chuck collapsed back into the chair. "Oh God, I feel so much better, especially seeing as I'm the executor and get paid either way." He wiped his brow one more time with his handkerchief. "I mean, the sitting here, knowing, while you had no idea . . ."

"You're lying," Ronnie snapped.

"I'm not. I have a copy here." The lawyer said looking at his stack. "Rayner was planning to use it . . ." He shot a look over to Julie. "For the show."

All eyes swiveled over to the producer.

She licked her lips, then shrugged. "We might have discussed something."

"I don't believe this," Ronnie said, still in her scary, quiet voice.

Julie shook her head violently side to side. "It wasn't supposed to stick, Ronnie. He was just going to use it to make you all talk. He really thought that one of you was trying to—"

Suddenly, laughter burbled up into the room. Ashley. "See, mom?" She threw her hands into the air, then let them flop onto the table. "This is where all of your hard work has gotten you."

"Boom," Kenny whispered.

Ronnie teetered on her heels. Stunned.

My eyes shot over to Brody to see how he was taking the news. But he wasn't. He was still looking out the window. Kyle, the youngest of the group, looked frozen in shock.

I leaned toward Julie and whispered, "I don't get it. It's not like she's destitute, right? She's got the show."

Julie looked back at me like she had just realized that I too was a terrible person. "It doesn't work like that. Judging rich people is fun. Judging poor people just makes you a jerk."

"Oh. Right." I tore my eyes away from her back to Ronnie.

"No. No," she said. "I don't accept this. Chuck there's got to be some way to fix it."

And just like that the lawyer looked sick again. He really hadn't thought this all the way through.

"Chuck?"

He shrugged and mumbled something under his breath.

"I can't hear you," Ronnie said, pushing up the sleeves of her catsuit. The muscles in her forearms rippled. Man, she must work out in that way rich women without jobs work out. And nobody works out like that. "Could you repeat that? A little louder this time?"

A tense, tense moment passed before Chuck finally said, "I don't think so."

"No. No," Ronnie said again, but in a faraway voice this time. "I was faithful. Rayner knew that. I mean, we had our problems, but he wouldn't do this to me."

The room fell silent as the once-fierce MILF fell back into her chair. I felt for her. I really did. I mean, it wasn't like I respected gold-digging as a profession per se, but . . . well, a deal was a deal.

"When? When did all this happen?"

"Just like a week ago," Chuck said.

"But why?" she asked. "This doesn't make any sense." She suddenly jolted up in her seat. "Who did he leave it to?"

"I can't tell you that," Chuck said, picking his papers up and folding them against his chest. "I'm sorry, but you don't have the right to that information anymore."

"You did not just say that to me," Ronnie said getting up again and taking a step toward him. Chuck shrank back even more in the armchair. "I don't understand what's going on right now. There's something you're not telling us."

He shook his head quickly, making the loose skin at his cheeks shudder.

"Why did Rayner do this?"

He shuddered again.

"Chuck . . ."

"He already told you," the lawyer said, gesturing at the head of the table where Rayner had been sitting. "You were here. You already know why."

Ronnie's brow almost contracted into a look of concentration. "That nonsense about one of us trying to kill him?"

He nodded quickly.

A confused look fell over her as she shook her head. "But that's crazy."

"I know!" Chuck said, putting his hand to his chest. "I told him the same thing. I said, 'Uncle Rayner, that's totally crazy.' Except now, he's—"

We all looked over to the afghan.

"—dead."

Chapter Seventeen

"Okay, that's it," I said, getting to my feet. "This has gone far enough. I think that until the police get here—"

"Why do you keep talking?" Ronnie asked, turning on me again. "This has nothing to do with you." Suddenly she froze. "Unless . . . were you sleeping with Rayner?"

"Wait, what?"

"Plot twist," Kenny whispered, swinging the camera in my direction.

"Why else would he pick this God-forsaken place?" She gasped loudly and pointed at me. "And he called you squirrel! And you liked it!"

I closed my eyes. Why? Why was this happening? "Okay, this is really getting out of hand. This is my mother's retreat, and I came for a visit. That's all. I promise. None of you were supposed to be here."

She continued to study me.

I looked to Julie for support, but she was busy texting. Probably her boss. Probably to see how this could be turned into a *Survivor*-type scenario. "And as for all this murder talk. Well, it's just ridiculous. You were all here. And I'm assuming that no one saw him murdered, right?"

They all looked a little unsure at that.

"Wouldn't you know if he was murdered right in front of you?"

Chuck groaned. "Well . . ."

We all looked at him.

"Obviously I've had a little more time to think about it, and . . ." He pointed at the half-filled glass of Scotch still sitting on the far end of the table.

"What? No way," I scoffed, planting my hands on my hips. "I mean, I've looked into some poisons lately, and—"

Suddenly I had everyone's attention.

"No," I said with a hurried chuckle. I even waved my hands in the air for extra innocence's sake. "It was for another murder—"

Rapt attention.

I dropped my hands. They weren't helping. "What I'm trying to say is that there are not a lot of poisons that can kill instantly."

Chuck let out a noise that sounded a little like a whine and tilted his head from side to side. "Cyanide can."

I stared at him for a moment then looked at the rest of the family. The mention of cyanide had obviously meant something to them. I dropped back into my seat and threw my hands into the air. "Okay, so which one of you just happens to have cyanide lying around?"

"Gramps did," Brody said out of nowhere.

Whoa, it was weird hearing his voice when it wasn't all shouty and filled with hysteria.

He turned from the window, still wearing his resting spooked face. "Around his neck."

I dragged a hand over my eyes before shaking my head in disbelief. "I'm sorry, what?"

"I can't believe I didn't think of it sooner," Ronnie said, suddenly looking a little spooked herself. "He always wore that fricking thing. Even during . . . you know." She pointed her finger down at the table and gave it a little swirl. I had no idea exactly what move that was supposed to represent, but I didn't want to either. "He thought it made the *act* more exciting."

A gust of wind rattled the windows.

"Why? Why would he do that? I mean aside from the . . . you know?" My finger almost made the same swirly motion, but I caught it just in time. "Who wears a cyanide necklace? Was he suicidal?" My face suddenly felt a little tingly. Oh right, I needed to remember to breathe.

"Ha!" Ronnie shouted. "Suicidal? That's *rich*." Saying the word looked like it had hurt her. "It was an artifact from the Second World War."

"He brought it out when he thought people were being sissies," Brody went on in a near normal tone of voice, which kind of made it even creepier coming from him. Especially given that his eyes were still way wide and still looking at things the rest of us couldn't see. "I was seven the first time he offered it to me. I was afraid of the tooth fairy."

"Well, that's just charming," I said, scratching my temple. "And you don't think he would maybe take it off given that he believed someone was trying to kill him?"

"I doubt it," Ronnie said. "It wouldn't have even occurred to him."

"Okay," I said, looking over to the body covered in the afghan against my will. "Well, have any of you checked to see if he's wearing it?"

Nobody said a word.

I looked at Julie. She held out a *be my guest* hand.

"Yeah, no way," I said quickly. "I was specifically told

not to touch the body, and, frankly, I have already touched enough of that one."

"Told ya she's a freak," Kenny whispered to Julie.

I shot him a look.

His free hand flew up. "I don't judge your necro love."

Julie whacked him and whispered, "Stop talking. Editing is going to hate you."

He shrugged.

"All I'm saying is that maybe we should leave the murder accusations to the police."

"Well, when exactly are the police going to get here?" Ashley asked, darting angry looks at her mother. "It feels like it's been hours."

I sighed. "As soon as they can."

Ronnie's eyes widened. "Oh my God! I just realized. You have no idea when they're going to get here, do you? They probably told you that too! And you didn't tell us!"

"I can't be trapped," Brody muttered, voice rising again. "No way, man. Not again."

"It's okay, baby." Ashley said, getting up, her mother's eyes narrowing with each and every step Ashley took over to the window. "Nobody's going to hurt you."

The look on Ronnie's face kind of suggested otherwise.

"Nobody is going to hurt anyone," I said in my most authoritative voice. "Look. We just had a nice calm dinner. We can't let this guy and his *conjecture* get to us," I said giving Chuck a pointed look. That's right. I knew lawyer speak. "We need to stay calm. The storm is keeping the police pretty busy, but they will come. And until we have concrete evidence saying otherwise, I think it's best to just assume the most likely cause of death was a heart attack."

Truth be told, I kind of wanted to know if I had just served dinner to a murderer, but I also didn't think it was a good idea for everybody else to know. This was a highly unpredictable lot. Too many people. Too many reactions. One small trapped space. This hypothetical murderer wouldn't have to do a thing, and we could end up tearing each other apart. If someone did in fact murder Rayner, that was terrible—regardless of his failures as a human being—but outing that person now wouldn't bring the old guy back. There would be time for that later, when we weren't trapped on an island in a storm. Besides, the cyanide necklace meant the killer had planned to kill Rayner specifically, and the rest of us probably weren't in any danger. As soon as I had the thought, a Klaxon alarm went off in my head reminding me of the broken generator that we thankfully didn't need, *yet*, but, well, I didn't have a super reassuring *but* for that, *but* the police would be here soon.

"Well, if you're so sure no one killed my husband," Ronnie said. "There's one way you can prove it."

I raised an eyebrow in question.

"Bottoms up," she said, waving a hand toward the glass still on the table.

My jaw dropped. "Well . . . you . . . you really are terrible people!"

"Told ya," Kenny said in a soft voice.

I dragged my wary eyes from her when I saw Brody on the move. He was headed for the body. "What are you doing?"

He stopped a couple of feet away, popping up on his toes to see over the dead man's shoulder. "I don't see the necklace," he said, quickly shaking his head. "I don't see it!"

"Calm down," I said again, wondering if perhaps *calm down* were the two most useless words in the English language.

"Seriously, dude!" Brody yelled. "It's not there!"

"How can you tell?" I tried. "He could be lying on it!"

Suddenly all eyes were on me again.

"No," I said, shaking my head vigorously. "I just told you that we are not supposed to touch the body."

"Well you don't have to give him a full pat down like the last time," Ronnie said, nodding knowingly at Kenny. He nodded in return. "Just check to see if the necklace is still there."

"Brody already kicked him off the chair," Chuck offered. "I don't see what difference it makes from a legal standpoint."

"Oh really, Mr. Lawyer," I said, shooting him a look. "Is that your expert opinion?"

He shrugged.

I rubbed my face roughly with my hands. "Is me flipping the body really what it's going to take for you all to get ahold of yourselves? Or . . . or . . . but . . . you're his wife, Ronnie!" I said flinging my hand out to her. "You should be the one to touch him."

"I really didn't *like* the thought of touching him when he was alive," she said with a sniff. "I like it even less now."

"I don't believe this," I muttered, slowing making my way around the table. "I so don't believe this." I turned to Kenny and said to his camera lens, "Rhonda, when you see this, know I had no choice."

"Don't talk to the camera," Julie whispered. "Remember. Natural."

I shot her the middle finger.

"Better," she whispered happily. "Better."

I turned back around, wiping my sweaty palms against my jeans, Rayner's body right in front of me. A cold gust of wind whistled down the chimney, making the fire crackle. Man, touching Rayner the first time had been bad enough, and then there had been a chance he was still alive. But I couldn't see what other choice I had. This group was right on the edge of losing it. Brody in particular, who was standing just to the side of me, one arm wrapped around his waist, the other's elbow resting on it, hand covering his mouth. He was barely hanging on. I needed to prove to them all that Rayner was not murdered.

But I really didn't want to touch him again.

In fact, my desire not to touch him was so bad that suddenly I found my toe inching forward to see if I could just tip him back.

"Don't use your foot!" Ronnie yelled.

I whipped around. "You said you didn't want to touch him!"

"Well, I know," she said folding her arms across her skin-tight mourning outfit, "but you can't treat rich people like that. Show some respect."

She was right. Not about the rich part. But the respect. My gaze suddenly landed on Kyle. I couldn't read his expression, but he was watching me so closely, I couldn't help but think he was struggling to put on a brave face. He was still a kid. And this was his father. I did need to show more respect. I sighed and crouched down placing my hands on the dead man's shoulder. A small shudder ran through me. He was warm . . . and loose. Man, how long did it take for rigor mortis to set in? And why did I have a life where that was even a legitimate question? I gave a small push, and the former Rayner Boatright rolled onto his back—the afghan still over his face.

I was going to either have to take the blanket off or reach my hand underneath and feel around. I definitely, definitely didn't like that second option.

"Wait!" I suddenly shouted, catching a glimpse of

something shiny in a little gap where the blanket draped. "It's all fine. I can still see the chain around his neck." I lifted it carefully with one finger. "It's right—"

Uh-oh.

Chapter Eighteen

I spotted a little ring sliding down the chain as I lifted
the necklace up. A broken little ring. That probably used
to hold a capsule full of deadly poison.

I looked over my shoulder to see Ashley holding
Rayner's glass up to the light. "Look."

A tiny voice in my head said, *Sure, now she thinks to
look in the glass.*

We all leaned forward to get a closer look.

There it was, swirling around the bottom of the glass,
dancing in the light from the fireplace.

The missing capsule.

You might be tempted to think all hell broke loose just
then. But it didn't.

Nope. Not even close.

There were no screams. No gasps. No sudden move-
ments. Instead, everyone just leaned back from the table—
almost in unison—as Ashley placed the glass carefully
back on the table.

It felt like a good three, maybe four minutes passed
before anyone said anything at all.

"So Uncle Rayner was right," Chuck said in a small voice.

I carefully sidestepped my way around the table back to the other side of the room. "Maybe . . . maybe it was an accident."

Ashley gasped. "It was when the power was out! Everyone was moving around!"

"Okay, just hang on," I said. "This doesn't mean anything. There's a reason why people don't go around wearing fifty-, sixty-, seventy-year-old necklaces full of deadly poison."

"She can't do math," Kenny said matter-of-factly to Julie. When he caught my look, he tagged on, "Sorry. It's cool. Math's hard."

"I think I heard him yell, *Get off of me!*" Ronnie took a few steps toward her daughter, but Ashley jerked away to stand by Brody.

"Somebody could have broken off the capsule and dropped it in his drink," Chuck said, finishing the thought everyone was thinking.

"People," I began, knowing it was useless, "let's not get carried away. I really think—"

"Stop telling us to calm down!" Ronnie shrieked. "If anything, we have been too calm. Here we are having dinner with a body on the floor. That is not normal!"

She had a point. And by the way my heart was hammering in my chest, well, it seemed to think so too. Still, I had to try to keep a lid on this. Rhonda had told me to keep them calm. This definitely did not feel calm. "Look. All I'm trying to say is that we should wait. We are not detectives. I know what can happen when you don't leave things to the professionals. Suddenly you're digging up graves in the middle of the night and—"

I caught myself too late. They were all giving me that look again.

"That was another situation entirely."

"Are you some sort of P.I.?" Kenny asked, peeking around his camera. Then he snapped his fingers. "Oh! Or vampire hunter?"

"Neither," I said closing my eyes and pressing my palms to the ground. "But I do know that this could all get out of control very quickly."

"Oh, so what should we do? Play Vegan Monopoly?" Ronnie asked, throwing her hands wide.

My mouth opened. Then shut. Then opened again. "I'm not really sure how that would be different from regular Monopoly, but no." I shot her a sidelong look. "I think we should all just sit quietly and—"

"You can't tell us what to do!"

"You're right," I said, looking around for something, anything, to help get ahold of this situation. Thankfully, my eyes landed on the camera. "But have you considered that everything you're saying right now is being recorded?"

Her near frozen face tried to contract again in question.

"Every word you say will be reviewed by the police." Oh yeah, I liked where I was going with this. Mental high five. "You wouldn't want anything being misconstrued. Like, say, toasting a dead man by calling him a son of a bitch."

"I have nothing to hide."

"Well, I'm a court reporter, and you might be surprised how things can get twisted." Okay, to be totally honest I really hadn't transcribed all that many murder cases in my circuit—as in under five, and they were all drug-related, but I had watched a bunch of real-crime shows on TV, so I was pretty sure I knew what I was talking about. Ultimately, I just wanted everyone to stop talking. This entire day had been surreal and pretty unpleasant, but now a new feeling of dread was settling over me. It probably had something to do with the poison in the glass and the dead man on the floor. I could feel small stirrings of panic in my chest at the notion of being trapped with a potential murderer, and panic was not what we needed right now. "Tell them, Chuck," I said, looking at the lawyer while shooting him a pretty serious *you had better have my back on this* look.

"She's right. You should all probably talk to a lawyer." He froze for a moment. "I mean, a good lawyer, not me. I mean, I'm a good lawyer, but I'm also a witness, so yeah."

"Fine," Ronnie said narrowing her eyes. "But first I'm calling the police."

I threw my hands in the air. "Please. Be my guest."

Julie grabbed Kenny's elbow. "We should call work. Figure out how they want us to handle this."

"Good. Good," I said as everyone dispersed to different corners of the room. "I have a few calls of my own to make."

I called Rhonda first, but she didn't answer. Then I texted her. Repeatedly. Still no answer. Hopefully she was on her way to speak with Lake Patrol. I then debated contacting Grady. I mean, I really, really wanted to talk to him, but if he was out on the water trying to find some kids, it didn't seem right to have him worrying about me. It's not as though he could leave and come get me. And as bad as this situation was, it seemed contained at the moment. So I settled on a text that read,

Call me the minute you can.

I waited a little while to see if he would call back, but when he didn't, I casually got to my feet and walked off to the darkened corner of the room nearest to the kitchen. Well, at least, I tried to walk casually. It's kind of hard when you have a room full of people eyeballing your every movement.

After a few rings, someone answered.

"Oh no. What happened? I thought this night might not go well, so I bought you some ice cream. I mean, let's be real, I would have bought ice cream anyway, but—"

"Freddie, listen, I've got a life and death situation here, and I need your help."

A moment passed as he inhaled deeply. "I love calls that start this way. How can Freddie help you?"

Just like with Rhonda, I filled him in on as much as I could as quickly, and as quietly, as I could. Truth was I needed someone to advocate for me on the mainland. Someone who could get the attention of the right people. And if there was one thing Freddie was good at it, it was getting people's attention.

When I was through, all Freddie said was "Erica" in a very surprised, scared, and somewhat-accusatory voice. Like I had gotten myself into this mess?

"I know," I muttered.

"What the hell?"

"I know."

"This is bad!"

"I know!"

"You're going to die."

"Wait . . . what?"

"I'm really sad," he said. "Who knew that when I bought the ice cream, it would be for me?"

"Oh my God!" I yelled in a hushed voice, peeking over at Kyle sitting by himself at the end of the sofa. He was throwing me looks again. This time like he had doubts about my ability to tie my own shoes.

"Okay, okay, you're right," Freddie said. "You're not dead yet."

I faced the corner of the room again and whispered,

"I'm not going to die! There was one maybe-murder here tonight. One. Maybe." I was still clinging to my accidental-poisoning theory.

"Sure. Sure. I'd totally agree with you, *but*," he said, raising his voice into quite the skeptical pitch, "the generator tells another story. I saw this movie last week where the killer sabotaged the generator right before he gutted—"

"Yeah, I've heard about that movie," I said, pressing a finger hard into the spot between my eyebrows. "That is not what this is."

"No, you're right. It's more like . . . like that Agatha Christie book with the offensive name!"

I was rubbing my whole forehead now. In fact, I couldn't quite seem to rub it hard enough to get rid of the tension building there. "What are you even talking about?"

A beat or two passed before Freddie said quite seriously, "Tell me you completed your assigned readings."

I chewed the side of my thumbnail and muttered, "Well, it's just that I've been really into romances lately, and it's hard to force a genre swit—"

"Sometimes you really make me tired," he said. "We are never going to get this business off the ground unless you—you know what? This is a conversation for another time. I'm talking about the book where they're all trapped on the island? In a storm? Sound familiar?"

I brought my hand away from my mouth. "That does sound a bit like my situation." I watched Ronnie pound her phone a few times before sliding it across the table. I didn't think 911 would be of much help. "Okay, so what do I do, Mr. Security Expert?"

"I'm not exactly sure," he said slowly. "Let me think."

"Well, what do the heroes do in the books?" I asked,

pulling back the curtain to peer into the darkness beyond the porch.

"I've got it!" Freddie shouted. "You need to kill yourself!"

I let the curtain drop. "I'm sorry?"

"Pretend you're dead so that you can investigate without anyone knowing."

"First, I'm not sure how I would do that, you know, like in real life. Second," I said dropping my voice again and shooting a quick look over my shoulder to Kyle. "I can't leave the kid alone."

"I heard that," Kyle whispered. "And I'm not a kid."

I threw him a pained smile and a quick thumbs-up before shuffling farther away toward the kitchen.

"Wait," Freddie said, dropping his voice. "Did you just say there's a kid?"

"Yeah," I muttered. "He's the one I told you about, who showed up late?" I shot another look over my shoulder. Yup, he was still listening.

"You didn't say he was a kid!" Freddie moaned. "Oh jeebus, now you're going to die for sure."

"What?"

"Seriously, Erica, you need to forget about the kid."

"I can't forget about the kid," I said tightly through my teeth. "The others"—I stopped briefly to flash another smile over my shoulder—"don't seem to like him too much."

"Not your problem! Look, this plane you're on is going down. You need to put on your mask first!"

"I'm not sure your airplane analogies are really help—"

"You listen to me, Erica Bloom. Kill yourself. Do it now. Or forget about investigating! Just go to the twins' place. You can make it. Forget about the kid."

I dropped my voice even lower. "I can't forget about the kid, okay?"

"You can't forget about the kid," Freddie repeated in a mutter. "You can't forget . . . you know what? Fine. But so help me, if you tell me next that there's a loveable golden lab with only three legs that needs saving too, I think we just have to accept that you're going to die."

"Can we please just focus? Phone service is not good, and my battery is getting low." And given the way the lights were flickering again, there probably wasn't any way I was going to be able to charge it. "What I really need you to do is find out what's happening on the mainland and impress upon them how serious—"

"Who can you trust?"

"What?"

"Of the group! Who can you trust? This is important."

"I don't know," I said, trying to casually run a hand through my hair as I looked around the room. "At first I thought, maybe the TV producer. She's not part of the famil—"

"Okay, so she's the murderer."

"What?"

"That's just how these things work. If you think you can trust her, she's the murderer. Plus she produces reality TV, so obviously she's super evil."

"No, well, she's definitely a little evil when it comes to the show," I said, casting a look over to Julie and Kenny by the fire. "But she really seems all about the show. What would her motive be?"

"All about the show, huh?" Freddie said knowingly. "All about it enough to kill?"

"No . . . at least I don't think so." I squeezed my eyes shut. "No, but—"

"And are you sure the old guy is really, really dead? Maybe you're just being punked."

"Nope," I said, popping my lips apart. "I've already explored that option. He's dead. But if you'd stop cutting me off, I was going to say"—I dropped my voice as low as I could—"a couple of times I kind of got the feeling that either Julie was hard of hearing or she wasn't using her real name."

Freddie was saying something in return, but I lost it when I caught sight of Kyle making a small waving motion at me with his hand.

When I met his eyes, he mouthed, *It's not her real name.*

I nodded quickly.

"Freddie!" I hissed, turning my face to the window. "I'm right. Kyle says it's not her real name."

"Well, did he say what her real name was?"

"Hang on." I looked over to Julie to make sure she wasn't looking. She wasn't. She and Kenny were watching something on his camera. *What's her real name?* I mouthed to Kyle.

He shook his head and shrugged.

I nodded again. "He doesn't know."

"He doesn't know? That's it?" Freddie asked. "Well, that's just great. Oh my God, I hate kids."

I sighed while Freddie let out a noisy breath right into his phone and out into my ear.

"Okay, well, that's obviously step one."

"What is?"

"You need to find out her real name and text it to me. I've subscribed to some databases for the business, and I'll find out who she really is."

"And how exactly am I supposed to do that?"

"You'll figure something out. And get her birthday too."

I almost snapped something back, but now that Kyle had confirmed my fake-name suspicions, I couldn't ignore this bit of information. "Okay fine, but, in the meantime, find Grady or Rhonda or somebody in law enforcement and tell them that things are going south here, and I'm not sure how long it will be before the paranoia kills us all. I mean, this still could have been some sort of accid—"

"Stop it with the accident!" Freddie said sternly. "Generator tubes don't cut themselves!"

I shook my head like he could see it.

"Listen, you can do this, Erica. The murderer didn't count on you being there with all your . . . murder experience."

I opened my mouth to say something, but nothing came out.

"You are the wild card in the anointment. I mean fly. Whatever. It's a house of cards and you are the wind. It's—"

"Freddie," I said, trying to regain my composure. I could hear how freaked out he was. He was really worried for me, which was really making it hard to not worry about myself! "I get it."

"Do you? Do you really?"

"I don't have much choice. Just try to get people here."

"I'm on it. I won't let you down."

"Okay," I said, squeezing my eyes shut again.

"Stay strong. And remember, you're Erica Doom."

A sad-sounding laugh escaped my mouth. I guess everyone really was calling me that.

"Okay, I gotta go. But don't die, all right?"

"All right, but—Oh! Wait! One more thing," I said quickly. "Before you go, how did the hero in that Agatha Christie book survive?"

Freddie made a hissing sound like he was sucking air in through his teeth. "Um, well," he said, trailing the word off into a pretty high pitch. "Spoiler alert, but . . .

you know what? I'm sure it won't end that way for you. Bye!"

I slid my phone back into my pocket. Okay, so while I wasn't exactly down with the whole pretending to kill myself plan, maybe Freddie was on to something with the idea of making a break for Kit Kat and Tweety's. I shot another look out the window at the swirling snow. Wow, it was really coming down out there, but I knew the path through the woods like the back of my own hand. I unconsciously cast a glance at the back of my hand. *Had that freckle always been there?* I gave my head a shake. I knew how to get to the twins'. The question was could I get there with a teenager in tow. Especially one who might start screaming, *Not my mother!*

Just then my phone buzzed again.

Text from Grady.

Sorry. Can't call. On the water. Rhonda said something was going on at the retreat?

I grimaced at the phone. How the heck was I supposed to answer that? All my previous arguments for not telling him still stood, but maybe his situation wasn't as bad as I thought.

Have you found the kids? Are they okay?

A moment later the reply came.

No. Parents are frantic.

Well, crap.

That message was followed up with,

You're okay tho?

I shook my head while my thumbs hovered over the screen.

Fine.

You sure?

I stared up at the ceiling. Now what? Grady had a bit of a thing about lying, but I didn't want to put him in the position of worrying about me when there was absolutely nothing he could do about it. Plus, he needed to focus if he was out on the water in this storm. I sighed.

I'm good.

I stared at the glowing screen hoping it could also tele-pathically send the message that I was super scared and needed him, but—

Okay. Good. Talk more later.

Apparently, the technology wasn't there yet.

I sighed again and looked out to the common room. Julie and Kenny were still whispering to each other on one of the couches. The way Julie was pulling her hair back, she looked pretty stressed, but Kenny was patting her knee. Ashley was standing protectively over Brody back at the table, hand on his shoulder—maybe trying to stop all the rocking he was doing. Ronnie had moved closer to Chuck by the fire, arms crossed over the bottle of wine she had clutched to her chest. No, it probably wasn't worth risking the storm just yet to go to the twins' place, but it was an option to keep in my back pock—

Suddenly Ronnie slammed the bottle on the table and lunged at Chuck.

"Hey!" he shouted. "What are you doing?"

She whipped the top stack of papers off of his pile.

Chuck planted his free hand on the armrest, struggling to push himself up. "Give that back! You just can't—"

She whipped a finger at his face. "Stay."

He dropped back down. "I already told you that Rayner—"

"Yeah, you said he cut us out, but you didn't say who he named as his beneficiary instead."

Back pocket options were starting to look a whole lot more necessary.

Chuck twisted his face up in fear. "Ronnie, I don't think now's the time—"

Ashley moved away from Brody, taking a step in her mother's direction. "What does it say?"

Ronnie's eyes moved over the first paper in the stack she was holding. She flipped that page, and then another, before she froze.

"I knew it." Her heavily lashed eyes slowly rose up from the will to land on . . .

"You little turd."

Chapter Nineteen

Kyle jumped up from the sofa toward me as Ronnie lunged around Chuck.

"Whoa!" I shouted. "Someone stop her!"

Thankfully, Julie leapt to her feet, barring the path. "Ronnie, you need to slow down."

I pushed Kyle behind me.

Ronnie took another step forward, but Julie held her ground. "You know, I love it when you get all crazy, but he's a kid, who I don't have a filming contract for, so let's think this through."

"I'm not going to do anything," Ronnie said again in that tight calm voice people use when they are really angry but want to sound rational. "I just want to know what he said to Rayner."

"I didn't say anything!" Kyle shouted from behind me.

"Oh, but you must have said something," Ronnie said losing a bit of the grip she had on her voice. "Something that made him make you the sole beneficiary of *everything*."

Everybody's eyes fell on me, trying to bore through to the teenaged boy standing behind.

"I swear, I didn't say anything!"

"Really?" Ronnie asked, slamming the will on the table. "Because I'm thinking somebody must have put all these ideas into Rayner's head about his family trying to kill him, and you have been spending a lot more time with him lately."

Ashley shook her head and fell into place behind her mother. "Sweet baby—turd!"

I pulled Kyle even more tightly behind my back. Wow, he was having quite the night. Not only had his father died, making him a multi-millionaire several times over, but now his family was threatening to . . . I don't know what they were threatening to do, but I knew it wasn't good.

"Don't listen to her," he pleaded. I peeked over my shoulder to see his big brown eyes turned up to mine. He looked a little like one of those scared cats with the round baby eyes. Still kind of sickly too. I never thought I had much of a maternal instinct before, but looking at Kyle, all scared and without attitude, I was a bit moved. I kind of wished Rhonda were here to see it. I was totally ready for a dog named Butch.

"Don't worry," I whispered. "I'm not going to let them do anything to you. I've got this." I turned back to the others. "You two are going to need to stand down." I kept one hand behind my back, shielding Kyle, while I raised the other to point a finger back and forth between the re-united mother-and-daughter team.

"We just want to talk to him," Ronnie said in the most terrifyingly sweet voice I had ever heard. "Come, boy. Come talk to your step-mother."

"Yeah. Okay," Kyle said. "Everyone heard you say you hate me."

"I don't *hate* you," Ronnie said. "I never hated—"

"Like it's my fault you couldn't give Rayner more kids."

And that sucked all the air out of the room.

"Oh my God, I hate you!" Ronnie screeched. "Come here you little—" She lunged around Julie, Ashley pushing at her back.

"Not helping, kid," I shouted, pivoting hard and herding Kyle down to the other end of the table. I shot a look back at Ronnie. Frick! She was right on our heels! Tossing chairs like a madwoman. And now we were running around the table—oh yeah, and hopping over a dead man's legs—because that wasn't ridiculous!

Julie had stepped back beside Kenny. Well, she had given it a shot. Chuck continued to cower by the fire. And Brody? Well, he was still off fighting the monsters in his head.

"Ronnie, just stop!" I shouted. "This is stupid!"

She tossed another chair from her path, never taking her eyes from Kyle. "I told you. I just want to talk to him. Let me talk to him please."

"Yeah, no." I pushed Kyle around the table for another lap. Any second, even with the alcohol consumed, Ashley and Ronnie would figure out that if they just split up and went in opposite directions, they would have us cornered. I needed to do something before that happened. "What do you even expect him to say?"

"I expect him to explain to me why I am not a rich bitch."

"Me too!' Ashley shouted.

I heard Kenny chuckle from behind his camera. "I mean, they're already halfway there, am I right?"

I glared at him as we passed by.

"You're right," he said. "Not cool."

"You're grown women!" I shouted. "This is ridiculous! You need to stop."

"Or what?" Ashley shouted.

"Or . . . or . . . you don't want to know what!" I really

had no idea what I meant by that threat, but I thought I could back it up given all the adrenaline singing in my veins.

"Okay, look," Ronnie said, finally slowing to a walk, forcing Ashley to slow down too. "I don't have a problem with you." Kyle and I mirrored their pace on the opposite side of the table. "I just want you to stop walking for a second . . . so I can kill that little jerk!" She launched herself into another sprint.

I grabbed the closet thing I could find to push her back.

Ronnie skidded to a stop just short of the rolled-up yoga mat pointed at her belly.

"Really?" she said.

"Yes really." It was kind of a go-to move of mine.

Faster than I thought possible, given how drunk she was, Ronnie snatched the rolled-up tube from my hands and whacked me with it. Hard. On the shoulder.

And just like that everything went red.

I blinked a few times.

Had she really just hit me with the mat?

I mean, really, really hit me?

Oh yes . . . she had.

Ronnie looked at my face, and her eyes grew wide.

Before I even knew what I was doing, I snatched the mat back, snapped it open, and stretched it between my hands.

Then I charged them.

"Holy crap!" Kenny yelled. "Fight! Fight! Fight! Fight!"

"Shut up!" Julie shouted. "Just film!"

Ronnie was strong, but she was drunk and wearing heels that were *stupid* high. She was going down. And she was taking her daughter with her.

Unfortunately, they took me too.

I landed on top of the screaming pair, hands still pushing them down with the thin foam mat.

"This all stops now! Do you hear me?" I said. I heard Brody move from the window. "You had better stay where you are, Brody, or I'll make you wish you were back in that toilet." He went quiet. "This is done. Are we clear?"

Ronnie nodded quickly, but Ashley had a strange little smile on her face. "We should totes go hunting together."

"No. No, we shouldn't," I said, shaking my head a little too wildly. "Do you want to know what we should do instead?"

Ashley started to say something, but her mother harshly whispered out of the corner of her mouth, "Stop talking. You'll only anger it."

"We should all just go back to sitting down and being quiet."

They didn't answer.

"Because none of this ridiculousness will change what's on that stack of papers over there." Besides, I couldn't keep them like this forever. Ronnie's fake boobs were feeling like rocks under my ribs. "Think about it. What are you going to do? Kill the kid?" I asked. "It won't get you the money back. It's over."

Then, something very strange happened, which was kind of mind-blowing given how strange things already were. I didn't exactly know what that something was, but everyone else in the room seemed to.

It was like I could feel them all thinking . . . the same thing.

Silence fell over the room.

In fact, the entire lodge had gone still.

Then I heard Kyle make a funny little noise. Almost like he was going to be sick.

"What?" I asked, turning my head toward him, keeping my eyes on Ronnie. "What happened?"

He didn't say anything. I took a chance and dragged my eyes from Ronnie to really read his expression. Whoa.

Okay, that wasn't good. His eyes had somehow grown even wider than when Ronnie had first jumped at him, and his head was shaking back and forth.

"What?" I asked, looking around, trying to read everyone's expression at once. "Why are you all freaking out? In the quietest possible way?"

Still nothing.

"I was being ridiculous to prove a point. Ronnie's not actually going to kill you. But if she were—as crazy as that is—I was just pointing out that it wouldn't get her the money back."

Kyle seemed to grow even more pale.

"Because it wouldn't, right? I mean, if you truly have the money, and God forbid you were to . . . die . . ." I licked my lips, as a horrible, sinking feeling traveled its way down from my scalp to my toes. "Kyle, I . . . I don't suppose you have a will?"

"I'm fifteen! What do you think?"

I swallowed. "Well, it doesn't matter." I craned my head. "The money would go to your mother, right?"

Please say right. Please say right.

"My mother died when I was two."

I closed my eyes. "So . . ."

"These people," he said, gesturing weakly around the room, "are my only family. It would all go back to them."

Chapter Twenty

"I'm dead," Kyle mumbled. "I'm dead. You've killed me."

"No. No. No." My cheeks suddenly felt very hot. Burning hot. "You're not dead."

"You are too." Kyle nodded, eyes still wide. "They're going to have to kill you too to get away with it."

I chuckled. "Come on. You're being silly." Then I realized I probably wasn't helping my point much by having two women pinned to the floor with a yoga mat. I struggled to get off of Ronnie and her daughter, but not before whispering, "You remember this next time you think about hitting someone with a yoga mat." Once I was on my feet, I brushed my hair back and said, "As I was saying, nobody's going to kill Kyle or me or anybody else, right?"

Nobody answered. I'm sure they were just shocked that I would even say such a thing and not, you know, thinking about the half a billion dollars suddenly back within their reach.

"See?" Kyle said, throwing a hand up. He whipped out his phone. "Excuse me for a second. I just need to change my status to dead."

"Okay, just settle down now," I said, looking around the room for more support and not finding any. "This . . . we are all getting carried away. This is what happens. It's cabin fever."

"It makes sense, you know," Kyle went on in an eerie faraway voice, like he had already crossed the great divide. "One of them probably knew ol' Rayner was going to change the will, and thought they could kill him before he got the chance. But they were too late."

"Okay," I said, looking around the room *again*. "Now's the time for all of you to jump in and say how ridiculous this is. Anyone?"

Still nobody.

"Way to go with the whole not letting anything happen to me," Kyle said, tossing me a weak thumbs-up while still texting. "You were right. You totally got this."

"Okay, that's far enough, Mister." Yup, that felt as painful as it had sounded. "They would have figured out the whole will thing without me."

"Yeah, eventually," Kyle said, sparing me a look. "Like tomorrow, after I hired my own security team!"

"Okay, I—"

Suddenly the lights flickered and then dimmed for a sickening moment before snapping back to full power.

"As I was saying," I said, shooting the lights a warning glare. "Ronnie is just upset, and maybe a little—no, make that a lot—drunk. And Ashley is . . . I think maybe she just can't help but chase when somebody runs. Nobody is really trying to kill you. Right, ladies?"

"Of course not," Ashley said. "It's a . . . what's that word? Commandment?" She almost looked to her mother for confirmation, but then quickly strode away, arms crossed over her chest. Guess she just remembered that she was mad at her. Ronnie shook her head while trying to poke a fake eyelash back into place.

"See? Nobody is going to kill you."

"Well, not yet," Ronnie said, pulling out the nearest chair and plunking herself into it. She then dragged the hanging lashes off her eyelid. "I haven't decided if it's worth it yet."

"I already told you I didn't say anything!"

"Can we agree," I said, putting a hand in the air, "that maybe now is not the time to talk about it?"

"She's right," Julie said. "Maybe we should all just sit back down and steer the conversation away from the kid to something we can tape and actually air. I mean, it seems like you could all use the money." She chuckled, but it died quickly. "Too soon?"

A tense moment passed, and I sat beside Kyle on the sofa, despite him sending me palpable *I can't believe how much you suck* vibes. Kenny slapped Chuck on the arm, who, at some point I guess, had positioned himself behind the armchair. "It's safe, dude. You can come out." Chuck scuttled back over to his place by the fire.

Silence fell again over the room. Suspicious looks ping-ponged from person to person. But after about ten minutes, I thought we were maybe past the worst of it. Of course, Brody was still occasionally moaning and rocking in his seat, but even that was a bit reassuring in its ceaselessness.

I wasn't sure how long this peace would last, but—
Thump!
Not very long apparently.

Everyone jumped. Brody nearly flipped out of his chair. "It's back!"

All of our faces snapped to the windows.

"What was that?" Ronnie hissed, gripping her armrests.

"Death," Brody whispered.

"I'm sure the wind just knocked something over," I whispered, not entirely sure why I was whispering if I believed that were true. "Porch chair maybe."

"Are you sure?" Chuck asked. "It kind of sounded like someone was out there."

I licked my lips. "There's an old camping saying. 'If it sounds like a bear, it's probably a raccoon. If it sounds like a raccoon, it's probably a squirrel. If it sounds like a squirrel, it's probably—' "

"What the hell are you going on about?" Ronnie hissed.

"It's just being in the wilderness, in the dark, your imagination can run away with you," I explained, still whispering. "But maybe someone should go and check it out."

Nobody volunteered.

We waited in tense silence a few minutes before Julie said, "It was probably nothing."

Just then the lights dimmed dramatically, then flickered on and off. All eyes turned from the window to stare at the wooden light fixture mounted in the center of the room. I jumped to my feet.

"Where are you going?" Julie asked.

"We have some lanterns in the closet." I pointed behind me. "I'm just going to—"

"But I thought you said this place had a back-up generator?"

My feet suddenly rooted themselves to the spot. "It does. It's just . . ." I stopped. I knew I had to lie. A sabotaged propane generator was not exactly what this group needed to hear right now. "It's totally fine." Unfortunately, I was also a terrible liar. "It's just when I went out to check it before, I noticed it was a little bit broken."

"What do you mean broken?"

"It's nothing," I said with what I hoped was a reassuring

smile. "It's this high-tech model, and you know how high-tech models can be."

"No. Tell me," Julie asked, rising to her feet.

"It's old. That's all."

"No, no," Julie said, pushing her glasses up. "I meant to ask you earlier. You looked really freaked out before when you came back in from checking the generator. Why?"

I took an involuntary step backward. "It's nothing."

"What's nothing?"

I didn't say anything.

"What's nothing?"

I let out a shaky breath. They had a right to know. "There was a small nick," I said, making an eensy weensy space between my thumb and forefinger, "in the tubing that connects the propane to the generator." I quickly darted my eyes around all the faces in the room. Man, there were a lot of faces, looking at me, seeing right through me.

"You mean," Julie said, "like it was sabotaged?"

I chuckled awkwardly and shook my head. "No."

I watched the group expression change from confused to something much, much worse.

Julie took a step toward me. "Why didn't you tell us this?"

I laughed. "Come on, are you seriously asking that question?"

Suddenly Brody jumped to his feet, sending his chair tumbling back.

"Don't any of you get it?"

Ashley rushed toward him, but he put up a hand to stop her.

"None of us are getting off this island! Ever!"

Chapter Twenty-one

"You're not!" He pointed at Julie. "You're not!" The finger moved to me. "Not you!" he shouted, finger whipping to Kenny.

"Hey," the cameraman said, sounding peeved.

"Dude, you're definitely not!" Brody yelled, pointing at Chuck. "We're all going to disappear! Just like your m—"

"What?"

Suddenly the power snapped off again. Fully and completely off.

Someone let out a scream and multiple chairs scraped against the floor. Then came the angry shouts.

"Move!"

"Out of my way!"

In the near darkness I could see someone lunging toward me. A second later, I was knocked into a side-table by Brody's shoulder as he ran past me.

"I can't be here!"

"Wait!" I yelled. "You can't! The storm!"

"I'm getting off this island," he shouted back.

"Brody, stop!" Ashley shouted from behind me. I think

he had knocked her over too, and she was still struggling to get to her feet. "Please!"

"It's coming for me, man. I gotta get out of here!"

"Stop. I have lanterns. Just calm d—"

Brody flung the door open. Bitterly cold wind ripped through the lodge.

"Shut the door!" Ronnie shouted, sounding annoyed. "It's freezing in here."

I couldn't let him do this. It was suicide. His clothes couldn't protect him from this type of weather. He'd die of hypothermia if he got lost out there, and the way the snow was driving, he'd get lost for sure. I tried to follow him, but Kenny and Julie were arguing in front of me.

"Follow him," I heard Julie hiss.

"It's too dark," Kenny said. "The camera's barely getting any of this."

"It's better than nothing."

"Move!" I shouted, trying to maneuver past them.

Kenny finally pushed forward, and we all stumbled out after him onto the porch.

With the darkness and snow, it was almost impossible to see anything, but . . . was that a light? Out by the trees?

I blinked hard, and when I opened my eyes again, the only light I could see was from the camera.

"It's too late," Kenny called out. "He's already—"

Suddenly the beam of light coming from the camera swirled violently in the air. A moment later, it was followed by a heavy—

Thunk!

Chapter Twenty-two

"Kenny!" Julie screamed.

I felt my way back around the bodies to reach into the hall closet. We needed real light now. I rummaged around the shelf above my head, articles of clothing falling on me. Where was that basket? I finally got the lip and pulled it down, only toppling a few flashlights onto my head. I grabbed the first two off of the pile on the floor and clicked them on, whirling their beams toward the door.

Julie was already on her knees by Kenny's side, clutching his lifeless hand. "You killed Ken—"

"What?" I shouted, fumbling with the lights.

"You practically pushed him out the door!"

"Me!"

Chuck dropped down beside Julie and put his fingers to Kenny's neck. "He's not dead," he shouted over the wind. "His pulse is steady."

"Okay," I shouted back. "Let's get him inside."

"Weren't you the one who said you weren't supposed to move dead people?" Ronnie called out from the lodge's threshold with . . . with Rayner's Scotch bottle in her hand? Fabulous. I had forgotten all about it. Obviously, Ronnie hadn't.

I dropped to my knees by Kenny's shoulder. "He's not dead, and we can't leave him out here in this storm."

"But it might help," she went on. "I read you can't die if you're still alive and frozen."

"Just stop. Everyone needs to help."

Chuck moved down to Kenny's legs, and Julie's eyes met mine. "I'm sorry," she said, glasses collecting snow. "I didn't mean to accuse you of anything."

"It's okay," I said quickly. "Don't worry about it." I felt bad for her because I knew she really cared about Kenny, but it was hard to feel really bad for someone when you knew they were lying to you. "Let's just get him inside. Everybody take a part."

Not surprisingly, nobody listened.

"Ronnie get over here!"

She took a step back into the lodge.

"Don't make me get the mat," I warned. "You too, Kyle. You can help. Where's Ashley?"

Just as I had said the words, she appeared in the doorway, pulling her heavy jacket on while keeping hold of the flashlight I had used earlier.

I rocked back on my heels. "Please tell me that you are just cold and you're not thinking—"

"I'm going after him. He needs me."

"Over my dead body, you are!" Ronnie shouted.

"Whatever," Ashley said, flipping the hood over her head. "Have another drink, Mom."

"Hey! In case you haven't noticed, I'm kind of having a bad night." Ronnie took a sloppy swig right from the bottle. "You, little liar . . . who lies . . ."

"Getting lost in the storm is not going to help Brody's situation," I said trying to meet Ashley's eyes, but she was scanning the darkness. "You don't know the landscape; you'll get turned around. You'll—"

"I know a little bit about surviving in harsh environments," Ashley said. And with that she reached underneath her vest and pulled out a long, serrated hunting knife.

I threw my hands up and closed my eyes. "First, a knife is not going to help you against a storm, and second," I said, snapping my eyes open, "why do you even have that thing?"

Ashley didn't have time to answer me because her mother had grabbed her arm. "You are not going after him. I forbid it."

"God, you just can't stop, can you?" Ashley said, yanking her arm away, sending her mother tottering back on her heels into the wall. "You don't get to tell me what to do. Not anymore."

One job. Rhonda had given me one job. Keep everyone calm . . . and together. Fine, two jobs. I swear, this entire group was going to knock itself off, and I'd be left trying to explain what happened. Yup, that's me. Erica Doom.

I reached for Ashley's arm as she stomped by. I needed to try one more time—

"Just let her go if she wants to!" Julie shouted. "We need to get Kenny inside."

Ronnie stumbled back onto the porch. "Stop! Ashley! Don't do this! You're too good for him."

Ashley stopped at the bottom of the porch steps and shot a look over her shoulder. "Go back inside, Mom. You're embarrassing yourself."

"Whoa," I called out, rocking back on my heels. "Easy. She's still your mother." They weren't exactly words that I ever expected to come out of my mouth, but it kind of felt like they needed saying. Maybe it was because I couldn't stop worrying about my own mother.

I hadn't realized how deep the snow was until I saw Ashley step into it, trying to awkwardly stomp away.

"At least follow his prints!" I shouted after her. She stopped and changed direction. Yup, prized trophy hunter my a—

"Come on!" Julie snapped. "She's made her choice."

"Okay, okay."

After a whole bunch of struggling, we managed to get Kenny onto the couch in the living room. I wasn't entirely convinced we should be moving him, but leaving him out in the storm wasn't an option.

I set a few lanterns on the table then found another blanket for Kenny. Julie was already on the phone with 911. I knew talking to them wouldn't get help out here any faster, but they could at least tell us what we could do for Kenny. This day . . . this night . . . it felt like a car rolling for the edge of a cliff—a car that I was trying to hold back with my bare hands. Didn't take a genius to figure out how that would end.

A moment later, I pulled out my phone and swiped the screen to text Rhonda again. I hesitated a moment, biting my lip. Maybe I should try calling first? I needed to impress upon her th—

Just then my phone buzzed in my hands, making me flip it into the air.

I might have screamed a little too.

Thankfully, I caught it before it hit the floor.

"Sorry everyone. Sorry. I was just—it's the police." I turned and walked toward the kitchen as I brought my phone to my ear. "Rhon—"

"Erica, thank God. When you didn't answer, I thought maybe I was too late."

"Too late?" I stopped walking and looked over my shoulder. Yup, everyone was staring at me. I lowered my voice and resumed my walk into the darkness of the kitchen. "What are you—never mind, listen things are going south. I think one of the guests has a concussion. Actually I know he has a concussion. He's out cold. And another guest took off into the storm, and now his girl-friend has gone after him, and—"

Rhonda let out a growl of frustration. "Okay, I'm on it. But you listen to me. You need to get out of there."

I blinked. "What are you talking about? I'm trying to keep people from leaving. The one guy doesn't even have a winter j—"

"That's really bad, and I'm doing everything in my power to get help out to you, not that it's doing much good, but you've got bigger problems."

I did not like the way that sounded at all. "What could possibly be worse than a dead body on the floor, a man with a head injury, and two people potentially lost in a snow storm?" But even as I was saying the words, a big part of me was pretty sure I didn't want to know the answer to that question.

"They may be safer than you are at the moment."

I peeked over my shoulder. "Rhonda, you're kind of freaking me out right now."

"Good," she snapped. "You need to get out of there. Take the kid. Go to the twins'. Go anywhere."

I walked farther into the kitchen. "Why?"

"Okay, well, I don't want to upset you, but . . ."

"Rhonda."

"I think you may be stuck on the island with a serial killer."

Chapter Twenty-three

"What did you just say?"

"It's kind of a long story," Rhonda said, words tumbling through my phone. "And I'm not sure how much time you have. Just go. I'll fill you in on everything when you're somewhere safe."

"That is not going to happen," I said, wrapping an arm tightly around my waist. "You tell me what's going on. Right now."

Rhonda growled in frustration again. Louder this time. "Why will nobody do what I say? I have a uniform!"

"Rhonda."

She scoffed. "Fine, so, since I last talked to you, I've been going back and forth with Lake Patrol about trying to get someone to go over to the island, but they were all like *It's suicide. No boat's going on that lake now. We can't risk our people for a dead body.* Blah. Blah. Blah. So I tried to explain to them about the generator, and the movie I saw last week with the killer who—"

I lost focus of her words for a few moments as a little bit of relief sprinkled over me. I knew what was going here. Rhonda had done exactly what she had warned me not to do—get carried away. Some people just shouldn't be allowed to watch movies.

". . . so after the donut, I calmed down and decided I needed to go talk to someone in person, but, you know, once I got in the jeep, it occurred to me that maybe I should swing by the marina to see if the bodyguard you said had left the island in Ted's boat had shown up yet. I mean, it's not like Lake Patrol is going to give me any updates. They're so *This is our jurisdiction and . . .*"

I lost focus again as I rubbed a hand over my face. As much as I liked Rhonda, and I really, really did—when she wasn't setting my boyfriend up with her cousin—I was seriously hoping that Freddie had found someone else to talk to. Grady, ideally. I mean, I could only imagine what Lake Patrol thought when Rhonda got them on the phone talking about movies with knife-wielding—a snapshot of Ashley's serrated blade popped up in my mind, but I quashed it pretty quick—serial killers. The real danger, right now, was the storm . . . and the paranoia.

"So the boat wasn't there and—"

"Oh no," I said, snapping back into the moment. "I mean, he was kind of a scary dude." And he kind of had the look of a man who could survive underwater for a year or two before rising up out of the lake to kill us all—which was a totally uncharitable thought to be having given the circumstances. "But nobody should be out on the water tonight. I hope he's okay."

"Yeah, well, you just hang onto your hope there for a minute until you hear the rest."

I squeezed my eyes shut and pinched the bridge of my nose. "Rhonda, can you please just tell me what it is you're trying to say. I don't need all the details. Can you just skip to the—"

"Serial killer part?"

I dropped my hand. "That would be great."

"Okay." I heard her take a breath. "Erica?"

"Yes?"

"Have you ever heard of the dark web?"

I threw my head back, smacking it against the wall. "What?"

"You know, the side of the Internet that you can't access with regular search engines? It's like a hidden part where all the illegal stuff happens. But you need a special browser or something to use it. I heard you can download it, but—"

A small sound escaped my throat. But I knew interrupting would just make it worse. She needed to tell the whole story. I had to let her. Otherwise we'd all die of old age before she was through.

"Okay, maybe I'm getting ahead of myself," Rhonda said. "Let's back up."

I threw my hand in the air for no one to see . . . except all the people once again looking at me from the common room.

"Okay, so, I went to the marina. There's no boat. So I decide I should probably check in with Ted. See if he had heard anything. And nope, he hadn't, but he tells me this bodyguard of yours gave him a bad feeling—not enough so that he wouldn't rent him the boat. I mean, he was paying in cash, so—"

"Rhonda, please, I'm begging you . . ."

"Right. Sorry. I'm really freaked out, and the longer I talk to you, the more freaked out I get because you need to get going! The killer could be on your porch right now looking at you through the window, but you can't see him because—"

"What the fricking hell, Rhonda?"

"Right. Anyway, Ted took a photocopy of his driver's license, so I decided to do some checking and . . ."

I pushed myself off the wall with my foot. Driver's

license. I could feel my panic level creeping back up again. "And?"

Rhonda made a scared humming noise before saying, "And it was a fake."

Okay, my heart really didn't like the sound of that, given the way it was banging against my ribcage . . . probably trying to escape. "Having a fake ID doesn't make you a serial killer," I said, over the thumbnail I was suddenly chewing. At least I hoped it didn't. What with Julie—or whoever she really was—in the other room.

"I know that! Don't you think I know that?" She took a noisy breath. "Sorry. Sorry. We're getting to the part where—" Suddenly she cut herself off with a surprised laugh. "My hands are shaking. They haven't done that since I was in training, and—"

"Rhonda! What are you talking about?"

"Amos."

"Amos?"

"The new kid at the station? You've met him. He's the one who nearly got fired for helping Shelley upload her booking photo to *Hot Mugs and Jugs* when we took her in that one time for—"

I tried to yell something, but I think it came out more as an angry stream of barks.

"I'm sorry! I'm babbling. I know I'm babbling! The sugar from that donut probably didn't help," she said, sounding more and more freaked out, which was not helping my level of panic one bit. "So, anyway, Amos saw the guy's picture on the driver's license and he ID'd him right away. That scar is pretty distinctive."

"ID'd him as who?"

"Oh, Erica . . ."

"Who is he?

"The Dark Web Assassin."

Chapter Twenty-four

I closed my eyes and pressed the palm of my free hand toward the floor . . . trying, I guess, to keep the crazy from rising up and swallowing me whole. "The Dark Web Assassin. The Dark Web . . . Rhonda, that is the most ridiculous thing I have ever heard." I said the words, but I was also suddenly remembering the feeling of dread I'd had when the bodyguard was standing—no looming—over me.

"I know, but dark web assassins are a real thing. And he's *The* Dark Web Assassin."

"Dark web assassins are not a real thing."

"How do you think people go about finding killers? Google?"

"I was going to say Craigslist."

"This is no time to be joking. Amos looked it up on the regular web and showed me the guy's picture. It's him. They think he has some sort of military slash mercenary background. He's wanted for multiple murders. In one case, he—" She cut herself off again.

"In one case he what?" I asked, eyes jumping around the empty room.

"You don't want to know."

"Tell me."

"I don't think it will help."

"Maybe you should let me decide what will help."

"No, I—"

"Rhonda!"

"He killed an entire family of five in one night."

I slumped back against the wall. "You're right. I didn't want to know that." Suddenly I felt very cold. "Are you sure? Like really, really sure? It's not like some grainy photo that could be anyone?"

"I'm like ninety-nine, okay maybe ninety-five, ninety-four—"

"Stop!" I snapped before dropping my voice. "The number's not important."

"I'm pretty sure."

I rubbed my hand over my mouth. "So . . . so one of the family did know Rayner was planning on changing the will . . ."

"Will? What will?"

I chuckled weakly. "I didn't tell you about the will?" I filled Rhonda in as quickly as I could.

"Holy crap, Erica!"

"I know."

"This is bad!"

"I know."

"You really are going to d—"

"So help me if one more person says I'm going to die, I will kill everyone here," I barked before realizing that that didn't exactly make a whole lot of sense. "And then, you know, it will be settled." I made a slicing motion with my hand at the fridge, just in case it was getting any ideas.

"Sorry. Sorry. But wait . . . this is actually good news, isn't it? I mean, if he's already killed the old guy, his job is done. He should be on his way to some tropical island by now. At least, that's what they always do in the movies. I think in real life, though, assassins would probably have trouble relax—"

"Stop! And no. The job's not done." I peeked back out to the living room. Hmm, they were huddled in a bit of a circle, tossing suspicious glances in my direction. Great. Good. Well, at least they were unified in their distrust of me. "Kyle has all the money, and he doesn't have a will."

"But the bodyguard left before he knew any of that."

I shook my head. "Everybody has a phone here."

"Huh." Rhonda made a clicking sound with her tongue. "So who stands to inherit if the kid is, you know, done in?"

"I'm sure they'll all make a claim in court. His nephew probably stands the best chance." The nephew who was currently missing and could be looking at me right now through the kitchen window! I whipped around to face the darkened pane of glass above the kitchen sink.

Nothing.

"But you saw the guard leave?"

"Yes . . ." I stopped and thought about it. "Well, I didn't see him leave with my own eyes, but the boat was gone."

"So, he could still be on the island."

I swallowed hard, letting that new reality sink in. He could very well be. I mean, if he wanted to use the boat as his getaway, it wouldn't be wise to anchor or just tie it off to some tree in this storm, but who knew what dark web assassin resources he had! I felt my eyes widen just before my brain caught up to a new thought. "We heard a noise earlier. I thought maybe something had just been knocked over in the wind, or maybe even Jake Day was trying to freak me out, but—"

"Okay, that settles it. You need to get the kid and go to the twins' place. Now."

"What about Grady? Does he know what's going on?"

"I'm having trouble getting through to him."

"But . . . if the killer's out there, aren't we safer in here?" I took half a step toward the window, peering again into the darkness.

"No," Rhonda said. "You don't know who you can trust. Besides, didn't you hear the bit about this guy murdering a whole family in one night?"

"I heard that," I said, placing my hand on the lip of the sink. "I really, really, *really* heard that."

"So don't make it easy for him!" She took a breath. "The best thing you can do is get the kid out of play. Actually it's the best thing for everyone. He might stop murdering if he can't get the kid first."

"I don't think it matters if he's supposed to kill every—"

Suddenly a new voice cut me off. "What's going on?" I heard Julie call from the other room. "When are the police going to get here?"

"Soon," I shouted over my shoulder, before dropping my voice again. "As I was saying, if he has to kill everyone, does it really matter what order he does it in?"

"Yes! Erica, listen to me. The kid is the most important target. The other kills are irrelevant if he doesn't get him. You follow?"

"I don't follow any of this." I was supposed to be with Grady right now . . . drinking wine, by the fire . . . maybe on the floor in front of the fire . . . a floor that didn't have a dead body covered with an afghan. "I don't know anything."

"That's why you are going to do what I say." Her voice sounded like it was giving me a good shake through the phone. "You can do this. You have been in tight spots before."

"With, like, amateur murderers! Not military-grade assassins!" I yelled, suddenly catching my own reflection in the window. Wow, that chick looked scared.

"Calm down."

"Oh my God, first you tell me I need to go, go, go because I'm trapped with a serial killer, and now you tell me to calm down? I will not calm down! I will not!" I suddenly understood Ronnie's feelings about those two words. They were really aggravating.

"You can do this. Just get the kid and leave. You have the advantage. You know the island better than anyone. I mean," Rhonda went on with a nervous chuckle, "unless this guy has night vision goggl—" She cut herself off again. "I guess it is possible that he has night vision goggles. Probable even. Kind of sounds like something a paid assassin would have."

My eyes shot back into the darkness, fully expecting to see the greenish glare of night vision goggle lenses on the other side of the window.

Nothing that I could see.

I backed away slowly to my safe spot by the fridge.

"Forget I said that last part. Just get the kid and go."

I peeked around the fridge to look back into the living room. Hmm, their huddle had grown tighter. I shot them a little wave in an attempt to ease some of the tension. Nope, by the looks on their faces, that hadn't worked. "Rhonda, it's going to be kind of hard to do that without everybody noticing. Are you sure we can't just wait for help?"

"Listen, I know it seems like you're only a fifteen-minute boat ride away from civilization, but with this storm, well, for Lake Patrol, you might as well be on the other side of the moon. I'd come myself," she said, voice full of emotion, "but they ordered me to stand down."

"But didn't you tell them about *The* Dark Web Assassin?"

"I tried. I mean I called them back. But I, maybe, sometimes, come off as a little . . ." She sighed, in a way that made me think she was frustrated with herself. "They didn't believe me." She paused a moment. "But you do, right?"

I shook my head. I didn't know what to believe. This was Rhonda. And Rhonda was . . . Rhonda. But she had come through for me at times in the past. And I did know with absolute certainty that her intentions were good. But dark web assassin?

I shook my head. Time to focus on what I knew for sure. There was a dead man on the floor. An unconscious man on the sofa. Two people missing in a storm. And a half a billion dollars on the line. The way things were going, anywhere was probably safer than here. "I believe you."

"Okay, so no more talking. Get going."

I swallowed hard. "Right."

"Tell me you can do this, Doom."

"I can do this," I mumbled over the thumbnail I was still working on chewing off.

"Say it again. With a little less fear this time."

"I can do this." I smacked the kitchen counter. Unfortunately, I didn't see the fork there that I sent flying into the air then clattering to the floor. Someone in the other room screamed.

"Good," she said, sounding more reassured. "Text me when you get there. I'll keep working on things on this end."

"Okay."

"Again with less fear."

"Okay!"

"Good luck. Oh! And don't move the guy with the head injury because—"

"Already did."

"Gah!" Rhonda hung up on me.

I shoved my phone back into my pocket, but didn't move. I *could* do this. I just needed to get Kyle and go. I had walked the path a hundred times. I could probably do it without a flashlight. Not that I wanted to try. I—

Suddenly I realized I was staring at something.

Something I had been seeing on the counter . . . without really seeing it.

A bag with a Third Act logo on the side.

Julie's bag.

I twisted my hair behind my neck. I should probably just get going, but there it was, just sitting there. It wouldn't take much for me to walk over and take a quick peek. Granted, if I did walk over, I would only be partially shielded from the view of the others. But if I was quick?

I chewed my lip. It probably wasn't worth it. I mean, I doubted she was a dark web assassin too, and how much worse could her secret identity really be?

But, then again, could I really be sure of anything?

I sidled over to the counter as quietly as I could, positioning my body to block the view. I reached up with one hand to make it look like I was going for something in the cupboard while my other hand dipped into the bag.

"Ow!" I hissed quietly. "Frick!"

The pointy end of some tweezers had dug under my fingernail. I brought it up to my mouth as I quickly shot a look over my shoulder to the living room. I could see Julie still. She was seated by Kenny on the couch, but the rest must have moved back to the table because I couldn't see them anymore.

I gripped the handle of a mug with my decoy hand as my other dropped back down into the bag again and rifled around.

Papers. Folders. A laptop. I felt around to the next compartment. Gum. Noisy, noisy keys. Tissues. Where was her freaking wallet?

I risked a look down. Oh crap. A pocket book with a zipper. A fiddly, little zipper.

"Hey, squirrel?" Ronnie's alcohol soaked voice called out again. "What are you doing in there? We want to know what the police said."

I thought I heard someone else mutter, "I'm telling you she's up to something," just before I heard a chair scrape across the floor.

"Hang on . . . uh . . . I just . . ." I almost had it.

"Are they on their way?" Chuck asked.

The freaking zipper was caught!

"They . . . uh . . . just said . . . mainly good, reassuring type things . . ."

I was going to hell.

Screw it. I grabbed the little pocket book with both hands, unzipped it, and . . .

Bingo! Driver's license!

"What do you think you're doing?"

Chapter Twenty-five

Crap! Julie! Right in the threshold!

"Hi there." I slowly slipped my hand out from its guilty, guilty hiding place. "I . . . I . . ."

Kyle suddenly came up to Julie's side. "I told you she was going to snoop around in your bag."

My eyes snapped over to him. "You little—"

"What?" he said. "I told you earlier that you wouldn't find any weapons in Julie's bag, but you wouldn't listen."

What? Weapons? My eyes darted from his face to Julie's then back to his.

"She's not trying to stir the pot," Kyle said, "by freaking people out with a gun. You're wasting your time."

My eyes met Kyle's. He widened them just a smidge, obviously trying to communicate the fact that he was saving my butt, and I was not making it easy for him. It wasn't exactly the best cover story, but then again, it was better than the nothing I had up my sleeve. "I guess you're right," I said, pushing the bag carefully back on the counter. "I didn't find any weapons."

"Told you," Kyle said matter-of-factly, but his shoulders dropped a fraction of an inch. Guess, he was a little worried about my ability to keep up. Hard to blame him.

Julie didn't say anything as she pushed her glasses up her nose, but the look on her face spoke to all sorts of suspicion.

"I'm sorry," I said quickly. "But, given the circumstances, I don't think it's all that surprising that we're a bit suspicious of each other."

She stared at me a moment longer, then shot a look back at Kenny. "Next time just ask. I've got nothing to hide."

"Of course."

She rubbed her arms. "Did you tell the police about him?" There was no denying that Kenny was more to Julie than just a co-worker. Man, all these secret romances would almost be heartwarming if we weren't about to die.

"I did. They're doing everything they can to get here," I said, but she was already moving back to her seat on the couch. Ronnie and Chuck turned away too. I shot Kyle a big smile and flipped my hand around to show him Julie's license while mouthing, *I got it!* with a big smile.

He shot me a wobbly thumbs-up.

I could tell he was impressed though . . . you know, deep down, in that place where teenagers still had souls. I stepped back into the part of the kitchen that was hidden from view and shouted loud enough for everyone to hear, "Kyle, hang on a sec. You can help me get some snacks ready."

"Okay," he said in a low voice, hurrying forward, "I know you think you're being subtle, but the entire time you were talking on the phone, Ronnie and Chuck were discussing whether you were just funny weird or like dangerous weird."

"I'm totally fine with that. Give me one second." I

pulled out my phone and quickly texted Julie's real name and birthday to Freddie. "Okay, there. So," I said, meeting Kyle's eye again, "We need to get ready to go."

Kyle's head dropped down to his chest. "What?"

"There's been a development."

"What kind of development?"

I studied his face a moment, debating how much I should tell him. Despite all of his sarcasm, he was still a kid. I couldn't have him freaking out. Not if we were going to make it to Kit Kit and Tweety's in this storm. But even more than that, there was just something inherently wrong with kids being scared.

"Well," I said, trying to buy myself more time. "We . . . we might not be as safe here as I would like."

He shook his head. "What do you mean?"

Just then my phone buzzed. I took it out and looked down at the message.

Kimberly Winters? Are you sure that's not the fake name?

I quickly typed back, *Nope, that's the real name.*

"Who are you texting?" Kyle asked.

"A friend. His name is Freddie. We, I mean, he has a security business. He's going to look into Julie's identity for us."

My phone buzzed again.

Wow. Very eighties soap opera. I like it.

I shook my head and shoved the phone back in my pocket. I felt a little weird about not telling Freddie about the maybe hired killer on the island, but I so didn't have time to deal with the fallout of that, so why worry him? "Okay, where were we?"

"You were about to tell me why you're acting like some kind of meth cat trying to get us to risk our lives in a blizzard?"

"Meth cat?"

"You know," he said erratically flailing his hand around the room. "A cat. On meth."

"Of course," I said with a little scoff. "But why would a cat be on meth?" I so did not understand this younger generation.

"It doesn't matter! Just tell me what's going on!"

"It's nothing." That wasn't a complete lie. It could absolutely be nothing. I couldn't even think the words *Dark Web Assassin* without tacking on a *Really?* In fact, the more I thought about it, the more ridiculous it all seemed. I mean, maybe Rhonda was still just getting carried away. And as for the new guy working at the station—Amos—well, I couldn't be sure he could be trusted to identify his own mother properly. Actually, that probably wasn't fair, but it sounded nice and reassuring in my head. I really didn't want to tell Kyle all of this if I didn't have to. "Well, it's like you said, you are now worth hundreds of millions of dollars." I gave him a little congratulatory punch on the shoulder before gesturing to the other room. "But they all are not." I ended with a nod and some pretty big *uh-oh* eyes.

He tilted his head. "I thought you were clinging to the whole *it could have been an accident* theory?"

"I am. I am," I said with my most convincing expression, which probably meant it looked painfully the opposite. "But that doesn't mean we can't play this safe."

"So what's the development then?"

Frick. I couldn't get anything past this kid. "Did I say there had been a development? I didn't mean—"

"I'm not three, okay? Tell me what your cop friend said, or I'm going to go into that room, and tell everyone that you're keeping something from us. Chuck may be an idiot, and Ronnie's getting close to passing out, but Julie already knows something is up, and if there's one thing she knows how to do, it's how to turn a group against someone." He pointed a finger at me. "So what's it going to be?"

My brow furrowed. Maybe Freddie was on to something with his whole dislike of kids. I planted my hands on my hips. "Are you sure you want to know?"

He went still a moment, brushing his heavy flop of hair back from his eyes, then nodded.

"Are you sure you're sure? Because I thought I was sure . . . and now I'm not so sure."

"If you want me to trust you, you need to tell me what's going on."

"Fine," I said, throwing my hands in the air. "Fine. Have it your way."

He waited.

"Kyle, have you ever heard of the dark web?"

The kid, perhaps not surprisingly, was really anxious to get going after that. If I had known fear was such a good motivator, I definitely would have used it sooner. We agreed, though, that we needed to be subtle about our departure. Even though I was feeling enormously guilty about not telling the others what Rhonda had told me on the phone, we didn't know who we could trust. Initially, Kyle thought that we should just slip out a window when nobody was looking, but we needed to protect ourselves against the storm, and our jackets were still in the living room. I also needed to sneak another flashlight out of the hall closet.

After a few minutes, we came up with a plan and headed back into the common room.

Julie hadn't moved from Kenny's side, but Ronnie was now peering through a window, swaying, most likely trying to spot her daughter. Chuck, meanwhile, had given up on all his paperwork and was sitting upright in an easy chair, hands pinned between his knees.

"Wow," I said, rubbing my arms. "It's getting kind of cold in here with the power out."

Nobody said anything.

Not even Kyle, who was really supposed to say something right now.

I shot him a side-eye, but he stayed mum.

"Don't you think it's getting cold in here, Kyle?"

He closed his eyes and shook his head. Huh, in a weird way it was almost like having Freddie with me. Always so judgmental of how I delivered our agreed-upon lines.

Finally, Kyle cleared his throat and said, "You're not my mother."

My eyes widened. That was not in the script.

He turned his back to the others and mouthed the words, *Play along.*

I jerked up straight. Oh, well, maybe he was better at this than I was.

"Fine," I said with probably too much indignant horror. I was still learning. "Freeze. I don't care. Julie was right," I said, catching her eye, "you are a—" I caught myself. Nope, still couldn't say it. "You can be a little bit *unpleasant* at times."

He rolled his eyes but carried on with, "Do you even have clothes that would fit me?"

"I'm sure I have something that would—"

"Why do you have clothes for teenaged boys?"

My mouth snapped shut.

"Are you like a cougar or something?"

I blinked. Rapidly. "I am not a—I don't keep clothes for teenaged—just get over here." I jerked a *follow me* gesture at him.

The others didn't say anything. They were too busy staring at us.

So much for subtle.

I couldn't worry about that though. As long as they

weren't getting in the way, we just needed to stick to the plan.

A couple of baskets had fallen from the top shelf of the closet when I had been searching for the flashlights. I dropped to my knees and grabbed a handful of knit hats, dumping them back into a container. Wouldn't want to trip running away from the assassin roaming the island. I passed one of the hats to Kyle before rocking back up to my feet to survey the other contents. Life vests, a couple of helmets for the ropes course, some snowmobiling gloves—

Wait a minute . . .

"Kyle, come here," I said, waving him closer.

"What?"

A moment later, I had him fully outfitted with all the gear I could manage.

"Are you sure this is enough?" he said, looking himself over. "I mean my legs are still pretty unprotected."

I nodded, maybe a little too quickly. "You're right. I think I may have some old goalie pads from—"

"I was kidding!" Kyle shouted.

"Of course," I muttered thoughtfully. "That's a stupid idea. You couldn't run in them anyway."

"Seriously, don't you think this is a bit of an overkill?"

I leaned in, whispering, "I want you to think about the last word in that sentence."

I knew I was acting a little bit crazy, but I couldn't help it. I had never been responsible for someone like this before. I mean, I had always been kind of responsible for my mother, but the trouble she got herself into was self-inflicted. This was a kid, and I was currently the closest thing he had to a guardian. I'd put him in a bubble if I could.

The thought of my mother felt like a shard of ice to the heart. Nope, I couldn't think about my mom right now.

"Okay, fine," Kyle said, twisting his hands into the air. "But do I have to wear the gloves? I can't even move my fingers."

I chuckled and folded my arms across my chest. "You obviously haven't seen hundreds of pictures of defensive wounds blown up to poster-board size, or you wouldn't be asking that question."

His eyes widened.

"Erica?" Julie's voice called out from across the room.

I whipped around, my eyebrows raised.

"Are you okay?"

"Um, yes." But given how my head was wobbling all over the place in an attempted nod, I could maybe see why she had asked the question. "I'm sorry. Did you hear that last bit? I mentioned I worked as a court reporter, right? I don't just go looking at pictures of defensive wounds for like fun."

"Right," she answered slowly. "But why do you have the kid dressed like he's headed into mortal combat in the first place?"

"Oh." My mind spun around in circles trying to find an appropriate lie, but it was really hard because the guilty, guilty part of me wanted to blurt out what I knew about the maybe assassin on the island, but I couldn't because I didn't know if I could trust them, especially fake-Julie, and the longer I took, trying to sort all this through, the guiltier I was looking . . . which made it even harder to come up with a lie! I just needed to say something. Anything. "I regret nothing."

Julie cocked her head, looking a smidge alarmed.

"Sorry. Sorry. You know what? Truth is. I'm worried about him, okay? This has been a strange night. But you don't need to be concerned about me. I'm not going to go all . . ." I waved my hands in the air, "Brody."

Ronnie looked at me, gripping the curtain for support.

"If you're doing all this because you think I'm going to attack the kid again, don't. I'm too worried ab—Whoa!"

Suddenly, Chuck jumped to his feet causing her to roll back in a wave down into a chair—a move that should only be attempted while drunk.

"What's going on?" I asked, tossing Kyle an old pair of elbow pads.

"I thought I saw a light."

Julie's head whipped to the window. "Where?"

I pushed past Kyle to look too.

"I'm going to be sick," Ronnie said, bringing the back of her hand to her mouth. "Where's the washroom?"

I pointed to the back hallway. "What kind of light? Like a flashlight?"

"No, farther out. Like on the water."

We all peered out into darkness. Maybe Rhonda had somehow managed to convince Lake Patrol to come out after all. Maybe Grady—

"Your mind's playing tricks on you," Julie said, slumping back down, body still leaning protectively over Kenny. The cameraman almost looked content in his unconsciousness. "You can't see anything out there."

She was right. All I could see was blurring snow.

Chuck ran a hand over his forehead. "But I could have sworn . . ."

"It must have been Ashley," I said, leaning away from the glass. "All the snow . . . the light from her torch just looked father away. I should probably call her. Get her to come back inside. Realistically, if she hasn't found Brody yet, she probably . . ." I let the sentence trail off as a new wave of guilt rolled over me. If someone truly had paid the pretend bodyguard to kill Rayner, the most likely suspect was Brody. He stood the best chance of inheriting. His craziness all could have been an act and that meant the people in the room right now were most likely innocent. I mean, Ronnie could have hired the assassin—the word still sounded weird in my head—to kill Rayner if she thought he hadn't changed the will yet, but now that she knew he had, she had nothing to gain from anyone else dying. She wasn't Kyle's blood. Ashley wasn't either. I didn't think step-mothers and step-sisters really stood to inherit that much, not when Kyle had blood relatives. Chuck was going to get paid either way. And when it came to Kenny and Julie—I mean, Kenny and Kimberly . . . aw, that was kind of cute—despite the fake name, I just couldn't see what their motive would be. At the end of the day, they all had the right to try to defend themselves, and I didn't know if I could live with myself if I didn't tell them.

"Everyone," I said, backing away from the window, "there's something I need to tell you." My eyes darted over to Kyle. Okay, he didn't look happy.

What are you doing? he mouthed.

I shook my head. I had to. I had to give them a fighting chance.

"When I was on the phone with the sheriff's department, I learned something that I think you all should kn—"

My voice cut off as all of our heads whipped back around to the window. The hair on the back of my neck prickled.

No . . .

I shook my head, but there was no denying it. We had all heard the same thing.

Not right outside. But not that far away.

A noise.

That sounded an awful lot like . . .

. . . screams.

Chapter Twenty-six

"You heard that, right?" Julie asked, keeping her hand on Kenny's chest but lowering to her knees on the floor. I guess she felt uncomfortable being so close to the window. "Do you think it was Ashley?"

I spun on my heel.

"What are you doing?" Kyle asked as I brushed by him. "You're not going out there?"

"I have to," I said, grabbing the biggest flashlight I could find from the box.

"But what about me? Aren't you kind of forgetting"— he shot a quick look back at the others before dropping his voice—"that I'm the target."

I stopped and met his eye as I pulled my hat down over my ears. "I won't go far. I just need to see if she needs help. Don't let Ronnie follow me," I said, looking to Chuck and Julie. I mean Kimberly. Whoever! "She's in no condition to be out there."

"Erica," Kyle said in a shaky voice. "Please don't leave me with them."

"I swear," I said gripping his arm. "You are my top priority. I'm just going to look. For all we know, she could

have fallen like Kenny. She may just need help getting
back inside."

"Please," Kyle said again in a way that made my heart
clench. I could see how hard it was for him to ask me for
help. He was so very caught in that space of feeling the
pressure to be a man. Too bad he wasn't old enough to
get that we were all afraid.

"It's going to be okay. Just wait here, and if you see
me running back"—I swallowed hard—"you know, hold
the door open." Suddenly I found myself wrapping my
arms around him and pulling him in for a hug.

"What are you doing?"

"Just giving you a hug. Is that okay?"

"I guess," he said, putting his arms around me. "Just
keep your hands north of the equator."

Stepping outside felt a lot like stepping into another
world . . . a dark, snowy world filled with hidden assassins. I didn't turn on my flashlight right away. If anyone
had been watching the lodge, they would have seen the
door open and shut, but I moved quickly in the hopes that
I would be lost in the darkness. I hustled down the front
steps, now covered in a few thick inches of snow, then
shuffled as quickly as I could in the direction I thought
I'd heard the screams.

While I couldn't see too far in front of me, overall vis-
ibility was better than I had thought it would be. All the
snow was reflecting the dim glow from the lodge, and
even though the wind was swirling the falling flakes into
funnels, everything else seemed deathly still.

I plunged one foot into the snow after the other, wanting to hurry, but the snow had drifted in places, nearly
reaching my knee. An incredible amount had fallen in a
short period of time. It was heavy, wet stuff too. I couldn't
imagine Brody being out here without a jacket. I felt

really sorry for him if, you know, he wasn't the one who had hired the killer.

The farther I walked away from the lodge, the more complete the darkness became. It was hard to even be sure I was going in the right direction, but my instinct told me I wasn't too far off. When I had first heard the screams, my instant thought had been *the canoes*. My mom stored a few under a little wooden overhang shelter near the tree line. I had to trust that. It was all I had to go on, and I didn't have much time. I needed to get back to Kyle.

Being out in the wind and the swirling snow, the grip I had on what was real and what wasn't slipped away from me again. I mean, this was an emergency, but there was an eerie calm that came with the stillness of all that was hunkered down against the storm. And no matter how hard I tried, it seemed like my brain was working on a time lag, like it just couldn't catch up to everything that had happened. It was still stuck on finding a way to make things right with Grady. It was nuts. I shouldn't be worried about my love life at a time like this . . . but somehow it just made it all worse. I wanted to go back . . . weeks . . . months. Right to the moment at the airport when he had disappeared behind the gate.

I shook my head. Now was so not the time. I would get my chance to explain everything to him. Make it right.

If I survived.

I moved to take another step, feeling snow fall into one of my too-short boots as I lifted it from the drift.

So many things I couldn't think about.

The worst?

My mother.

In fact, it was taking everything in me not to think

about my mother . . . because the moment Rhonda had told me that there might me a killer on the island, a little thought trail had started deep in my consciousness that began with my mother not going to Arizona, and it ended with her . . . nope.

No.

Definitely not.

But I couldn't pretend that when Brody was shouting, just before he left, saying we were all going to disappear, well, I could have sworn he was going to say, *Just like your mother.*

No. No. I refused to believe that. Besides, he wasn't exactly a reliable source.

I just needed to worry about me and Kyle.

Everyone else was fine.

I clenched my fists and pushed forward. Just a few more steps. Then I could go back inside knowing in my heart I had tried.

Just a few more steps into the terrifying darkness . . .

Suddenly my phone buzzed. I jerked so hard I nearly cracked my spine.

Maybe it was Grady.

Please let it be Grady.

Nope.

"Freddie," I said as quietly as I thought I could while still being heard over the wind. "I'm kind of busy right n—"

"Why didn't you tell me about the assassin!"

I grimaced. "Oh, you talked to Rhonda."

"Yes, I talked to Rhonda! But I should have heard it from you!"

"You're right," I said, blinking snow from my eyes. "But can we talk about this later? I'm kind of—"

"Where are you? Are you outside?"

"Yeah."

"Where the assassin is?"

"Maybe."

"Why? Why would you do that?"

I shook my head. Suddenly I couldn't remember why. "We . . . we heard screaming." Oh yeah, that was it.

"Oh, well. What the hell is the matter with you? I told you to forget about the kid!"

I scanned the darkness in front of me and mumbled, "It's not the kid. It's the hunter girl, Ashley."

"What? That's even worse!" Freddie had yelled so loudly, my ear was ringing. "Go back inside. This isn't your business! Let Mother Nature have her revenge."

"I will. I will. I'm just going to look by the canoes," I said, suddenly keenly aware that the glow of my phone was probably lighting my face up like a target. I shoved it up my hat a little. "Freddie, be quiet for a second. I want to see if I can hear anything. But . . . don't go. It's kind of creepy out here."

"You think?" Freddie let out a rough breath but quieted down.

I squinted against the snow in the direction of the canoes. I so badly wanted to shout Ashley's name, but I couldn't find the nerve. Maybe if I just turned on the flashlight for a second? I could sweep it in the direction of the shelter, maybe see something that would tell me if it was worth going any farther. I wasn't that far from the lodge. I could make a run for it if someone suddenly jumped out of nowhere. Not that running in deep snow would be that much use against a gun . . . but then again he was probably already watching me with his night vision goggles, so did it really matter?

"Okay," I whispered. "I'm going to turn on my flashlight."

"What? That has to be the stupidest—"

"Shush!" I took a breath of icy air.

Freddie kept mumbling something, but not loud enough for me to hear.

"Okay, here goes nothing." I clicked on the beam.

At first I couldn't see anything through the swirling snow, but a second later I was able to pinpoint my surroundings. I was faced too far toward the lake. Jeez, I had grown up here and had still managed to get myself turned around. I tracked the light slowly toward the shelter, but before my beam landed on any canoes, it caught something in the snow.

"What do you see? What do you see?" Freddie asked, reading my mind.

"Um . . ."

"Um, what?"

"Footprints. I see footprints."

I had forgotten to look for them too.

"Well, they're probably hunter girl's, right?"

"Right." I swallowed hard as I swept the flashlight back in the other direction following the trail . . . but deep down I already knew where they led.

You see, there wasn't much in the front clearing of the lodge. In the summer, there were a few picnic tables, a couple of half-barrel planters for flowers, sometimes a volleyball net . . . but this time of year, there was just the one thing.

A boulder.

Big enough that I would climb on top of it as a kid to gain a couple feet to see up over the trees to the lake . . .

. . . also big enough to hide behind if you wanted to watch the lodge hidden from view.

My heart thumped again against my ribcage. Not because of the size of the boulder. Although that was bad enough, given the whole hiding situation. But still, that wasn't what had me worried.

It was how close it was.

I bit my lip.

Twenty feet? Thirty, if I was lucky.

Those footprints could be Ashley's or Brody's. But I knew better. I just knew. They had no real reason to hide.

"Erica?"

I edged my beam closer and closer to the rock, and just as I caught its edge . . .

. . . a figure rose up from behind.

Chapter Twenty-seven

I did what any sane person would do.

I screamed and fell backward into the snow.

My phone was screaming too. Maybe even louder than I was.

My flashlight dropped into a drift, causing me to lose sight of the head that had been rising up from behind the boulder. I scrambled backward, turning at the same time to get to my feet. There was no time to get my flashlight back, but I didn't need it. I could see the lodge glowing maybe a hundred yards away. I just had to get there.

My feet pounded through the snow, slipping back with every step.

I wasn't going to make it.

He was right behind me.

I shot one look over my shoulder and screamed again.

I could barely hear Freddie shouting, "What's happening?"

"Assassin! Assassin!"

It was definitely him. I couldn't make out anything but his size, but that was all I needed—unless there was another seven-foot man on the island. Any doubts I had about Rhonda's story spun away with the whirling snow.

I pushed forward. Harder. Faster. My lungs burned with the cold as my mind screamed for me to keep running, but my legs were heavy and slow.

Come on, Erica. Don't give up. Come on!

But just then, my right foot landed in a deep patch of snow, and when I pulled my foot back up, my boot was left behind.

Didn't matter. Didn't matter. I just needed to get away. Needed to get to the lodge. I couldn't feel anything anyway . . . until the hand landed on my back.

The weight of it knocked me to the ground, taking my breath away. Snow pressed into my eyes and mouth. I flipped over again and scrambled backward in a crab-walk, phone still in my hand. I couldn't get up this time though. Not with the man looming over me, covered in white, looking almost like a snowman. A seven-foot-tall murderous snowman with a crescent-shaped scar. Yup, I'd be seeing that in my dreams. If you had dreams when you're dead.

I shuffled back some more. Every time my hand came out of the snow, I could hear Freddie yelling.

"Don't you touch my fr—"

Dunk.

"I'll hire twenty assassins! Fifty! If you so much—"

Dunk.

"Get ready for the dark web of Freddie, psycho! Population, y—"

Dunk.

I didn't dare turn to run. I needed to see if the man looming over me was going to move to hit me again.

But he didn't. He just kept walking forward with every move I made back.

What was he doing?

More important, what the hell was I going to do?

"The police know you're here," I shouted into the wind.

"Yeah!" I thought I heard my phone shout distantly.

"They'll be here any second. Looking for you."

"Any second!"

The man didn't say anything.

"You're a business man. It's time to cut your losses."

Nothing.

"Think about it. Are you even getting paid to kill me?"

Still nothing.

I crab-walked back another step, leading with my hands, snow burning my wrists.

This time he didn't follow.

I moved back again.

He stayed in his spot.

I slowly got up to my feet, and took one step back. Then another.

I thought I heard, "Erica?" muffled through my snow covered phone.

The man didn't move.

Didn't have to tell me twice. I pivoted hard and ran for the lodge.

I didn't hear him following, but I also didn't dare look back either until I was up on the porch.

Nothing but darkness. Almost like he too had been whirled away in the snow.

"Freddie! I'm okay. I'm—" I grabbed the handle to the front door and pushed. Its lack of give nearly sent my face careening into the wood.

"Okay," I shouted. "Who locked the door?"

Chapter Twenty-eight

"So let me get this straight," Ronnie said, pointing at me with the Scotch bottle in her hand. "You think this dark webbed assassin—"

"Web!" Julie said for the fourth time. She was sitting back on the couch with Kenny. We decided it best to close all the curtains. "Web. Like the Internet?"

"Web," Ronnie corrected, rolling her eyes. She was barely holding onto consciousness. "And he wants to kill us?"

"Guys, we don't have time for this. There's another cabin on the island. We'll be safer there." Maybe. "We need to go. Like now," I said, hopping while trying to pull on one of my mom's way-too-small boots. And yes, I was still trying to save these people even though they had temporarily locked me outside. They had claimed that it wasn't really me they were locking out. They were just scared. It was hard to blame them. "We are fish in a barrel in here." I had ended the call with Freddie pretty much as soon as I got inside. He was off to find help anyway.

"Wait. Wait. Wait," Ronnie went on. "So there's an assassin, and you think he's going to kill us."

"Yes!" We hadn't told Ronnie about the screams we had heard earlier, but I was getting close. I couldn't speak for anyone else, but it seemed cruel to tell her when we didn't know for sure what we'd heard. Plus, there was no way Ronnie could go looking for her daughter herself, and I couldn't do it for her. I looked over to Kyle. He was sitting in the corner of the room against the wall still dressed in winter clothes, a helmet, and hockey pads. He had gone very quiet and was doing a good job of staring at the floor. I think he was trying to block out everything at this point. The stuff going on in his head was probably more than he could take. "Now get ready. We're going."

"But he's not trying to kill me, right?" Ronnie said, before taking another swig from the bottle. "Or Ashley? Because we probably won't get a dime—"

"I think we have to assume we are all at risk," I said again. "They'll have to construct a crime scene that makes sense and that will be hard to do with witnesses. Right . . . Chuck?" I looked around the room. "Where's Chuck?"

"He's a . . ." Ronnie said, meshing the words together into a *za* sound, "Washroom! I saw him when I was done with the . . ." she waved her hand around her mouth in a puking motion. "Where's Ashley? I need to talk to her. She said some mean, mean things to me." Suddenly Ronnie looked like she might start drunk weeping. "Ashley?" she shouted, stumbling off toward the kitchen. "Baby?"

I closed my eyes, wondering if I could just knock Ronnie out and throw her over my shoulder.

"Why didn't he kill you?"

I opened my eyes. They landed on Julie. "What?"

"Why didn't he kill you when he had the chance?" Wow, she was not happy. Those two spots of color were back on her cheeks, and her eyes had an angry sparkle to them. I couldn't blame her. Julie was smart, and she was worried about Kenny, worried about herself, and here I was adding an assassin to the mix. Then again, I couldn't know anything for sure about Julie, could I?

I shook my head and looked down at my hands. "I don't know." It was the truth. Maybe what I had said about making sure he got paid had had an effect. But it still felt like I was missing something. "I don't know."

"Are you all right?" she asked me again.

I flicked my eyes back up to hers. She didn't try to hide her expression one bit. She wasn't asking out of concern. She was really asking me if I was going to be a problem. Yeah, right back at ya.

"I'm fine." Okay, that may have been a little bit of a lie. I hugged my jacket closer to my body. I just could not get warm.

"And who do you keep texting?"

"Oh," I said looking up. I hadn't even realized I had pulled out my phone again. "I have lots of friends in the sheriff's department. I'm just checking to see if we're any closer to help arriving."

She nodded, but didn't look all that convinced.

"Are you coming?" I asked.

She shook her head. "I can't leave Kenny."

I ran a hand over my face.

"What can I say? I might even be . . . in love with the guy." She looked down at him, and brushed some hair from his brow. "How ridiculous is that?"

A heavy tumble of emotions fell over me. Fake name or not, it was hard to imagine Julie being behind all of this. She was clearly in love with Kenny, and you could tell it was the kind of love that hoped for a future, a future that wouldn't be risked for money. Then it again that was the kind of future I wanted with Grady, and I was messing that up all the time. I sighed. "It's not ridiculous at all."

She met my gaze again. I guess she saw something there because she nodded.

I turned away quickly, taking a step toward the back hallway. "How long has Chuck been in the bathroom?"

"I'll go check on him," Kyle said, jumping to his feet.

"No!" I shouted. "You stay here. We're just about to leave."

"I'll be right back. I can't just sit here anymore. Waiting."

"Kyle," I said, reaching out in his direction, right as Ronnie stumbled back in the room blocking my path. "So let me get this straight . . ."

"Oh God," Julie moaned.

"So you think . . . you think it's Brody who hired this assassin?" Ronnie suddenly gasped and flung her arms into the air, which sent her tumbling down into a dining chair like a clumsy praying mantis. "That's why he left! He didn't want to be here for the actual killing! He's probably having hot chocolate somewhere . . . while we all get." She made a horrible screeching noise, while cutting a sloppy finger across her throat. "Where's Ashley?"

I frowned at her, worried she was circling her way closer to remembering that Ashley had gone after Brody. No telling what she'd do then. Just like Kyle, I kind of wished I could put her in a bubble too. A bubble that I could put in a box. With a lock. Maybe in a sealed basement until help arrived. "Again, I don't know that Brody is the one who hired him. I—"

"I do," Kyle suddenly said. He was standing by the table where Brody had been sitting, thumb scrolling over a phone.

"What?"

"It's Brody's," he said looking up at me. "He had his banking app open."

I took a step toward him. "And?"

"There's a . . ." he looked down at the screen and blinked. "A pending transaction here for fifty thousand dollars."

"Come on," I said moving around Ronnie's legs. "Let me see that."

He offered the phone up to me like it might explode.

I speed read the little screen. Definitely a bank transfer. The money was being held, though. Something about a waiting period for large transactions. I scrolled down. But who was it to?

The words, "Oh crap," came out before I could stop them.

"What?" Julie snapped. "Truth this time."

"It is a banking transaction for fifty thousand dollars."

Kyle scoffed. "Yeah, that's kind of what I said."

"Fifty thousand, smifty thousand," Ronnie drawled.

"She's right. That's not a lot of money for this family," Julie began. "He could have just—"

"Fifty thousand dollars to be transferred to a Swiss bank."

Chapter Twenty-nine

"What should we do?" I asked, looking to Julie. She was the only other functioning adult in the room.

"What can we do?"

"I don't know," I mumbled, but my fingers seemed to have an idea.

"What are you . . ." Kyle began, panic filling his voice. "Are you sure that's a good idea?"

"Nope." My thumbs darted around the phone. When I was done, I dropped it on the table and took a step back.

Kyle leaned over to look at the screen before turning some very wide eyes back on me. "You cancelled the transaction."

"Yep," I said, pinching my lips together.

"You did what?" Julie shouted. "Why?"

"Not exactly sure," I said with a shrug.

"What if . . . what if that just makes him mad?"

I nodded, but I was starting to see the logic in my thumbs. "But if he's not getting paid, he has no reason to kill us."

"But," Kyle began, shaking his head in jerky motions,

"now Brody will just come back looking for his phone and—"

"No problem," Ronnie said, throwing herself across the table. "I got this." She snatched up the phone, dropped it to floor then stomped on it with her heel.

"Um, okay," I said, meeting her proud smile. "Good job."

We all stared at the broken pieces on the floor.

"Now what?" Julie asked quietly.

I pushed my bangs back from my forehead with both hands. "Now we go."

"We need a gun," Ronnie said thickly. "Where's your gun?"

"I don't have one. I—"

"Erica?" Kyle interrupted.

I shot him a quick look. "Hang on a sec."

"What about your mom?" Ronnie asked, pulling herself up. "We can go hunt this sucker down." She had taken a few steps before she realized she was headed directly for Rayner. She tried to do a quick about-face, but smacked herself into the wall. "Right," she said, patting the wood a few times. "Now, where's your mom's gun?"

"She doesn't have a gun." Even if she did, there was no way I was giving it to Ronnie in her condition. Or any condition.

"Erica?" Kyle said again.

I half-looked at him but held up a hand, "Did you check on Chuck? Where is he?"

"She doesn't have a gun?" Ronnie yelled. She was working on a couple seconds delay. "What does she do when, like"—her hands flailed around the room—"the wildlife attack!"

"Erica?"

"Kyle, please, just get Chuck. We need to go." I turned

back to Ronnie before I thought to add, "And stay away from any windows."

He huffed a breath, pushing himself away from the table toward the hallway.

"There has to be a gun here somewhere," Ronnie went on. "Stupid airport wouldn't let me take mine." She lifted a cushion off a chair as though she just might happen to find a weapon hiding there. "I'd have taken out that sucker by now and had the pic up on my fan page."

Just then Kyle walked back in the room. "So I went to check on Chuck . . ."

"And?"

"He's—"

Suddenly there was a loud bang outside. All eyes snapped around to the lodge's front windows.

"Gone," Kyle finished, taking a nervous step back in the direction of the hallway.

"It might just have been the wind," I whispered, side-shuffling toward him. "Wait, Chuck's gone?"

"Bathroom window's open. Chuck's gone."

"Why? Why would he—"

Bang!

There was no mistaking that sound for the wind. That was definitely a person . . . this time banging on the door.

Ronnie crept forward a few steps. "Ashley?" she whispered in that really loud way drunk people do.

"Quiet," Julie hissed.

I licked my lips. "Maybe it's the police?"

"Wouldn't they just say, 'This is the police'?" Julie snapped, crouching back down to the floor, hand still on Kenny's chest.

"I don't know."

The door handle rattled. This time I was really glad Kyle had decided to re-lock it.

The knock came again . . . but quieter this time.

I took a single step toward the door.

"Don't!" Ronnie shouted, making a wild swing for me. "It's not Ashley. I know it's not Ashley. She'd be yelling by now. It's the murderer. Normal people don't knock that way."

I stared at her. "You know how murderers knock?"

She nodded up and down in a big movement. "That first knock was all *Bang Bitches! You're all going to die!* And when that didn't work, the knock was all *Little Pig. Little Pig. Let me come in.*" She rolled a hand in the air. "But just like . . . in reverse."

I stopped walking. It had sounded a little like that.

"Open the door!" a voice shouted, but it was almost a half-shout, like whoever had made it wanted us to hear but was hiding from someone else.

"Is that Brody?" I whispered looking around at the others.

They all shot me uncertain looks.

I took a step forward.

"Don't!" Ronnie shouted. "I'm telling you. It's a trap."

I shook my head. I was kind of thinking the same thing, but . . . "We don't know anything for sure."

"What about the bank account?" Kyle asked.

I froze. "Oh yeah."

"You open that door," Ronnie said sharply, "the assassin comes in."

"Please," the voice called again. "Let me in!"

I took another step, Kyle grabbed my arm. He had his big, big eyes going again. "You said you would protect me."

"I know. I know." I squeezed his hand. "I'm not going to open the door. I'm just going to take a peek and—"

"Get shot in the head!" Ronnie finished.

"Please! Hurry!" I could hear the panic rising in the voice on the other side of the door. "He's out here."

"I know what it's like to be out there. I'm just going to talk to him," I said to Kyle. "Go over and stay with them."

Julie held a hand out to him, but he didn't move.

"Look, I could be wrong about"—I shook my head—"everything. But we can't just leave him out there to be killed. Not without at least asking him a few questions."

Kyle held my gaze a moment then moved to crouch by Julie. I wiped my hands on my jeans and looked back at the door.

"She's going to die," I heard Ronnie moan. "She's going to let the webbed killer guy in, and we're all going to die."

"I'm not going to let him in!" I shout-whispered.

"Please. He's coming!" The shout was followed up with a scream and a whole bunch of thumps on the porch.

I launched myself toward the door, got up on my toes, and peeked out through the small window at the top. I couldn't see anything.

"Brody?" I called out.

Nothing.

"Brody?"

Oh God, what if he was crumpled in a heap at the foot of the door?

Or waiting to shoot me in the face.

I reached out for the door handle.

"Don't do it!" Ronnie yelled.

I yanked my hand back.

Just then Brody's face popped up out of nowhere on the other side of the glass.

I yelped and spun around so that my back was against the wood.

"Please, don't let me die out here."

"Brody," I said, gulping a breath. "I'm going to have to ask you a few questions."

"What? Just let me in!" He hit the door again, hard enough to bounce my shoulders on the wood.

"Brody, focus. Where's Ashley?"

"I don't know. I don't know, man. I heard her scream."

"What?" Ronnie shrieked.

"Let me in!"

I shook my head like he could see me. "I don't think I can do that, Brody. Not yet."

"Why not?"

I pulled my bottom lip through my teeth. "Why do you think someone is after you?"

"I saw him! Just a minute ago! The big dude. The bodyguard Gramps hired, who took our boat!"

I backed away from the door and rubbed my hand over my mouth. I looked over to the group. Julie was practically sitting on Ronnie to hold her down. "What do you guys think?"

"He's lying," Julie said.

Kyle nodded.

"Let him in!" Ronnie shouted, smacking the floor with her palm. "If he did something to my daughter, I'll—"

The producer plunked her weight more squarely on Ronnie's back.

"Brody?" I called out, stepping back toward the door.

"What?"

"Why did you transfer fifty thousand dollars to a Swiss bank account?"

"What are you talking about? Just let me in!"

My eyes flashed over to the others. "What am I supposed to tell him?"

"Nothing! Anything!" Julie shouted. "Who cares?" I couldn't blame her for feeling that way. She was now pulling Ronnie back from the table by her bodysuit while Kyle was trying to yank his step-mother's outstretched hand away from a steak knife.

I turned back to the door. Problem was, I cared. Kind of. It really did look like Brody was guilty . . . in a really circumstantial way. What if we were wrong? What if I was wrong? I had started this whole thing. It hadn't seemed like Brody was faking all his crazy stuff earlier. If we were wrong about this . . .

I should at least maybe give him a little heads-up instead of letting him bang on the door out there like some blue-highlighted sitting duck.

"Brody?"

"Thank God, you're still there. Let me in!"

"Yeah, about that."

"What?!"

I took a step back. "We took a vote."

"You took a vote and what?" Brody shouted.

"We took a vote," I began again, "and we decided that certain parts of your story are troubling, and—"

"And?"

I shook my head at the wooden planks in front of me. Man, it was hard breaking this kind of news to a door. "We decided that those of us in here . . . are more comfortable with you being out there."

I looked back at the others. Julie mouthed the words, *Good. Good,* while she and Kyle still wrestled with Ronnie.

I looked back at the door. It hadn't said anything.

I couldn't help but think that probably wasn't a good sign.

"Brody?" I called out. "Did you hear me?"

Nothing.

"Brody?"

I scurried back around to the couch and leaned across, planting my hands on the back of it to peer out the window.

It was hard to see anything in the dark, but . . .

"Guys," I said in a whisper. "I think he might be gone."

And that's when I heard the window in the kitchen shatter.

Chapter Thirty

"Oh no. Oh no!" I screamed flinging myself away from the window.

"What's happening?" Julie shouted.

"I think he's coming in the kitchen!" I yelled, yanking Kyle up off the floor. "We gotta go people! Now!"

"Oh, I'm not going anywhere," Ronnie said lurching herself forward to snatch the knife off the table.

"Your choice."

Julie stood motionless by the couch.

"Come on!" I shouted. "Last chance.

"I'm not leaving Kenny," she said, shaking her head. "He can't defend himself. He wouldn't leave me. We're a team."

I thought about arguing even more with her, but by the sounds of the grunts coming from the kitchen, Brody was about halfway through, and the look on Julie's face was resolved.

I shook my head at them both.

"Go!" Julie said. "Protect the kid."

"I got this," Ronnie said, swirling the knife to point at the kitchen, fumbling it, then re-establishing her point.

"At least, take this," I said, rushing to hand Julie the poker from the fireplace.

She took it with a nod. Now that the decision had been made, fear slipped through her steely look.

"Good luck," I said.

"You too."

I yanked Kyle toward me, grabbing a flashlight from the table. "Stay close." A loud thump sounded on the kitchen floor just as I whipped the front door open. Icy wind barreled into the lodge. "Don't let go of me."

Chapter Thirty-one

We pushed our way out the door and stumbled down the front steps into the snow. I felt Kyle fall behind me, but he didn't let go of my jacket. I could barely keep my eyes open against the driving wind and now . . . blinding sleet? I crossed my free arm over my forehead, taking a moment to orient myself. There was no way we would make it to Kit Kat and Tweety's. We wouldn't even find the opening to the trail.

Now what?

The shed!

The lodge had a rusted-out old shed in the back for the lawnmower my mom never used.

It was worth a shot. With the flashlight, I was pretty sure I could get us that far.

"This way!" I shouted, but the wind tore the words from my mouth. I grabbed Kyle's wrist with one hand and dragged him forward, while bracing myself against the wind with the other.

We made it just a few steps when I heard Kyle scream something. I stopped, feeling for his shoulders to bring his face closer to my ear.

"I think I saw someone!"

"Who?"

"I don't know. I just saw a light!"

"Forget it! We have to keep going!" I clicked off my flashlight. If Kyle could see somebody's light, that probably meant somebody could see ours. We needed to do this blind.

We trudged across the lawn for what felt like hours before I clicked my beam back on again, grateful to find it bouncing off the aluminum siding of the shed. Tears of relief flooded my eyes.

"Hang on!" I yelled back to Kyle. I gripped the cold metal handle of the shed door and gave it yank. Didn't even budge. I jerked it again, putting more weight behind it. Not an inch. The top of the flimsy door had a lot of give, but the bottom wasn't moving.

I grunted and gave it a good kick.

"What's going on?"

"It won't open. It's wedged in the snow!"

"Just hold the top down," Kyle yelled. "I'll slide in, then hold it open it for you!"

"Okay!" I pulled as hard as I could on the door, creating a sliver of space from the top of the threshold to just under the door handle. Kyle turned sideways and with a big step climbed in. Once he was through, I passed him the flashlight, and he pushed against the top of the door, creating the same space for me to follow. Mirroring Kyle's move, I stepped over the closed part of the door and slid my body halfway through when—

"Ow! Son of a—"

"Sorry! Sorry! Sorry!" Kyle yelled, bringing his hands to his mouth. "I slipped!"

Kyle had been pushing so hard on the top of the door, he'd lost his footing. His hands slipped off the slick metal, allowing the sheet to snap back on me—which would have been okay, if an errant nail or a screw hadn't driven its way into my back.

"It's fine," I said trying to choke out the words without screaming in pain. I was really starting to rethink my desire to have kids. "A little help, though?"

"Oh, damn!" He launched himself back at the door, hands outstretched to give it a pretty good hit . . . taking the nail and my flesh with it.

"Sweet mother—" I cut myself off as I hit the dirt.

Kyle dropped to his knees. "Are you okay?"

"Yup. Good," I said through my teeth. "Just really in need of a tetanus shot."

"I'm so sorry. I—"

"No, it's fine," I said, hauling myself up into a seated position. "Really. Fine."

I dragged myself toward the back of the shed on my hands and knees, resting my shoulders against the one bit of wall that wasn't covered with rusted-out equipment left behind by the previous owners . . . fifty years ago. Yeah, it wasn't creepy at all in here. Well, except for maybe that scythe hanging on the far wall. That was a bit disturbing. Kyle huddled in beside me.

This night. This freaking night!

Nope, a part of me still couldn't believe this all was happening. It was just too crazy. I clutched my shoulders to warm my trembling arms, but I knew I wasn't shaking from the cold.

We sat in silence a good moment listening to the wind screech and pound against the thin metal walls. The noise drowned out any real possibility of conversation, so both Kyle and I stayed quiet, falling into our own thoughts.

How could this have happened? How could any of this be happening? If only my mother hadn't—

And there it was again.

My mother.

I couldn't stop myself from thinking about her anymore. My mom . . . she wouldn't have left a bunch of strangers alone in the retreat. Especially not members of an estranged family. She would have felt it her duty to stay and help. I had known that all along.

So, where was she?

I closed my eyes.

And what was happening at the retreat right now?

Was Brody telling the truth? Did it matter? Had the assassin gone in after him? Had I left them all to d—

Nope. Nope.

Even if I could have helped them in any kind of meaningful way, I didn't have a choice. I looked sideways at Kyle. He was hanging in there, but by the looks of it, just barely. He caught me looking at him and said, "You okay?" in a voice loud enough to compete with the sleet that was battering the old tin roof like a million tiny drums.

I nodded at him. The glow of the flashlight illuminated his face. For the first time, he suddenly seemed a lot older, like he had aged about a decade in one night.

"Look," I shouted. "We're safe now. We'll just wait the whole thing out in here. Help will come. We're going to make i—"

And that's when someone crashed into the door.

Chapter Thirty-two

"Erica!"

Kyle clutched at me, his hard, bony fingers digging into my bicep. I had told him to keep his snowmobile gloves on!

"Don't worry! They're not getting in." I lurched forward and grabbed the handle to the door. I felt the person yank at it on the other side. But there's was no way they were getting it open. I ground my feet into the dirt floor, holding the door back with all of my weight.

The person yanked at it again with a yell this time, and I felt it jerk a bit, but my grip was holding. Uh-unh. No way they were getting in. Not with me—

WHAM!

My hands flew in front of my face as I fell back into Kyle.

"Erica!"

I tried to scream back, but my throat wasn't working. Nothing was working.

My body had shut down the moment I saw the blade of the ax rip into the door.

"They have an ax!" Kyle screamed again, shaking my arm.

"I know," I moaned, but I doubted he heard me.

"Do something!"

He was right. I knew he was right, but I just couldn't seem to move. We'd lost. We had hung in there as long we could, but Brody was right. No one was getting off this island. And I was tired. I didn't have anything left. I just—"Ow!"

Kyle had slapped me.

Okay, apparently I wasn't completely numb. I hopped to my feet and lunged for the scythe. I yanked it off the wall, but it dropped from my hands to the floor. Wow, that was heavy. Okay, probably not the best defensive tool in this cramped space.

Another deafening WHAM! exploded behind me followed by an ear-splitting metal on metal screech as the blade cut a strip down the door.

Okay. Okay. I whipped back around, my flashlight dancing spastically over the wall. Weapon . . . weapon . . . garden sheers! Okay, maybe not the best match against the ax, but all I needed was one good strike to the belly. Oh God, could I really do that? Stab someone in the belly? It seemed so—

WHAM!

I could do it. Totally. No problem.

"Kyle! Take the flashlight!"

I tossed it behind me, but it tumbled to the floor. Didn't matter. The shed was small enough that the beam still cast enough light regardless of where it was pointed. I grabbed the rusted shears from the nail on the wall, gripping the handles in my hands.

WHAM!

I spun around, pointy end out. "Kyle!" I screamed. "Get behind me."

The last ax strike had torn a good shred out of the door right at face height.

I raised the shears.

A hand reached in to pull the cut metal down.

That's right, I thought. *Get just a little closer.* I didn't want to waste my one surprise shot on an arm wound.

Hands gripped the side of the metal, and a face loomed forward just as Kyle pointed the beam of the flashlight up and—

"Rhonda?"

Chapter Thirty-three

Rhonda's glowing white face popped in the space cut into the door.

"Hey, guys."

I dropped the shears and collapsed back down again to the dirt muttering something like "Ohmygod. Ohmygod. Ohmygod." And then, "I could have stabbed you in the belly."

"What?" she yelled, looking at my garden shears.

"Well, you were all coming in here with an ax! What was I supposed to do?"

"I tried knocking," Rhonda said, shaking her head tightly in the gap. "You didn't answer. I thought somebody might be hurt."

I didn't say anything.

"Are you okay, Erica?"

I nodded. Probably too quickly. My stomach lurched. Rhonda squinted. "Are you going to help me get in?"

"Right. Right," I said, trying to get to my knees. Apparently all my adrenaline had exploded and laid waste to my muscles. I felt very floppy.

"Who is she?" Kyle asked, helping me up.

"She's our freaking salvation."

Both Kyle and I pushed at the ruined door while Rhonda pulled from the other side. With just a few good yanks this time, we got the door a foot open. Rhonda slipped inside and pulled it half-way shut behind her. It was the best she could do.

I couldn't help it. The minute she turned around, I threw my arms around her.

"There. There. Doom," she said in my ear. "You've done good."

"I'm so happy to see you," I said barely able to get a sound through my too-tight throat. "How? I thought Lake Patrol—"

"Bah. They were being jerks."

I pulled back to look her in the eye. "You mean . . . ?"

She shrugged. "I'm in big trouble back on the mainland, but I knew you were in even bigger trouble here. Besides, it seemed like there was a small break in the storm when it changed from snow to freezing rain. I decided to go for it."

"How did you know we were in here?" I asked, giving my face a wipe. Not that I was crying or anything. "And where did you get the ax?"

"The ax was leaning against the shed," she said. Huh, kind of wished I noticed that before I chose this as our hiding spot. "I was coming up the steps just as you ran from the lodge. I'm surprised you didn't see my flashlight."

"He did," I said, gesturing back to Kyle. "But I thought . . ."

She nodded and looked over to him. "Oh, there you are." She flashed him a smile, but it looked a little . . . pained? "And how are you doing, young man?"

He blinked at her, then looked to me for answers. I shrugged. It wasn't so much what Rhonda was saying. It was how she was saying it. Like she was talking to someone who had just woken up from surgery and needed Jell-O.

"How are you feeling?" she went on. "You feeling okay?"

I squinted at her. Maybe teenagers made Rhonda awkward too?

"You feeling good?"

"I'm fine," Kyle said. "You know, given everything."

"Good. Good," she said, nodding, but not taking her eyes from him. "That's good."

Rhonda suddenly grabbed my arm and put up a *hang on just one minute* finger to Kyle. She then yanked me back toward the door . . . because, you know, there was so much more privacy two feet away. She gave Kyle one last smile then muttered close to my ear, "Has he been okay?"

"Um, what do you mean by okay? His father's dead. He just found out he's crazy rich, and someone might be trying to k—"

"No," she said with a quick shake of her head. "I mean, physically okay."

My eyes jumped around her face. "Well, I did think he might be coming down with something earlier. He was pretty pale. Why?"

Rhonda bit her lip. "I made some calls earlier because I saw a weird report when I looked up Rayner Boatright in the system, and, uh, just before I left, a detective in Miami called me back."

Kyle took a step toward us, but I shot a *Stay!* finger over at him.

"What kind of report?" I mumbled.

Rhonda grimaced. "A toxicology report."

I waited, not liking where this was headed.

"Well, you know how Rayner thought someone was trying to kill him?"

I nodded.

"Well, he wasn't just worried about himself."

"You don't mean—" I jerked my eyes in Kyle's direction.

Rhonda nodded.

"Well, what did it say?"

"The detectives there thought Rayner was paranoid, but they took some blood to have it analyzed, and . . ."

"And what?"

Rhonda pinched her lips together and shook her head. "Someone's been poisoning that kid."

Chapter Thirty-four

"Arsenic."

"Arsenic?" I whispered, feeling the blood drain from my face. "Come on. You can't be serious?" First cyanide and then arsenic? Talk about weird choices for a modern-day killer. "How bad?"

"They're surprised he's still standing. He needs to see a doctor." She jerked her thumb toward the door. "Like now. Or at least the minute the lake is passable."

I felt Kyle take another step toward us. "What are you guys talking ab—"

"Shush," I said whipping another finger around at him. "Adults talking."

"Okay, so here's the plan," Rhonda said, grabbing my shoulders and looking into my face. "You need to get Kyle to the boat."

"Wait . . . what?" I asked. "What do you mean *you*? What about *we*?"

Rhonda set her jaw.

"You're coming with us, right?"

"I took the police boat with the cabin. It will give you some shelter."

I cocked my head at her. "What exactly are you planning to do?"

Her eyes darted to the side as she went on. "You're going to need to hurry. I saw another light. There's a good chance someone knows we're in here."

"Well, you've got a gun," I said, pointing to her hip. "And an ax. Let's all stay here. Together."

"I'll get you guys to the top of the stairs and—"

"Rhonda! No! Do not finish that sentence. Let's just stay here, and you shoot anyone who comes to the door."

"Erica," she said shaking her head, "You know I can't do that."

"Why not?" I yelled, voice cracking.

"There are innocent people back inside, right?"

"Oh my God! No!" I yelled, bringing a hand to my head. "I mean, yes, maybe, but . . . Rhonda! You can't. They might already be dead. And . . . this killer . . . you don't get paid enough. I'm not going to let you do this."

"Has anyone else been hurt?"

My hand dropped to the side of my face. "I don't know. People keep disappearing, and then Brody came crashing through the window, and—"

"Okay. Okay. I need to get over there," she said, still looking at me with that serious expression I was not used to seeing on her face.

"I'll go," I blurted out, surprising myself. "You take Kyle."

"No. No way," Kyle said.

"Erica," Rhonda said, face dropping. "Come on."

"Let me do it. I can—"

"No. This is my job."

"You've done enough tonight. You're a hero for making it across that lake," I said with a defeated wave of my hand. "I can't let you—"

"Okay, Ms. Untrained Civilian," Rhonda said with a

goofy smile. "Take this." She pulled something out of her pocket and pressed it into my palm. It was a set of keys. "There's a shotgun in the locker under the rear seats in the cabin. As I said, I'll get you to the steps at the top of the hill, then you guys head for the boat."

"Rhonda . . ."

"Can you make it to the boat?"

"Yes."

"Good," she said, straightening her jacket.

"What are you going to do?"

"I'll handcuff everybody, get them secure, and then wait for back-up. I'll come get you when I can."

My eyes dropped to her belt. "I see only one set of cuffs on your hip."

"I'll figure it out."

I looked up to the rattling ceiling, shaking my head. "I don't like this plan at all."

"You and me both, right?" she replied. "But it's my duty. Now, I almost didn't make it across the lake, but if someone comes after you, well, you make the call."

"Rhonda we're not leaving you on the island."

"You gotta protect the kid," she said. "Now no more talking. We're wasting time. I'll give you my flashlight. It's better. We all go together to the top of the stairs. Understand?"

"Come on. Please. Let's talk about—"

She cut me off with a look, then said slowly and carefully, "Do you understand?"

I sighed. "I understand."

"Good. Let's go."

Chapter Thirty-five

The three of us pushed our way back into the horror of the storm, the sleet nearly pelting us to the ground.

"Come on!" Rhonda shouted.

I covered my forehead again with my arm, hand gripping the flashlight. I grabbed Kyle's jacket with my other hand.

The one thing working in our favor was that we could still see the dim light coming from the lodge. It was a blur though. If this storm got any worse . . . I didn't want to think that all the way through. I had never experienced weather like this before. It had me believing in things like angry gods . . . with ice hammers. Why were so many things trying to kill us?

We kept moving forward, this time trying to resist the thrust of the wind at our backs. A lifetime later, we made it to the top of the stairs. Rhonda turned, bracing against the gale.

"First thing, you get the shotgun," she yelled. "You understand me?"

"Rhonda—"

"None of that. Good luck, Doom!"

"Good luck—"

But she had already turned toward the lodge. She never heard me.

"Come on," I shouted, yanking at Kyle. "Watch the steps."

Saying watch the steps was one thing. Trying to actually do it was another. The sleet was creating a layer of ice over the snow. Kyle lost his footing a couple of times.

Get to the boat. Get the gun. Wait for Rhonda.

I could do this.

When we got to the bottom of the steps, we had to slow almost to a stop. The dirt path leading to the dock was now an icy mudslide. Water rushed by my boots, and I felt the first little trickle of frigid water find its way through the seams. If the temperature dropped any more, I'd probably lose a couple of toes . . . but, you know, better that than a head. Funny how when you are stuck on an island in a storm with a paid assassin, everything becomes relative.

A few seconds later, we figured out how to slide-walk our way forward. "We're almost there!"

The dock posed a whole new level of difficulty. It was swaying and rocking in the water in a way that just shouldn't have been possible. Some sort of support must have gone. I could see the police boat bobbing up and down just beyond. I had never seen the water like this before. Maybe on the bigger lakes, but not here.

At least it wasn't far.

"I have to let go of you!" I shouted at Kyle. "Stay low. The water's not deep, but it's rocky here."

He nodded.

I took one step onto the planks of the dock. Holy crap, the whole thing felt like it was going to give any second. I inched forward slowly, the beam of the flashlight dancing wildly as I tried to keep my grip on it while shuffling forward.

"I've changed my mind," I shouted back into the wind. "You should go first."

Kyle's eyes went wide. "Why?"

"So I can see you! I'll steady you if you start to slip."

"That boat looks like it's going to sink. Let's just hide in some trees or go back to the shed!"

"It's dry in there," I shouted back. "And there's probably blankets. Maybe even spare clothes. We need to get warm."

He stared at me, uncertainty all over his face.

"Just go slow."

We traded positions, and Kyle took a hesitant step forward onto the wood planks of the dock.

"That's it. Keep going," I shouted, following his steps.

"I don't like this!"

"It's not far," I yelled, feeling around with my boot for a spot that felt more like crunchy snow and less like wet glass. "You're doing great."

"It's too slippery!"

"I know. Just—"

"Erica!" Suddenly Kyle's arms flew into the air as his feet slipped out from underneath him. I shot out my hands to push him back away from the edge, giving him just enough resistance to drop safely onto the dock . . .

Too bad doing that also sent me spinning for the water.

Chapter Thirty-six

Cold. Cold. COLD!

My feet were in the water. All the way in the water. And here I thought I couldn't feel anything with my mother's boots being so tight.

"Erica!"

I couldn't scream back. The cold of the lake had paralyzed my lungs.

"Erica!" Kyle screamed again, grabbing at my shoulder. "Come on!"

Thankfully we hadn't gotten very far, so the water was shallow, but the rocks were slippery. I tried to haul myself up too quickly and smashed my chest right up against the dock.

Kyle reached for me. "Grab my arm!"

My limbs felt heavy and stiff, but I lurched forward again, slapping my hand down on Kyle's arm. It was just enough leverage that I could pull my chest up onto the heaving planks of the dock. I pulled my knee up after, and before I could stop it, the motion pushed my phone up out of my pocket, sending it tumbling into the water.

"No!"

"What?" Kyle shouted.

"My phone!"

He grabbed my leg, pulling it all the way onto the dock. "Forget it!"

I collapsed completely onto the swaying boards. I tried to pull my knees up underneath me, but I just couldn't seem to make anything work.

"We have to get to the boat!" Kyle screamed, staying on his hands and knees. "Get up!"

Right. Get up.

Now how did I make all of my body parts work again?

Suddenly I felt a hard slap on my butt.

"Get up!"

I clenched my teeth together and hauled myself up to a four-legged position. "Okay, let's go." Thankfully I still had the flashlight. I think my hand had frozen into a clawlike grip around the handle.

Just get to the boat. Just get to the boat. The words kept rolling around in a loop in my mind. We just needed to make it to the boat. The boat would have blankets . . . and a change of clothes . . . maybe a bottle of seized alcohol that I could pour over my socks . . . and then light with a match. Actually that last bit didn't sound so nice. *Just get to the boat.*

When I got to the end of the dock, I pushed myself up with my stiff muscles, looked around, and groaned.

We'd have to jump to get onto the heaving vessel. It was too high. There was a metal railing that ran all the way along its edges, which wouldn't have been a problem if the lake was still—and I had any blood flow left in my limbs—but, as it stood, this, this might be the thing that killed me.

I passed the flashlight to Kyle.

He nodded, holding the beam on me.

I gripped the metal rod of the uppermost railing with

both hands and lifted one foot on the edge of the boat. Now, if I timed it just right with the rocking of the waves, the force should lift me up and over.

Almost. Almost . . .

Now!

I hauled myself up and—

"Freaking! Stupid! Nutballs!" My foot had slipped, slamming my shin on the hard fiberglass edge of the boat. How was it even possible that I could still feel that?

Oh, that was it!

That was so it!

Something hot ran through me, filling up my muscles with energy—enough energy to launch me up and over. I whipped around, hand gripping the metal railing.

"I've had it!" I yelled into the wind. Sleet battered my face. "You want to go?" I threw my free hand up into the air. "Let's go! Let's do this thing!"

The storm raged back at me, but that just made me even angrier.

I was so pissed. Beyond pissed. In fact, I was pretty sure, somewhere in a distant corner of the universe my rage had given birth to a brand-new solar system.

I let out another scream, barely resisting the urge to beat my chest.

"Um, Erica?" Kyle called up to me.

My eyes flashed down to him. I had barely heard his voice over the wind . . . and the hot, angry blood rushing through my ears.

"Who are you yelling at?"

"I don't know!" I roared. "The storm? The killer? The Gods!"

He nodded. "Can we at least, you know, get the gun, before you call anyone else out?"

I stared at him hard a moment.

He cocked his head and yelled, "Is that a yes?"

My shoulders slumped, then I nodded.

"Are you sure?"

"I'm sure," I muttered, leaning down to take his hand.

He reached up for me. "And I already know all the swear words, okay? You don't have to do that thing with the nutballs."

"Whatever."

Being a guardian sucked.

Chapter Thirty-seven

Once I got Kyle into the cabin, I pushed the door shut behind us, and slid to the floor, curling into a tight ball.

Thankfully there was a heavy police slicker hanging on a hook above me. I yanked it down and wrapped it around my shoulders. My fingers ached with the cold, but I had just enough rage-y adrenaline left to get my mom's boots off—a doubly impressive feat, given that the boat was tossing us around like clothes in a dryer.

Man, how had Rhonda made it across the lake? This was insane. I could only pray that her luck stayed with her up at the retreat. I shook my head. I couldn't think about that. I just couldn't.

Kyle collapsed onto a bench. "I can't believe we made it."

"I know," I said trying to squeeze some warmth back into my feet.

"I also can't believe you lost it like that," he said with a pained laugh. "You wanna go?" He shook his fist weakly in the air. "Let's go!"

"Yeah, thanks. I was there."

"Why? Why would you do that?"

"I don't like being scared," I said, finding a black knit hat in the pocket of the jacket. I whipped my wet one off and yanked it over my head. "I don't like smashing my shin either. And now I need a new phone."

"You can use mine," Kyle said pulling it out of his pocket. He poked at it a few times, then said, "Or not. It's dead."

"Figures."

He smiled again. "You were so mad. You probably could have taken Brody, the bodyguard, whoever."

I blew some air out of my lips as the faces of Julie, Kenny, Ronnie, Ashley, Rhonda . . . my mother . . . flashed through my mind. "I'd like to try." I wiped the last bit of wetness away from my face and looked around the cabin. "But you're right. It would have been better if I had the gun first."

Suddenly a horrible thought occurred to me. I mumbled *please, please, please*, as I slid my fingers into my jeans pocket for the keys Rhonda had given me. They hooked around the metal ring, and I yanked them out, waves of relief rolling over me.

Unfortunately, it was a short-lived sensation.

"Erica," Kyle said, and there was just something in his voice. I turned my flashlight to look where he was pointing.

The bench had a locker underneath the seat. An empty locker. Pried open with a crowbar, by the looks of it.

"Oh, come on!" I shouted. I flashed my beam over to the boat's dashboard. Smashed. Along with the police radio.

"Who would have had time to do that?" Kyle asked, his face dropping.

I shook my head. I already knew. Assassins were efficient like that.

A moment or two of silence passed before Kyle said, "I don't think I can stay here."

"I know the rocking is bad, but Rhonda said—"

Just then he let out a horrible, gulping cough . . . and retched all over the floor of the boat.

Swear to God, I would die to protect this kid . . . but . . . just kill me now.

"Kyle?"

He straightened back up, wiping the back of his hand across his mouth. "I can't stay here."

"We don't have a choice," I said, steadying myself against the wall, keeping a careful eye on the floor. "There are worse things than being seasick." I was having trouble thinking of any of them at the moment, but, you know. "We need to stay here. It's safe-ish, and we can't cross the lake yet."

"Are you sure it's safe? Somebody broke into that gun locker."

"I don't know. Give me a second," I said, roughly rubbing my face with both hands. "I just need to think this through."

I didn't like staying here either. Eventually whoever had done all this would come looking for us, and we wouldn't see them coming. But on the other hand, we had shelter, and if help ever arrived, we'd be right here to welcome it.

And maybe it would be Grady.

I was working so hard not to think of the worst case scenario of this night, but it was always there. Right on the fringes. Man, there was so much I wanted to do if we got through this. First and foremost, I'd make things right with Grady. No holding back this time. Rhonda was right, he deserved somebody that was all in. And it was time that somebody was me. Next, there was my mother. We certainly had our issues, but in a moment like this, I needed to know that she knew I loved her. And we could find a way to do this whole mother-daughter thing better. As for Freddie . . .

Nah, Freddie and I were good.

I squeezed my eyes shut.

Please, just give me one more shot.

"Hey," I suddenly said, tuning back into the moment. "You okay over there?"

Kyle nodded.

I had just remembered what Rhonda had told me about the arsenic. Maybe Kyle's being sick had more to do with that than the motion sickness. I needed to get him to a doctor. But the lake was just too rough to cross. I'd end up killing him before we made it to the hospital. "Don't know if it will help you, but just now I was thinking about what I'm going to do when this is all over. It might help to keep your spirits up."

Kyle made a noncommittal noise.

"Seriously, what's the first thing you're going to do when you get home?"

"I don't know," he said with a painful-looking shrug. "Take a whole bunch of money out of the bank, put it on my bed, and roll around in it?"

I chuckled. "Fine. You're right. It's not my business."

"No, I'm being serious."

I dropped my chin to my chest.

"Well, it's not like I have any family anymore. Rayner's dead. The rest want me dead."

"What about on your mother's side?"

"Nobody. I've been in foster homes since I was two," he said, face devoid of emotion. "Then, you know, Rayner found me."

"Wow. I take it he didn't know about you before that?"

"No," Kyle said, eyes looking faraway. "I think he did. He just wasn't interested until he knew Ronnie couldn't have any more kids. I think bringing me into the picture was his way of sticking it to her."

"What? Kyle, that's terribl—"

Suddenly a bang sounded in the distance. I jumped to my feet to stare out the window into the darkness. It could have been lightning. Maybe. It was possible. This storm was crazy like that.

But I knew better.

Rhonda.

Frick! Frick! Frick!

"Erica?"

"Okay, Kyle," I said turning back around. "I think you're right. Maybe we need to keep moving."

He raised his eyebrows, still looking nauseated.

"I told you there's another cabin on the island."

He nodded.

"I thought we couldn't make it before, but now I think it's time we go for it. Who knows when help will get here. We can't stay."

He put up a finger for me to wait, swallowed, then said, "Okay, where is it?"

"We have to go back up the steps, past the retreat, to get to the trail."

He smacked the back of his head against the seat. "Can't we just go by the shoreline?"

I shook my head. "The brush is too thick. The trail is our best bet."

He looked at me a second then said, "Tell me the truth."

"What?"

"The gunshot," he said weakly, pointing a finger at the window. "You're going to stow me away in this place, then go after your friend."

Well, crap. This kid was too smart for his own good. That's exactly what I had planned. I couldn't stand the thought of Rhonda being up there by herself. If I could just get Kyle someplace safe, then I could help her.

"Kyle . . ."

"I'm coming with you."

"No way."

"You're the one who keeps saying someone planned all of this. If they did, they know about the other cabin. I'm in danger there too."

I sighed. He had a point.

"I say it's time we fight back."

I held up my hands. "Okay, easy there, Rambo."

He looked at me quizzically.

"Rambo? Sylvester Stallone? Anything? How old are you?"

"You're so weird." Kyle closed his eyes and clutched his stomach before he added, "There were lock cutters in that shed."

"Lock cutters? You mean for a weapon?"

"No, to open the safe in your mother's office. Unless you have a key."

I felt my eyes narrow. There was a safe in my mother's office. An old safe with a padlock on the floor behind her desk. "How do you know about the safe?"

"Because it's where she put Brody's gun."

Chapter Thirty-eight

"You saw my mother?" Something both hot and cold surged through my body.

"No. I heard Brody talking about it to Ashley," he said, gripping the edge of his seat. "I tried to tell you before Brody came smashing through the window, but you were all *Adults talking, Kyle.*"

"Oh, sorry about that." So my mother had been at the lodge . . . maybe was still there somewhere. "And wait, Brody's gun? Brody has a gun?"

"Your mother took it from him. Said it was a rule or something for the retreat."

Yeah, it was. I wrapped my fingers around a hand grip as the boat tipped over another small swell. My mother did not like guns. I didn't either. But what if Rhonda needed my help? "Kyle, I'm not taking you back to the lodge. I can't. It's too dangerous."

"But we need a gun."

"And what? You think we're just going to waltz into the lodge with a big pair of lock cutters, and the killer isn't going to notice?"

"No," Kyle answered. "You know this place. We scope it out and sneak in."

I didn't say anything, just buried my free hand farther under my armpit, shivering.

"Besides, maybe we don't have to do anything. Maybe your cop friend has already been shot by the murderer."

"Hey!" I said pointing a finger at him. "Not cool. Don't even say that."

"I'm sorry, okay!" He shook his head, then clenched his jaw like he might be sick again. "You said you don't like being scared. Well, you're not the only one. You keep telling me to trust you, but I don't know anything about you. You want me to feel safe? Then let's get the gun, lock ourselves in a room at this other cottage, and point it at the door. That's what will make me feel safe. Or at least let me do that and then you can go get your friend or whatever."

"I still don't know about all this."

"Look," he said. "I'm going to fill this whole cabin with barf if we don't get off this stupid boat. Let's just go up to the retreat and see what's going on. If it looks bad, we go to your neighbor's cabin."

"I just can't help but think—"

Kyle's stomach clenched again as a disturbing burp escaped his mouth.

"Okay, fine!" I said, throwing my hands in the air. "You win. Let's go."

Chapter Thirty-nine

Kyle and I battled the storm once again on the steps. Going up was definitely harder than getting down, and that was saying something. Before we crested the hill, I turned off Rhonda's flashlight. I'd had it half-shielded by my jacket because I didn't see the good in advertising our position, but we'd needed it on the stairs.

Once we made it to the top, I scanned the clearing, and for a second, I thought I saw something by the canoes; but the canoes were near the boulder, so I wasn't about to investigate.

In minutes, we had made it back to the shed and got the lock cutters off the wall. Either the storm was easing up or we were just getting better at navigating in the dark. It had to be after midnight now. Maybe hours after midnight. Time didn't seem to make sense anymore.

I took Kyle in a wide circle by the tree line to the rear of the lodge. I was planning on eventually creeping up onto the back porch because even with the wind, I was worried someone might hear me if I got too close to the busted kitchen window.

After a few more minutes of walking, I yanked Kyle down to crouch with me under a cluster of small trees.

"Okay," I said in his ear. "You stay here until I check it o—"

Suddenly a tree cracked right above our heads.

We clutched each other, falling to our bellies.

I blinked my eyes open to see Kyle's face just inches from mine.

He mouthed the words, "Yeah, no."

I let my forehead thunk onto the ground.

"Listen," I said, before having to stop and spit out the dirty snow I had just taken in. "I need to keep you out of harm's way. The odds of you getting hit with a tree are small. The odds of you getting murdered if we go up there are pretty good."

Just then another gunshot sounded, and I caught a flash of light from inside the lodge.

"Your friend must still be alive," Kyle said looking back at me. "And she's in trouble."

God, what was I supposed to do? What if she did need my help?

"Okay," I tried again. "I'm gonna go check it out. You wait here."

"No way! Not going to happen!"

"I won't be long," I shouted, getting to my knees. "Wait for me to come back or . . . or if you see me stand up in front of that window," I said with a point. "That's means it's safe. You come."

"Erica—"

"I'm not arguing with you anymore."

"But—"

"Stay put!"

"I—"

That time I just cut him off with a look.

He didn't try again.

I pushed myself up to my feet and crouch-ran across the lawn. I stayed low, and when I got to the back steps, I climbed up them on my hands and knees. After that, I stayed on all fours and crawled over to the closest window, which was my mother's office. I wanted to peek up into it, but I was really afraid that when I did, someone might be looking back at me with a gun pointed at my face. I suddenly understood why snails had eyes on top of those long tentacle things on their heads. They would be really useful right now. I turned my face to the side and slowly inched up to look into the room.

Nothing. Empty.

I eased back down and—

"Kyle!" I shout-whispered. "I told you stay in the woods!"

"I thought you stood up!"

"You just—argh!" I resisted the urge to grab him by the collar and shake him around. Why didn't they make inescapable playpens for teenagers?

I gritted my teeth and sharply waved my hand for him to follow me. We crawled slowly down to the corner of the lodge. I peeked around. Nothing. The one window on this side was my bedroom's. It was still dark. I risked a look in anyway.

Nothing.

I dropped back down and continued the crawl.

When we made it to the end, I stopped and put my hand up for Kyle to follow suit.

The front stretch of the porch would be the most dangerous. We had to be careful.

I peered around the corner. The light from the inside of the retreat cast enough of a glow that I could see the porch was empty.

I brought my face up close to Kyle's. "You stay here this time, or so help me, I'll be your biggest problem on this island." I guess my eyes had finally achieved the level of scary I was going for because Kyle nodded tightly.

I nodded back and slowly edged my way around the corner. I crawled underneath the bottom of the first window of the common room. I reached one hand up to grip the window sill, pausing to close my eyes and take a breath.

There was no telling what would be waiting for me in there. Seeing the body of a stranger was pretty freaking bad, but if I saw Rhonda . . . after she had tried to save me . . .

No.

I blinked my eyes opened and slowly eased myself up to peer into the room.

It was exactly as we had left it.

The fire was still casting flickering shadows over the walls. The electric lanterns were still glowing their harsh light. Kenny still lay unconscious on the sofa, but . . .

Everybody else was gone.

Chapter Forty

I dropped down, leaning my back against the wood of the lodge.

No Rhonda. No Julie. No Ronnie.

Where did they all go?

I eased myself back up again.

Nope. Still empty.

I sank back down, furiously trying to think through what this all meant. Ronnie I could see not being there. She might have decided to go look for Ashley. Rhonda, maybe, had gone after the bodyguard. But Julie? She wouldn't have left Kenny. At least not by choice.

I scuttled back over to Kyle around the dark side of the porch.

"You don't look good," Kyle said in my ear. "Is your friend . . . ?"

"No, it's not that. Everybody's gone."

"What do you mean gone?"

"Gone. Kenny's still there, but everyone else is just . . . gone."

Kyle nodded. "Please tell me this means we are going to get the gun now."

"We're going to get the gun now."

Chapter Forty-one

Kyle and I hustled back around the porch to my mother's office, and I peeked in the window.

All quiet. Kind of like a graveyard.

Now was the time.

I debated once again trying to convince Kyle to stay hidden somewhere outside, but I knew there was no point. He had imprinted himself to me like a baby duck—a baby duck who had half a billion dollars on his head.

"Are you sure nobody is in there?" Kyle whispered.

"Nope. Not at all," I said, struggling to push the near-frozen window up as quietly as possible. Once I had it, I dropped back down and closed my eyes for another moment. I couldn't help but wonder how bad of an idea this really was. Going back into the lodge right now could get us killed, but if we got to the gun, we'd have a better chance surviving this night. I didn't know what the right move was, and it wasn't just my life at stake. Kyle was—

Suddenly my eyes popped open.

Kyle was already inside.

Okay then. Decision made.

I climbed in the window after him, sliding the window shut behind me.

Kyle and I stared at each other a moment. Both of us frozen.

"It's so quiet," he whispered. "I mean compared to outside."

I nodded.

He chewed his bottom lip as his eyes trailed around the room. "It's kind of freaking me out."

"You and me both." I shuffled my way over to the safe on my knees and set about adjusting the blades of the lock cutter around the small metal loop of the padlock.

"No, I mean like it's really freaking me out," he went on.

I didn't say anything, just fiddled with my hold.

"It's kind of feels like someone is listening to every sound we make," he whispered. "Like you're making a ton of noise right now."

"Kyle!" I hissed.

"What?"

"You're not helping."

"Sorry.

"Just hold the flashlight up a bit will you?"

He tilted the beam.

Now, you would think a tool with a name like *lock cutters* would just cut through locks, no problem.

Well, it didn't.

I wrestled with the long, awkward arms for about five minutes before realizing that it was hopeless.

"What's wrong?" Kyle asked.

"It's no use," I said, wiping my brow with the back of my gloved hand. "I'm not strong enough."

"What if I take one side?" Kyle moved to push at one

end of the lock cutters while I pushed the other, but that only resulted in us both doing the strange lock-cutter dance.

"They're rusted out," I said, shaking my head. "Probably haven't been sharpened in about fifty years."

"Well, now what are we going to do?" Kyle asked, suddenly looking really put out.

"I don't know. Maybe we could . . . wait!" I pushed past him toward one of my mother's double-stacked bookshelves.

"What are you doing?" he asked coming up behind me.

I reached up, stretching my hand over the top of the bookshelf and patted around. "One year my mother's psychopathic cat—"

I dropped back down for a moment and looked around. Again, where the hell was Caesar? Not that I didn't have enough to worry about, but surely the killer wouldn't have . . . ? No. No. I shook the thought away and resumed my pat down of the bookshelf. Satan would never let harm come to one of his own.

"Um, hello?"

"Oh, sorry," I whispered. "One year my mom's cat found a nest of baby foxes under this evergreen, which caused all sorts of drama. She didn't want babies there the next year, so she got a saw to get rid of the lower branches, and my mom never puts anything away so— Bam!" I shout-whispered bringing the handsaw down.

Kyle threw me an unimpressed slow-blink. "You could have just said there was a hacksaw up there."

"You so need a nap."

I hustled back over to the lock and dropped to my knees. The lock was flimsy enough that it just might work. I planted the fine teeth of the saw on the nick I had made earlier with the cutters and gave it a pull back.

"That's really loud, Erica," Kyle hissed in my ear.

"I know," I said, keeping my focus on making a deeper groove.

"Well, saw faster! Somebody's going to hear us."

I tried to pick up the pace, but that just made the teeth of the saw jump, and now would be a particularly bad time to lose a thumb.

A few moments later, I stopped dead.

"What?" he asked. "What's happening? Why aren't you sawing?"

"Do you hear that?" I asked, rocking back onto my heels.

"Hear what?"

I whacked him gently on the arm. "Listen."

We both fell silent.

A moment later, Kyle and I jumped up, clutching each other.

Oh, there was no mistaking it now.

It sounded like . . . scratching?

"What is that?" Kyle whispered.

"I don't know," I whispered back. "But I think . . . I think it's coming from over there." We hustled over to the back corner of the room. I crouched down and put my ear close to the wall—then sprang back like it had burned me.

"What?"

"Something's there!" Thoughts raced through my mind as I brought a hand to my mouth.

"What?"

"Get out of the way," I said pushing past him.

"What about the gun?" Kyle half-yelled, stamping a foot.

"We'll come back for it," I said already at the threshold. My heart banged in my chest while my mind started up the mantra, *Please. Please. Please.* "Come on."

I stopped and peeked out the hall, head swiveling side to side.

Nothing.

I hurried the few steps over and whipped myself into the next room.

My mother's room.

A small cry escaped my mouth.

Kyle fell in beside me. "What is . . . are you kidding me right now?"

I couldn't answer him. I was just so—

"We stopped trying to get the gun for that?" Kyle hissed throwing a hand forward. "The world's fattest cat?"

I eyed Caesar planted on the floor, one leg up in the air, licking his crotch. He rolled his extremely disinterested eyes up to mine.

"It's a cat, Erica," Kyle repeated. "We have bigger problems."

I hesitated one moment longer to look at Kyle and say, "It's not just a cat," before launching myself at the closet.

"Then what? Why are you—?"

"It's my mother."

Chapter Forty-two

"Erica, seriously, have you lost it again? We don't have time for this!"

I grabbed the handle of the closet and gave it a good yank. It didn't budge. What the . . . ?

My eyes trailed down to see a walking stick wedged between the bottom of the door and the floor.

"Wait!" Kyle clutched my arm. "What if it's a trap?"

I dropped to my knees and grasped the thin piece of wood. "How could someone trap themselves in there with a stick?"

"I don't know," he moaned. "But what about your friend, Rhonda? What if she found the bad guy and put him in there?"

"What if it *is* Rhonda?" I shot back. *It's not though.* I yanked again at the stick, wedged in tight. The stick that was making me insanely mad because it was keeping me from my—

"Erica, stop!" he said, pulling my arm. "Let's just think this through."

"I'm sorry, Kyle," I said, popping to my feet and giving the stick a good kick. "I have to."

I rammed the thin piece of wood with my toe, and it finally popped out.

I whipped the door open.

"Mom!" I threw myself over her even though she was buried in a big pile of junk. "Oh, thank you. Thank you. Thank you."

She wasn't moving.

"Mom?" I shook her shoulder gently as my eyes darted over her limp form. Her scarves! Someone had taken her silk scarves as used them to bind her hands and feet. Another covered her mouth. I quickly moved to get them off of her then gave her another shake. "Mom! Please. Wake up!"

She moaned. "Erica?" she said, blinking her eyes. "What's . . . what's going on? How did I get in here?"

I leaned back, threw a coat off of her, and grabbed her arm to help her up to a seated position. "You don't know?"

She clutched her head as Caesar walked nonchalantly into the closet, climbing up into her lap, rubbing his face up against her chin. She smiled before spitting out some cat hair. "Has no one given you your supper, baby? You must be starving. What time is it?"

"Mom, focus. What's the last thing you remember?"

"I was . . . I had just put a gun in the safe." She squinted then blinked a few times. "A guest had brought it, and then I went to my bedroom to . . . I can't remember why, but I thought I saw someone, outside, through the window, on the porch." Her voice sounded unsure. "I thought maybe it was one of the guests. I opened the window and . . . I don't remember much after that." She reached a hand up to touch the back of her head.

I put my fingers around to feel the spot too. Definitely a lump.

"Maybe I came to the closet to get something . . . and

something else fell on me?" she said looking around at the mess. "And maybe the door swung shut?"

"And you tied yourself up? I don't think so." I shook my head. "Was it a big man that you saw?" Maybe she had seen the assassin in the process of sabotaging the generator.

"No, I just caught a glimpse," she said eyes faraway. "It might have even been a woman." Suddenly her eyes snapped to mine. "I remember turning around because it sounded like other guests had arrived, and . . . I don't know."

My guess was that whoever was on that back porch came through the window and knocked her on the back of the head. "It's okay, Mom. I'm just glad we found you."

"Erica, who is this young man?" my mother asked, sounding more alert. "And why are all the lights off?"

"Mom, you have to keep your voice down."

She shot me a quizzical look.

"A lot has happened. This is Kyle. He's part of the family who rented the retreat for the night."

"I'm sorry," she said shooting me a pained face. "I tried to cancel, honey. The money they were offering was . . . well, it was tempting at first, but I knew how important this night was for you and that"—she rolled her eyes—"—sheriff of yours. But they were the types who just would not take no for an answer."

"Wait," I said, cocking my head. "You tried to cancel? For me?"

"Of course, darling. Your hopes and dreams are my hopes and dreams, regardless of how terribly misguided they may be."

I blinked. "Really?"

She blinked back. "Of course."

"Aw, Mom," I said reaching forward to hug her again. "That's just so—"

"What are you two freaks doing!" Kyle shout-whispered. "We're about to die!"

My mother pulled back. "What is he talking about?"

I took a breath. "Well . . ."

"Where are the rest of the guests?" she asked, looking to the door. "Are they in the living room?"

"One is. Actually, two." I had forgotten about Rayner there for a moment, but I guess he still counted. "In a manner of speaking."

"What does that mean?" she asked. "Erica, what is going on?"

"Well . . ."

"Why aren't you dead?" Kyle asked suddenly.

My mother's eyes blinked a few more times, then widened. "I beg your pardon?"

"Kyle!" I snapped.

"What?" he asked turning to me. "Everybody gets it but her?"

"We don't know that anybody but Rayner has . . . gotten it," I said, struggling to keep my voice hushed. "And what does it matter? Maybe he was in a hurry. Maybe—"

"Nothing's quicker than a *Bam!*" he said, mimicking a gun with his hand. "Two to the back of the head. I can't trust her. I don't even know if I can trust you!"

"Okay, calm down," I said. "I haven't killed you so far, right?"

He didn't look reassured.

"Let's just focus now. We need to get the gun and—"

"Gun? You mean the one I put in the safe?" my mother asked, heaving Caesar off her lap. "Erica, you know how I feel about guns."

"I know, but—"

"I told that jittery young man that it was more likely he'd shoot himself with that thing before anybody else." She reached down to her hips. "I had the key . . ."

I grabbed her hand. "Look Mom, again, a lot has happened. Nothing fell on you. Somebody hit you over the head and stashed you in this closet. And that somebody is probably still around. We need to get moving."

"So, you're telling me," she said, popping to her feet with a surprising ease given she had been locked in the closet with a head injury for hours. "That someone locked me in this closet all because they were afraid I would force them to face their inner truth in front of their family?"

"What? No!" I practically shouted. "I didn't say that at all!

She leaped past me. "You didn't have to."

"Mom, listen to me." But she was already in the hallway. Damn her yoga limberness.

"Erica, honey," she said, throwing her voice back to me. "I appreciate your protectiveness for your mother but, really, a gun is too far."

"Mom! You don't understand what's going on here. You—"

Kyle grabbed my arm, cutting me off. "I think maybe she needs to see this, don't you?"

It didn't matter if I agreed or not. My mother had reached the mouth of the common room and had stopped dead. Her back straightened as one hand moved to her mouth.

I raced to her side. Oh boy, someone had thrown the afghan off of Rayner.

"I'm sorry. I wanted to warn y—"

"We need a gun."

Chapter Forty-three

"I have the key here somewhere," my mom said again as we hurried toward her office. "Maybe it fell out in the clos—"

Suddenly a thump sounded on the front porch.

Footstep thumps!

"Someone's coming!" Kyle hissed.

I grabbed my mother's arm and pushed Kyle back into the office in front of us. I didn't get far though. My mom had stopped moving.

"Where's Caesar?" she asked, craning her head to look back toward her bedroom.

"Forget Caesar!" Somewhere, far off in my mind, a part of my consciousness was laughing, hysterically, because those really were the two most useless words I had ever said. Even more useless than *calm down*. It wasn't a child, or a loveable three-legged golden lab that was going to be the death of me, but a psychopathic cat who had been playing the long game all these years to get me killed. The rest of my mind was just screaming.

Thankfully Caesar had been following us, probably

expecting to get fed, so my mother spotted him quickly and scooped him up.

"Erica!" Kyle said. "Come on!"

But suddenly I had stopped too. It turned out that other corners of my mind had been doing more than just screaming. When I had pulled my mother away from the mouth of the common room, I had seen something. A purse. Ronnie's purse on the floor with a phone sticking out the top!

"Go!" I hissed. "Go out onto the back porch!"

"What about the gun?"

"Just go!"

I darted down the hallway, casting a terrified peek into the room. Empty. I swung around the threshold and lunged down to scoop up the bag lying on the floor just underneath the table, the entire time thinking, *Don't look at Rayner. Don't look at Rayner.*

Gah! I had looked at Rayner.

My eyes then shot over to Kenny, still helpless on the couch.

"I'm so sorry," I mumbled, getting back up to my feet, pivoting hard to face the hallway. I sprinted on my tiptoes—which was as useless as it sounds—taking one look back at the doorway.

It was opening!

I gripped the doorframe of the office to slingshot myself back into the room, and gently closed the door behind me. But whoever that was out there could have totally heard that and—

"What are you two still doing here?" I hissed. "Get out that window!"

Kyle obeyed, but my mother just looked at me and said, "You first."

"I have to get the gun. I almost had it before."

My mother nodded, then moved—the opposite way! Back toward the door!

"What are you doing?" I threw up my arms football-style to block her.

She veered to the right, still holding Caesar, positioning herself by a small bookshelf, pushing at it with her hip.

"Good idea!" I threw the strap of the purse around my neck and helped my mom slide the small, but heavy piece of furniture in front of the door.

"Now go!" I said, shooing her toward the window as I dropped to my knees in front of the safe.

"Are we sure it's the killer?" my mother whispered.

"No," I said quickly, positioning the saw back in place. I was almost there. The teeth now bit deeply into the groove I had made earlier. I was so close. "But we're not taking any chances."

I was praying that it was Rhonda's footsteps I was hearing walking down the hall—*right now!*—but I knew it probably wasn't. She'd announce herself or—

Suddenly the doorknob jiggled.

We all froze. I gave my mother another frantic wave to get out. She actually listened this time and moved toward the window—trying to take my arm with her. I snatched it back, dropping the saw. I could probably snap the lock now. I just needed to—

Thunk!

We all screamed as what sounded like a fist collided with the door. Luckily my full body jolt snapped the lock off in my hand.

I whipped open the safe just as the bookshelf holding the door shut made a horrible screech against the floor.

"I got it!" I shouted wrapping my hand around the gun. "Go!"

I didn't need to tell my mother again. She was side-stepping out the window, enormous fur bundle still clutched in her arms.

The bookshelf slid a bit farther in, but then rocked to a stop, its foot catching on one of the uneven planks of the floor.

I pushed my mom's hips out the window then swung a leg over, my free hand shakily pointing the gun back into the room.

The door shuddered with another hit. The bookshelf rocked on its feet a moment then toppled over with a bang.

"Shoot him!" Kyle cried.

I couldn't though. I didn't know for sure who was on the other side.

Suddenly the door banged again, and I saw big male fingers grip its edge just as—

I toppled backward out of the window.

Chapter Forty-four

"Oof!"

I landed hard on my shoulders, smacking the back of my head against the wood planks of the porch floor. But I didn't have time to be stunned. My mother was already pulling me up by my jacket. She probably could have gotten me up faster if she had dropped Caesar, but, you know, whatever.

I struggled to my feet, trying to blink the stars out of my eyes. "Let's go!" I shouted over my stomach somersaulting its contents way up into my throat.

"Where?" my mother yelled already moving to join Kyle who was hustling down the porch steps.

"Kit Kat and Tweety's."

I don't know how long it took us to find our way to the opening in the forest through the wind and sleet. At times it felt like we'd never make it. That we'd just end up frozen to the ground like a weird band of ice topiaries. But we hung in there and eventually found the path.

About halfway down the trail—which was now more of a giant mudslide—my mother had fallen, meaning that I had to take Caesar from her despite the fact that I was still holding the gun. My fur brother apparently didn't have much faith in my ability to carry him safely, so he had dug his claws into my neck for added security.

After what felt like both seconds and years, we were standing at the front door of the only other neighbors on our island. I brought some tentative fingers to touch the side of my neck. I was mildly concerned that I might be bleeding to death.

"How do we get in?" Kyle shouted over the howling wind. "Do you want me to break a window?"

I shook my head and bent to retrieve the spare key under the giant clay jug by the front door. A moment later we were all inside.

Except we weren't alone.

There was a small fire going in the wood stove.

And a bag of chips opened on the chair moved in front of it.

And a big lump standing behind the curtains . . . shuddering.

"Chuck?"

Chapter Forty-five

I knew it was him, and it wasn't from the chips or the shuddering.

No, it was the briefcase on the coffee table that gave him away.

"Dude, we know it's you," Kyle called out. "Learn how to hide."

Chuck's face peeked around the curtain.

"How did you get here?" I asked.

"The footpath through the woods," he said untangling his mud-caked shoes from the drapes.

My eyes narrowed, "But . . . how did you know about the path?"

"I researched your island before we came," he said with a jerky shrug. "And I took a course. Orienteering."

I arched one eyebrow—a move I could only accomplish when it came from a genuinely suspicious place. "Why didn't you tell anyone?"

"Well, why didn't you tell anyone about The Dark Web Assassin?" he asked, raising his own eyebrow to a level of accusation that matched mine. "I heard you talking with the boy in the kitchen." He ended his volley with a *dead to rights* point at the both of us.

"I had to look out for Kyle," I said, reaching for my charge to pull him into my side. But he had wandered off. Actually he was in the midst of a staring contest with a stuffed raccoon. I sighed. "Okay, I guess we're all just trying to survive here." I could be wrong, but my gut instinct told me Chuck was a bit of a coward and not much else.

"Is this your mother?" the lawyer asked, looking around me. "Summer Bloom? We spoke on the phone?" The tone of his voice almost sounded *hopeful*?

"Oh yes, of course," my mother said, floating forward. Oh sure, Kyle, Caesar, and I all looked like drowned rats, but my mother still managed to look like a butterfly. "Charles, I am very upset with you. I thought we agreed that your family wouldn't come."

"I tried! I really did!" Chuck said. It was hard to tell in the gloom, but he looked like he might be blushing. "I am so sorry. I told you my uncle could be, well, I shouldn't speak ill of the dead."

My mother nodded. "Of course not, but remember we spoke about the importance of standing up for oneself?"

Chuck nodded eagerly then added, "You look just like your picture on the retreat's website."

Oh, for the love of—

Kyle stepped over, thankfully, distracting me from whatever this was. "Are you sure we're safe here? The place kind of has a murder room vibe." He jerked a thumb at the eternally hissing fox."

"Honestly, I have no idea." I put the gun on the table before lifting the purse off from around my neck. I almost thought about sticking the gun in my waistband, but I was worried about the possibility of shooting myself in the butt.

I stripped off my wet jacket before I set to rifling through the contents of the purse. Wafts of Ronnie's rose perfume filled the air. "Bingo," I said under my breath, thrusting the phone into the air. I swiped the screen, and it beamed to life. "Yes!"

Then I realized I didn't know her password.

"Try 1, 2, 3, 4," Kyle said.

I squinted at him.

"Seriously, it's worth a shot."

I tried it . . . and wouldn't you know. "Good call, kid."

"So what's the plan?" Kyle asked. "Who are you calling?"

"The police first. Then Freddie." I turned my back to him and walked a few steps away toward the back hallway, poking at the phone's screen.

"You know all of this would be over if you had just shot whoever was coming after us back at the lodge."

I shook my head, but I couldn't say the same thought hadn't crossed my mind. "Sorry, Kyle. I'm just not all that comfortable shooting people hidden behind doors."

"You seem angry," my mom suddenly said. I almost answered her when I realized she was talking to Kyle. "And maybe a little afraid?"

The teen rolled his eyes so violently, I wasn't sure they were going to make it back down from the top of his head.

I half-smiled as a thought occurred to me. "She's right, you know."

Kyle's eyes snapped over to me.

"You two should talk as I make the calls," I said. "You have *feelings* that need a voice." The only cure for a grumpy teenager was an equally oblivious mom. "Do you think you could help Kyle with that?"

"Of course," my mother said coming up behind him, dropping her hands on his shoulders.

"She's right," Chuck called out. "Talking about your feelings is healthy. I read about it for this—"

Kyle managed to trip Chuck up with a look.

"Never mind."

He then turned back toward me and mouthed, *Help me,* as my mother draped an arm around him.

"You'll be fine."

I walked off into the darkened hallway of the small cabin toward the back den, grabbing a throw off the sofa and wrapping it around my shoulders. The room was just as cluttered as the rest of the house but had a door leading to the woods and no insulation by the feel of it.

I called Grady's number, but after ringing twice, the call cut off. I then sent him a text, but it bounced back saying it couldn't be delivered. I sighed. Maybe it had something to do with the storm?

I almost tapped Freddie's number before I opted to use video chat. I wasn't entirely sure why I had decided to go that route. Maybe I just wanted to convince myself that there was still a real world outside of this storm.

The phone trilled a few times before the screen popped to life.

"Erica?" Freddie asked. "Is that you? Where have you been? I've been calling and calling!"

"I dropped my phone in the water."

"You what? You look terrible. Where are you now? It's all dark."

"Kit Kat and Tweety's. Where are you?"

He didn't answer. Instead he just leaned in closer to the screen and squinted his eyes.

"Freddie? What's going—"

The look on his face sent cold fear rushing down my spine. His eyes widened, showing me a lot of white, but he wasn't looking quite at me . . . more . . . beyond me.

"Erica," he whispered. "Don't freak out, but I think there's someone behind you."

I went completely still.

The killer had known about the twin's place too. Of course he had. He was a professional! He—

I slowly turned my head and—

—jolted when I met the eyes of a deer.

"Jesus," I snapped, collapsing way deep into the seat of an old armchair. I had to clutch the armrest to stop myself from getting stuck in the springs. "It's a mount."

"Sorry. Sorry," Freddie said. "I can barely see you. I saw the eyes, and . . . it doesn't matter I'm just a little freaked out."

"Where are you?" I asked again, looking at a file cabinet off Freddie's shoulder. "Is that the sheriff's department?"

"Yeah, I came looking for Grady, or someone who might know where Grady is, but nobody's here. I can't find anyone. It's really starting to creep me out. I feel a little like I'm at the beginning of a zombie apocalypse movie."

I shook my head. "Relax. It was just Rhonda holding down the fort, and now she's here."

Freddie cocked his head. "What?"

"She's here. On the island."

"What?" Freddie asked again this time bringing the phone way too close to his face so that his left eye was peering into me. "How the hell did she manage that?"

"She took one of the police boats. She made it over when there was a break in the storm." I smiled weakly and shook my head, trying to push away the thought of where she might be right now. If something happened to her . . . "Lake Patrol said it was too dangerous, but she did it anyway."

"Seriously?" Freddie asked, still squinting at me through the screen. "Rhonda?"

"Yes, Rhonda." I squinted back at him. "You sound disappointed."

He leaned away from the phone and looked off to the side. "No. No. It's awesome. Rhonda, the hero. I mean, it does feel a little like she's throwing some shade on the rest of us in law enforcement, but—"

I smacked the phone against my forehead.

"All right, settle down," Freddie said. "Where is she now?"

"We got separated. Actually, I think she went after the killer," I said, blowing out some air. "I don't know what's going on. Everybody else has disappeared."

"That's not true," a voice said from the doorway.

"Is that the kid?" Freddie asked.

"Well, it's not. There's still Chuck and the doughy cameraman."

I rubbed my face with my free hand. Seriously, was this what being a parent was like? I couldn't even make a phone call.

"What?" he asked walking toward where I was sitting, plunking himself on the armrest. "It's true."

"Go back in the other room, Kyle."

"Is that your friend?" he went on, pushing his face toward the screen. "He's not what I pictured." An awkward moment passed. "You know for like being in security."

Freddie's mouth dropped open then shut. I could tell he wanted to say something, but he couldn't get the words out over his indignation.

"Please," I said. "Just go back into the other room. I'll talk to you in a second."

"I'm sorry," Kyle went on. "But that guy looks like he'd lose a wrestling match with a marshmallow. No offense."

My eyes widened as Freddie rattled off a string of half-shouted sentences that didn't quite make sense, but certainly got his point across.

I closed my eyes and took a breath.

He's just a kid. He's scared. He just lost his father.

A moment later, I opened my eyes just as Freddie had calmed down enough to clearly say, "Let him die, Erica."

"Kyle," I said before taking another breath. "Please go back into the other room."

"But I—"

"Go."

"Fine," he said, getting to his feet and throwing his hands in the air. "Not like you're the first person to not want me around."

He almost got me with that one, but I held firm. I waited for him to leave before I looked back down at Freddie.

"Seriously, Erica. Let him die. You'd be doing the world a favor."

I smoothed the hair back from my face with my free hand. "He's scared, and he's just a kid."

"He's a little bast—"

"Oh my God! You can't call kids that!" I yelled. "Especially when the father wasn't officially marri—doesn't matter. You can't call kids that." Why was I the only one who understood this?

"Yes, you can, Erica," Freddie said with all sorts of certainty. "You can. Say it with me. This is a safe space. No one will judg—"

"Erica!" my mom's voice shouted from the other room. "Stop calling Kyle names this instant! You too, Freddie Ng!"

"Oh my God!" Freddie whispered, ducking his head down into his shoulders. "Is that your mother? Where did your mother come from? I thought she was in Arizona?"

"We found her knocked out in a closet."

"Is she okay?"

"So far."

"Oh, good," Freddie said nodding. "That's great. I'm glad. But a little heads up she's around would be nice, you know?"

"Sorry," I mumbled. "I didn't think she could hear us. I forgot she's got ears like a bat."

Freddie nodded and sat down at what looked to be Rhonda's desk. "Okay, so what next?"

"You need to call Lake Patrol. Go talk to them in person if you have to. Tell them Rhonda's not crazy."

"Already tried that. Their best boat is over at Honey Harbor for some reason. And they're not going to risk their people in any other craft." He shook his head. "I still think Grady's our best bet. I mean, I get that he dumped you and all, but he would not want you murdered. Where is he?"

Suddenly I felt tears come to my eyes. I quickly blinked them away. "I thought I told you before. He's at Honey Harbor, too, trying to find some kids on the wat—"

"Are you kidding me? More kids!" Freddie yelled. "How many people have to die before we see the danger?"

"Freddie . . ."

"No! No. I am so tired of hearing *oh, I can't let the killer murder him; he's a kid*," he said in what I could only guess was an Erica imitation. An unflattering one. "Everybody treats kids like they're so special. You know, one time this kid came to my door asking for candy. Can you believe it? And—"

"Was it Halloween?"

He laughed. Then sighed. "I've been saving that joke all night. Then I realized this would probably be the last time I saved jokes to use on y—"

"Still not dead, Freddie."

He nodded like he didn't quite believe it but was putting on a brave face.

"Besides"—I moved to the back corner of the room and whispered—"it turns out the kid may already be dying." I filled him in on what Rhonda had told me.

"Oh, well," Freddie began before pausing a moment, "way to make me look like a jerk."

I snorted a breath.

"Okay, I'm going to go find Grady for real this time, and let him know what's going on." He scanned the desk. "He'll find a way to get us over there. With all his muscles, he should be able to swim to the island with me on his back." Freddie shook his head. "Maybe *his* musculature will reassure the little—"

"Please." I closed my eyes and shook my head.

"There has to be some way I can get in touch with him. Police radio, maybe?"

"Hey!" I shouted suddenly remembering something. "What about the walkie talkie thing they gave you for the fair?"

He scoffed. "They took it back. Said it was for official police business, and I wasn't a—" Suddenly his eyes darted side to side. "Wait! Forget it! Listen, you need to save the battery on that phone. Just stay safe, and I'll find Grady, and if I don't . . ." I watched his eyes trail off.

I suddenly knew what he was thinking. "Don't you come across that lake, Freddie," I said. "Rhonda barely made it."

"Sure. Sure," he replied, turning down the corners of his mouth in the most insincere expression ever.

"I mean it Freddie. Don't you—"

"Bye! Don't die!" He then ended the call, but not before he mumbled what I thought might be, "Nobody puts Freddie in a corner."

An hour and a half later, we were still in the cabin. No one had come to rescue us. But no one had come to kill us either, so all things considered, we were doing okay. I had tried calling both Grady and Freddie again, but I couldn't get through to either one. I wasn't sure what to make of that. I just hoped Freddie had listened and wasn't trying to make it across the lake.

After Kyle escaped my mom's therapy session, he went back to sitting on the couch, jumping at various noises, while my mother tended to Caesar and chatted with Chuck. The two quickly found a lot of common ground in the area of self-improvement and seemed almost content with the way the evening was shaping up.

I wasn't so lucky. In fact, I was finding it pretty difficult not to slip too deeply into my own dark thoughts. But the harder I tried to resist, the more questions popped into my head. Meaning-of-life type questions, like, what I would do differently if I made it through this night alive? What would I change about my life? What did I want to live for? Worse yet, if I died, what would I really leave behind? My mother would be devastated, of course, but if I was killed, she probably would be too, so I didn't really need to spend too much time on that scenario. I mean, Freddie would be upset. No doubt. But he was young-ish and resilient-ish. He'd move on. Eventually find a new best friend. Probably drive him or her nuts by saying things like, *Well, Erica would have let me have the last slice of pizza.* So I guess that was a bit of legacy. But not really the impact I wanted to leave behind on the world. I guess when most people think of legacies, they think of their children or the work they've left behind. As a court reporter, really, my death would just leave scheduling difficulties. And as for children, well, I'd need a father for that. Well, not according to my mother, but, I guess I was a traditionalist. And that of course led me to . . .

Grady.

Why did I keep messing things up with him? I had him right where I thought I had always wanted him—asking me to stay with him. Have a relationship. Be together. And I had blown it all up. Again. I mean, the obvious excuse would be to blame it on my upbringing. Growing up in a spiritual retreat for women, I had attended hundreds of divorce-recovery type sessions by the time I was twelve. That does something to a person. Then there was the whole my-mother-refusing-to-talk-about-the-identity-of-my-father thing. When I was really small, for a while there, I thought I might have been conceived through a Wiccan ritual. These are not normal thoughts for a child to have. And yet that didn't explain everything. Not really.

A few times, I wondered if maybe deep down I believed Grady wasn't the man for me, and that I was sabotaging the relationship to get away. But that wasn't it either. Truth be told, I think maybe Matthew was on to something. I had just been a coward. Our being together—just happy and together—seemed like a dream come true, and I couldn't let myself be vulnerable enough to enjoy it. Trust it. Because what would happen if it all went away? That's why I had put off the decision to move home. Made excuses. And hurt Grady a whole lot with all my mixed messages.

I just needed one more chance to make it right.

I closed my eyes and prayed again to the powers that be . . .

Please just one more chance.

I shook my head. If only it worked that way.

But, still, the thought of never being able to say I was sorry . . .

Wait.

Suddenly I shot up from the chair I had been sitting on at the kitchen table and looked around.

"What?" my mother asked, eyes widening. "Did you hear something?"

"No. I was just looking for—aha!" I grabbed a pad of paper off the kitchen counter then rummaged around in the drawer underneath for a pencil. Got it.

"What are you doing?" Kyle asked.

I settled myself back down at the kitchen table. "Writing a letter."

"A letter? How is that going to help?"

"Mind your business," I mumbled, face already turned down at the page.

Now, how to begin?

Dear Grady.

Nah, that didn't sound right. I crossed it out. It didn't feel like us. Too formal. I wanted this to be personal.

Grady.

Nope. I crossed that out too. That just sounded like I was mad at him. I tapped the end of the pencil on my chin.

Hey Babe.

Definitely not. That sounded like I way too cool given the situation . . . or high. I ripped the paper off the pad and crumpled it up.

"What about starting with *Good-bye cruel world*?" Kyle offered. "Seeing as, you know, we're all going to die. Not that you could tell with all the letter-writing and discussion of vegan recipes going on right now."

I shook my head. Man, he really did need a nap.

"I'm sorry, okay?" he said with enough force that I had to turn to look at him. "I just want this all to be over!"

"Come sit with me," my mom said, patting the spot beside her on the sofa.

He slumped, but shuffled in her direction. "Fine. But I don't want to talk about why my family hates me anymore."

"I know. I know," she said, pulling him down on the couch. "But it might do you some good."

I rolled my shoulders and tilted my head side to side a few times before looking back down at the page.

Dear Grady,

Yeah, that was fine.

If you are reading this, I am probably dead.

I looked at the words. Definitely clichéd. A bit melodramatic. Wait, no, not melodramatic, because they were true. Besides how often does someone get to write those words and really mean it? If I was going to die, I might as well live a little.

I am really sorry things have turned out this way. Not just about my being murdered—although that really sucks—

I decided to throw in a little smiley face. I thought he'd want to know I kept my sense of humor to the very end.

—but about how things turned out between us. First, you probably know this, but it was never about you. It was about me. And you were right. I was afraid. Not about you. Or about the commitment.

Hmm, suddenly my throat felt tight.

It was about believing it could really happen, and being afraid of how good it could be. And I know that now. I know I could have counted on you. And me. I just needed to jump off the dock.

I drew a little heart there. Not that I was a heart-drawing type of girl, but docks had special meaning for us.

If I could go back, I would do it all so differently. And I'm not writing that to make you feel bad about dumping me—especially now that I'm dead. You were totally right to dump me. I would have dumped me too. I just wanted you to know that.

I pulled back.

Why was this so hard for me?

Just write it, Erica!

I meant the words today. I meant them that day back in the airport . . .

I could still see the smile on his face. The smell of his aftershave. The sound of his voice . . .

I love you, Erica.

Yup, he had said it. Those three little words everyone wants to hear. Four, if you count my name, which totally made it even better because, you know, there was no confusion about who he was talking about.

And he was so happy when he said it.

I was too!

And I was so ready to say the words back to him. They had been right there in my head, but they just wouldn't come out. I had even opened my mouth, and—

It's okay.

He said those two words without his smile faltering a bit.

I know it's going to take you some time.

But it wasn't okay. It really, really wasn't.

Then he had turned, bag on his shoulder, smile on his face, and he had walked through the gate, throwing me a wave.

At the time, I had nearly convinced myself that everything was fine. Better than fine. I had always wanted to hear him say those words.

And for a little while, everything was still great.

But those were heavy words to sit between two people. Open-ended. Hanging like an unspoken question.

And there were so many times I was going to say it. I was ready to say it. I knew it was true. But every time I went to . . . well, it was either over the phone, or the moment didn't seem quite right. And then the pressure grew, and the silence of not saying them was deafening. And then he kept asking for more details about when I was moving home . . . if I was moving home . . . if he should look into moving to Chicago . . . and I didn't have any of the answers. And I didn't want to say it then because it would have just seemed like I was saying it to hang onto him, and that wasn't it at all.

And I didn't want to ruin the moment.

Because those three words should be good, happy words. Like they had been for him in the airport.

I had missed my chance.

Well, I wouldn't make that mistake again.

I stared at the sheet of paper lying on the table in front of me. This might truly be my last chance to tell Grady how I really felt.

Come on, Erica, I thought, gripping the pen. *Do or die time.* Or do because you're going to die.

I love you.

I dropped the pen like it was hot and leaned back in my chair.

Wow, that really hadn't been *that* hard. In fact, all of a sudden, I wasn't quite sure what I had been so afraid of.

I quickly signed my name at the bottom of the page, then folded the paper up, wrote Grady on the front, and shoved it in my back pocket. Wasn't very likely it would get bloody back there.

I stood up and gave my spine a stretch before I jolted

when the movement opened up the scratch I had on my back from the nail in the shed door. Despite the searing pain, I was feeling much better about things. That had been a big step, and if we did in fact manage to survive this thing, which was looking more likely with every passing minute—

Suddenly my mother jumped to her feet, sending Caesar scurrying.

"Do you smell smoke?"

Chapter Forty-six

"I do." I inhaled deeply. "That's definitely smoke."

We had purposely let the fire Chuck had started die out because we didn't want to attract the killer's notice, but suddenly I was more worried that the killer might be trying to attract ours.

"What do we do?" Kyle asked, eyes darting around the room. "Where's it coming from?"

"Stay calm," I said, darting from window to window then down the hall. Flames! Big flames! Rippling in the wind from the now open window in the back room! "We got to go!" I shouted running back down the hall.

"We're trapped!" Kyle was at the front door, holding a doorknob up in the air. "I can't get it open."

I ran over to him, coughing. The smoke was thick already. I tried to pry the door open by squeezing my finger into the small gap between the door and its frame, but it was no good.

"Do something!" Kyle shouted. "We're going to die in here!"

"No. We are not." My eyes jumped around the room

until they landed on my mother over by the fireplace yanking at something.

The old shotgun mounted on the wall!

Good call, Summer.

I snatched Brody's gun off the table and passed it to Kyle before gripping the rungs of one of the kitchen chairs. I hoisted it up, and I hustled over to the window, shouting, "Watch yourselves!" I swung the chair sending its legs crashing into the glass.

It must have been a pretty good swing because the entire window shattered, driving big shards of glass to the floor.

"Let's go!" I shouted, waving Kyle forward.

He shook his head no.

I coughed, waving my hand at the smoke. "Come on!"

"He's out there!"

I looked back into the dark beyond the window. He had a point, but we didn't have a choice. We at least had a shot out there. If we stayed inside, we'd die for sure. "Kyle, I know you're scared, but—"

"He lit this fire to get us out there," Kyle snapped. "As soon as we step out that window. He'll pick us off. One by one!"

Suddenly the sound of a shotgun being loaded snapped our heads around. "Then he can start with me," my mother said.

"Mom?"

"Erica, grab the cat and your gun. Kyle, hold the flashlight." My mother marched toward the window, barrel of the gun leading the way. "Chuck, follow me."

"Anywhere," Chuck said, scurrying after her.

Kyle scooped up the flashlight from the table. "I still don't like this."

"Hey, at least you're not carrying the cat." I heaved Caesar up into my arms. I cradled him with my gun hand then waited from him to secure himself with his claws. *Yup, there we go,* I thought, hissing the pain out. The cat was secure.

"Ready?" my mom called out from the window.

Kyle and I nodded.

"We head for the old stone shed out back."

"What if the killer's in there?" Kyle asked.

My mom cocked the gun. "Then we end this thing."

She stepped through the window first, followed by Chuck.

"What's going on with her?" Kyle yelled over the wind, now howling through the room. "Is she in shock or something?"

"No, she's good," I shouted back, blinking my eyes in the swirling smoke. If nothing else, Summer was a woman of extremes, especially when it came to my safety. "Sometimes you just don't want to mess with her."

He shot me a confused look then—

BOOM!

Chapter Forty-seven

My mother fired the shotgun into the air before waving us through the jagged frame, shouting, "Go! Go! Go!"

Kyle went first. I hobbled after him with Caesar.

The wind howled around us, pounding and rattling the tin roof of the porch.

"Let's go!" my mom yelled, pushing us forward. "Kyle, hold that light up!"

Kyle fumbled with the flashlight. "But he'll see us!"

A horrible metal screech ripped through the air as the wind tore the porch roof up and away. "We can't stay here!" I shouted. "Let's go!"

Kyle pointed the flashlight as we pushed against the wind toward the side of the cottage. I tilted my face down and away from the onslaught. With the light of the fire growing by the second, I could see what I hadn't been able to before.

The boat.

Ted's boat from the marina. The bodyguard had known about the twins' place all along. He had done his research. I thought about trying to get the group to head there instead, but the shed was closer, and I didn't like how exposed we were. Besides, judging by the way the boat was rocking, it was going to be on its side any second.

As soon as we stepped down from the porch away from the security of the cottage, the full wrath of the storm hit us. Rain and dirt whipped my cheeks. A bright flash of lightning cracked overhead. Lightning. Sure. Why not?

"There!" I shouted. The tiny stone shed appeared in front of us about a hundred yards away. "Kyle! Keep the light on it!"

We pushed step after impossible step forward.

Somewhere in my consciousness, I knew we should still be afraid of the murderer, but even with all the killer had in his unknown arsenal, it was nothing, nothing, compared to the power of this storm. We were all meaningless in this moment. Bugs washing away into the gutter.

"We're almost there!" my mother shouted. "Hang on!"

She stopped just at the entrance, planted her left foot on the ground and kicked the wooden door. It flew open, door latch dropping to the ground.

Oh, thank you, I thought, staring into the little dirt room illuminated by the weak beam of Kyle's flashlight. Empty.

Then the light was gone.

We were plunged into darkness again. The glow of the fire barely reaching us.

"Kyle?" I shouted. "Where's the light?"

Nothing.

"Kyle! Stop messing around!"

I whipped around trying to see . . . something . . . anything . . .

My voice dropped. "Kyle?"

But he was gone.

Chapter Forty-eight

I dropped Caesar and took off blindly in the direction I had last seen Kyle. Frick! I was going to fall. I could barely see the ground. The glare of the fire was messing with my eyes.

Wait? There!

Was that a light?

I spotted a glimmer just around where I thought the trail back to the retreat should be.

I took another hurried step forward, but the ground rolled under my foot, dropping me on my back.

The flashlight! I had tripped on Kyle's flashlight. I ran my hand over the mucky earth until I found the metal cylinder and flicked it on.

"Erica! What is going—"

My mother's voice cut off sharply with a yelp.

"Mom?" I jumped to my feet and spun the beam of the torch around. She was collapsed on the ground, holding her ankle, Chuck kneeling beside her.

"Summer!"

"Are you okay?" I asked rushing to her side.

"I think I just wrenched it," she shouted.

"I'm sorry. I'm sorry," Chuck moaned. "I got scared, and I fell on her."

I shone the light down on her ankle. Oh, sweet lady marmalade, that was *not* a sprain.

"Get me up. Let's go after him," my mom shouted in my ear.

"You're not going anywhere," I said, wrapping my arm around her waist, lifting her to her good foot. "Let's get you in the shed."

"What? No. I'm fine," she shouted. "Look, it's just a flesh—" Just then she looked down as the bouncing beam of the flashlight hit her dangling foot. "Oh dear. That's not good."

"No. No, it isn't."

"It's all my fault," Chuck moaned.

"No, it's not," my mother yelled. "This never should have happened. Not with all the kale I have been eating."

"But all calcium aside, I weigh a good two hundred and seven—"

"Not important!" I shouted. "Hurry! I need to go after Kyle."

"But how do you even know where he is?" my mother asked, hopping toward the shed, Caesar was waiting for her at the mouth of the door, looking just fine.

"He's at the retreat." It was my only guess. I couldn't help but think that whoever was doing this, Brody, I guess, was still trying to get away with it, and that meant he still had to stage a crime scene. I hoped . . . otherwise I was already too late.

No. No way.

A familiar heat suddenly swelled in my chest.

The kid was my responsibility.

I had promised that I would take care of him.

I had *promised*.

I felt my heart rate pick up.

I was so tired of this night. This storm. This killer.

But more than anything, I was tired of being afraid.

I needed to go. Now.

"Erica," my mother said as I eased her to the dirt floor. "You are not going up there. I won't have it."

"Sorry, Mom," I said straightening up. "But I'm going. He's a kid."

Her eyes rounded. "But you're my kid."

I gripped the flashlight, knuckles burning with the cold. "I have to try. He doesn't have anybody."

Chuck eased my mother's back against the wall of the small stone structure, placing the twins' shotgun on her lap. "I'll take care of her. You don't have to worry about that."

Just as I was about to leave, my mother grabbed my wrist. "Stop. Just slow down a second. I know that look on your face."

I didn't have to ask her what look. She was probably seeing all the rage threatening to blind me.

"I'm sorry, Mom," I said, taking a step back, making her drop her grip. "I love you, but I have to do this."

"And I'm so very proud of you for that." She shook her head, all sorts of pleading on her face. "But I love you, too, honey. And Kyle, I'm sorry, but he could already be gone."

"I have to try."

"Erica, please listen. If this person after us really is a trained killer . . ." She shook her head again. "With your temper? I just don't want you to . . ."

"What? You don't want me to what?"

The struggle to find the right words warred across her face. "I don't know. Poke the bear?"

"Poke the bear? Poke the bear? Me?" I patted my chest. After this night of poison, and guns, and concussions . . . and snow, and ice, and sleet . . . oh yeah, and vomit, I couldn't forget about the vomit . . . after all of that, she was nervous about me poking the bear? "You don't need to worry, Mom."

"Why not?"

"Because, right now, I am the fricking bear."

My mother dropped her face into her hands. "Goddess, help us all."

Chapter Forty-nine

Oh, I was angry. So very, very angry.

In fact, I was so angry I wasn't even registering the storm anymore, or if I was, it was just making me madder. Oh sure, this assassin most likely had a lot of advantages over me. But here's the thing: He also most likely had a vision of how this was all supposed to go down—kind of like a trail of dominoes around a room—to cover up who was behind all of this and make his getaway. But the problem with dominos is that it only takes one missing piece to stop the whole thing in its track—and I knew with every part of me, if I could just get close enough, I was about to toe punt the whole friggin' lot of them!

Once I made it to the top of the trail that opened to the grounds of the retreat, I clicked the flashlight off and crouch-ran toward the back of the lodge the way I had seen professional military types do in the movies. It probably didn't look at all like it was supposed to, given the fact that I was trudging through heavy, wet snow, but it felt right.

I had almost made it to the back steps when I heard something strange.

I froze.

There it was again.

It almost sounded like a distant—

"Help!"

A woman's voice. And it sounded like it was coming from somewhere near the canoes.

I clicked on my flashlight, but kept it pointed at the ground.

"Help!"

Crap. I didn't have time for this, but maybe it was Rhonda.

"Please!"

I trudged my way through the snow, about half the distance, then lifted my flashlight. I saw something move, but I couldn't quite make it out. I took a few more steps forward then my beam hit someone's knees? Under a canoe? I yanked the light up and—

"Ashley?"

Chapter Fifty

The beam from my light caught Ashley's miserable face. Her mascara was smeared in black clouds under her eyes, and her lips were almost blue. The top part of her body was huddled under a canoe on two saw horses, but her lower part was sticking awkwardly out in front of her, and . . . wait, was that Ronnie sprawled across her lap?

"What are you two doing here?" I yelled, shooting a look back at the lodge. "Is your mother . . . ?"

"Passed out. She came to find me." Ashley shook her head, looking even more miserable. "Even after everything I said. She still came to find me." She tightened her hold on her mother's shoulder. "She probably saved me from freezing to death."

Ronnie did look kind of like a blanket spread across her daughter's lap. A heavy, snoring blanket.

"But why here? Are you hiding?"

Ashley looked at something on the ground. I followed her gaze with my beam.

"Holy crap! Is that your knife?" Cause there was definitely something sticking out of the top of her cute, little boot, right in the laces.

"You were right, okay?" she said, shaking her head. "I dropped it. I was chasing after Brody, and I slipped."

"Wow." I knew I should probably try to morph my expression from its horrified state to something more neutral, but it was really bad! And it's not like I wanted this to happen. Not like the hyena probably looking down at us right now. Laughing. "Have you, uh, tried to, you know . . ." I yanked my own foot into the air.

"It hurts too much to move."

"Okay, listen, now that I know you're here, I'll try to get you help," I said dragging my eyes from her impaled foot. "But I have to go find Kyle first. Have you seen anyone else go by?"

"I thought I saw two people," she said, shaking her frozen braids. "They were fighting, so I didn't call out to them."

"Was it Kyle?"

"I don't know. It's hard to see with the storm."

"Okay," I yelled turning back. "I have to—"

"Wait! My mom was mumbling something about an assassin? That you think Brody hired him?" She squinted up at me. "He didn't. He wouldn't. You need to find him."

"Ashley, I—"

Just then Ronnie groaned and put her arm more tightly around her daughter.

"Stay put," I said before looking back down at her foot. "I mean . . . I'll be back."

I ran back over to the lodge's porch and crept up the back steps, once again dropping to my hands and knees to do a sweep of the place. I hated wasting time, but my mom was right. My getting killed would not help Kyle, especially if he was already . . .

Nope.

I had to be smart.

I stopped again at the front of the lodge, leaning my

back against the wall just underneath the window. I carefully placed my flashlight on the planks of the porch to get a two-handed grip on the gun. I slowly inched up and cranked my head to get a peripheral view into the room.

I tilted my gaze down.

Kenny was still on the couch.

My eyes swept the rest of the room.

Empty.

No Kyle.

Crap. I couldn't see any other way around it. I had to go inside, despite that slippery feeling in my gut that seemed to suggest my stomach, at least, was really, really against the idea.

Just then a blue light poured up into the darkness of the kitchen, catching my eye.

What the hell was that?

My mom's phone! Who would be calling my mom's phone?

I had forgotten all about it. I felt around in my pockets for Ronnie's cell, but I had left it back at the twins' in the craziness of the fire. What if someone was trying to get me and was calling or texting her number as a last resort? Rhonda? Or Freddie? What if they needed to tell me something? Like *The killer's right behind you!* I whipped around. Nope. But it could be something else important . . . or it might a subscription renewal email from Vegans R Us.

I chewed my lip. It didn't matter what it was. I was going in either way. I was Kyle's only hope. If he still had one. I had to at least look. Maybe he was tossed into a closet too.

Unfortunately, most of my anger had drained away. My inner bear had gone all bunny rabbit.

I clenched my fists and scurried over to the front door. It was slightly ajar, shuddering in the wind. I pushed it open and slid inside, quietly side-shuffling toward the phone still glowing on the counter, my gun pointed to the floor. Someone could still be in here. I couldn't take any chances. My eyes jumped to Rayner's body still lying in the same position. I then looked over to Kenny. Nope, he hadn't moved either. Not that Rayner could move. I mean—

Focus, Erica.

I hustled over to the counter. I wasn't really expecting to see anything useful, but when my eyes dropped down to the screen.

The glowing snippet of the new message made my insides sink.

It was an email from Freddie. The subject line all in capitals.

I shook my head.

No. No way.

I quickly swiped the screen and scanned the contents before whipping back around to look at Kenny . . . and the person slowly rising up from behind the couch.

I yanked my gun into the air.

"You're . . . you're another love child."

Chapter Fifty-one

"Just wait," Julie-Kimberly said raising her hands in the air, "I need you to listen to me." The gesture of putting her hands up would have been much more reassuring had she not been holding a gun in one of those hands.

But at least it wasn't pointed at me. Yet.

Where did she get the gun?

Why did everybody have guns?

"It isn't what you think."

"I can't believe you just said that," I spluttered, raising my gun an inch higher. "That's what every guilty person says."

"I can explain."

I waved the gun at her face. "Making it worse."

"I was just hiding back here" she said, patting the sofa. "I don't know what you think you know, but—"

"I know that you hired a lawyer and that"—I stopped to catch a breath—"that lawyer just filed, proceedings, today, to get a court-ordered paternity test."

"Okay, that's right. I am Rayner's daughter. My mother never told him. He never knew." Her eyes darted over to the body still on the floor. "I was going to tell him to-night."

"Tonight?"

"Yeah, it would have been the most epic season finale ever."

"What would be? You killing everyone? Is that how you win the money?"

"No!" she yelled with a lot of indignation—which meant absolutely nothing to me. Whoever could do all this was pretty twisted. Being a good liar would have to be on his or her short list of skills. "Don't you see? When they were all dealing with the fall-out of Rayner changing his will, I was supposed to hit them with papers of my own."

"That's insane."

"And pretty great television. Think about it," she said, shaking her head. "Why would I go through all the trouble of hiring a lawyer to start proceedings if killing everyone was my plan?"

"To make yourself look innocent. Like you're doing right now," I pointed my gun at the *right now* spot on the floor—before I jerked it back up! *Keep the gun pointed at the murderer, Erica.* "I don't buy it."

"Look, everybody at work was in on the plan. How do you think I got this big of a job at my age?" she asked. "I just wanted to meet my family and maybe advance my career at the same time! Whoever came up with this murder scheme—"

"Interesting that you would use the word scheme," I said pausing to bite my lower lip. "You mean, scheme, like lie about your identity to a whole bunch of people, come up with an elaborate ruse about doing a TV show so that you could then wait for just the right moment to—"

"No!" Her face twitched. I guess that had pissed her

off. "This was how Third Act wanted it to play out. That's all."

"I don't believe you. I don't." Actually, truth was, I didn't know what to think. She had lied. She had motive. But was that enough for me to . . . what? Shoot her? "What happened with Brody when he broke in through the kitchen?" I asked jerking my chin into the air.

"He broke in," she said. "He ranted around for a while, fought with Ronnie, but then he left again. He got spooked. Said he heard something outside. He thought the killer was coming. Tell her, Kenny!"

My eyes widened then whipped down to the unconscious form on the sofa. "Kenny?"

He didn't move. Uh-oh, was Julie-Kimberly having conversations with unconscious people now? Because—

"Kenny!" she hissed.

"She's telling the truth," he mumbled out of the corner of his mouth.

"Oh my God!" I stepped back toward the kitchen, moving the gun back and forth between the two of them. "How long have you been awake?"

He mumbled something.

"How long?" I shouted.

He shot up on the couch, "Does the exact time really matter?"

"What? Why would you . . . ?"

"It seemed like a good way to live." He dropped back onto the sofa and muttered, "Still does."

Julie-Kimberly-looked down at him, a strange new expression of her face. "He wasn't awake when you all were still here—"

"Well . . ."

"Kenny?" she snapped, color rising in her cheeks. "You said—"

"I didn't want to embarrass you after"—he paused as

he scratched the stubble at his chin, eyes still closed—
"you confessed your love."

Her eyes widened. "You heard that?"

"It's okay, Julie, Kimmy, whatever we're calling you
now," he said, peeking one eye open. "I am very lovable.
I can see why you both fell for me."

"Son of a—"

"Stop it! Stop talking!" I took one hand from my gun
and clutched my forehead. "What is the matter with all
you people?"

"I didn't know that numbnuts, here, was conscious
until after you left, Erica," she said, sticking out her non-
gun holding hand. "Swear to God."

"Like that means anything to me!" I took a quick,
shaky breath. My face was tingling again. "So what happened after Brody left?"

"Ronnie went after him to find Ashley. And then your
cop friend showed up."

"Where is she?" I said jabbing the gun at her. Then a
horrible thought hit me. "Is that her gun?"

"It is," she said, nodding, then slowly moving her
free hand to push her glasses up her nose. "She gave it
to me."

"Why? Why would she do that?"

"I wasn't going to leave Kenny, and she said she
needed to go back and check on you and Kyle at the boat.
She didn't want to leave me without any way to protect
myself. I was in the military. I know how to handle a
weapon."

"The military? Come on. You're asking me to believe
you went from the military into reality T—" I shook my
head. "Actually, never mind, that doesn't sound too far
off." I didn't know what to make of any of this. Giving
Julie-Kimberly the gun did sound like something Rhonda
might do. She would sacrifice her job and herself before

leaving someone else in a dangerous situation unprotected. "But I heard gunshots!"

"I can explain those," she said, shaking her head, hands back up. "Kenny startled her one of the times. I think she thought he had come back from the dead, and the other, she thought she heard someone outside, on the porch, and she wanted to scare him off."

"Where is she now? That was a long time ago."

"I don't know. But I swear, I didn't do anything."

I cocked my head to a dangerous angle. "Then where is she?"

"I don't know! Maybe the assas—"

"Don't you dare finish that sentence!"

"Okay. Okay," she said, jerking her hands even higher into the air. "Maybe she saw something. Maybe she found Ashley and Ronnie. She could be chasing shadows, for all I know," she said half-turning to the window.

I pinned my lips together. I wasn't exactly at the *sharing information* trust level with these two yet, but it was possible Rhonda had seen the fire and went to investigate.

"Erica, you have to believe me—"

"Where's Kyle?"

"What?"

I threw the question at her not really thinking she would have the answer—or tell it to me if she knew—but I had to try.

"Where's Kyle?"

"I'm here!" a voice called out from the back of the retreat. "I'm here!"

I caught the look of surprise on Julie-Kimberly's face. "Kyle? Where are you? Are you all right?"

"I climbed in the bathroom window! But he's coming! We need to go!" I heard him rushing down the hall.

"Stay there!" I snapped. "Don't come out here!"

"Why?"

I held my gun on Julie-Kimberly, but turned a little to shout, "Did the man say anything? Did he tell you who hired him?"

"He talked to someone on the phone. I thought I heard him say the name Katie."

I didn't move.

"Or maybe it was Kimberly."

Chapter Fifty-two

The producer whipped her gun at me faster than I thought possible.

"But I don't know who that is," Kyle went on. "Erica?" I heard his footsteps in the hallway again.

"Stay in the other room."

"But—"

"Stay in the other room!"

"Erica," Julie said calmly, gun pointed at my face. "I am saying this for your own good. You do not look comfortable with that firearm, and I am a very good shot."

"She is," Kenny said. "I've seen her shoot. She'll take you out. And can you guys just hang on a moment till I get out of the crossfire?"

"I wouldn't get cocky," I said, keeping the gun steady on her, well, as steady as I could what with all the shaking in my hands. "How hard can it be? People accidently shoot people all the time."

"Look, this is getting way out of control. I don't know what Kyle heard, but I am not working with the assassin," she said moving out from behind the sofa—which I did not like at all—but she was also lowering her gun.

"I'm going to put this down now." She turned the weapon sideways and placed it on the table, sliding it toward the far end. "Let's figure this out."

Suddenly the front door swung open, crashing into the wall . . .

. . . and an enormous silhouette filled the threshold.

I'd like to say I stayed cool. I'd like to say I raised the gun and took a deliberate shot.

But I didn't.

The shock of the door slamming open spun me around, sending me toppling over a chair. My gun skidded across the floor.

On some level I saw—heard—Julie go for her weapon, but the man fired at her. Wood splintered at the wall near her head. He fired again.

She screamed and hit the floor.

The man's arm swiveled toward me.

He was moving so slow.

But at the same time too fast for me to even—

BANG!

Chapter Fifty-three

I had just enough time to put up my forearms before the man's enormous body hit me, crushing me against the floor. He wheezed a breath into my ear, right before his weight slumped.

"Erica!" Kyle shouted. "Are you all right?"

I squeezed myself out from underneath the man, and pushed myself to my feet. I grabbed Kyle and hugged him to my chest. "You saved my life."

He mumbled something, but I couldn't make it out. His face was buried in my armpit. I jerked him away when I realized how dangerous the situation still was. We both stepped over the man's legs toward the door. "How did you . . . where did you get the gun?"

Kyle shook his head. "The table. I just grabbed it."

"Oh my God! Julie!" I spun around. Sure, I had just been holding her at gunpoint, but that didn't mean I wanted her to actually get shot. At least, I didn't think I did. Everything was so confusing!

Kenny had her in his arms on the floor. She was clutching her shoulder. Blood seeping out from between her fingers. "I'm okay. I think. I—"

"Everybody freeze! Police!"

All eyes whipped to the door as Rhonda came barreling in, flashlight pointed at us.

Kyle and I jerked our hands into the air . . . for the flashlight's sake?

Rhonda lowered the beam as her eyes trailed over the scene. "Whoa, Doom. What did you do?"

"Me? Nothing!"

She pointed to the man on the floor. "Is that . . . ?"

"Rayner's bodyguard. The assassin."

She wasn't listening though. She was too busy picking up the hitman's gun off the floor and securing it in her holster. She then pressed her fingers against his neck.

"Careful," I said.

"I can't feel a pulse," she said, shaking her head. "You've still got my weapon?" she asked, looking over to Julie-Kimberly.

"Kyle used it to shoot the . . . him," the producer answered, briefly dropping her eyes back to the enormous man.

"Good job, kid," Rhonda said as Kyle passed her the gun.

"Thanks," he mumbled.

She stood and moved to holster her gun too, but couldn't find a free place to stick it, giving me time to say, "You might want to keep that one out a little longer."

Rhonda froze and looked up at me, "Why?"

"Julie, here, is actually Kimberly Winters, and it turns out she's another love child of Rayner's."

I felt Kyle startle at my back. "What?"

"Yup."

Julie didn't say anything.

"Wow," Rhonda whispered under her breath. "So she hired this guy?"

"No!" Julie shouted.

Rhonda looked to me.

"I don't know."

"Right, well, maybe we should sort this out back on the mainland. Like with a chart. It's hard to keep track of all these Boatrights." Rhonda took one last look around, then said, "Okay, well, no point staying here with all . . . this. The storm's quieted some, and you both need medical attention." She made eye contact with Julie-Kimberly and then Kyle.

"*I* need medical attention?" he asked.

Rhonda flashed me some *uh-oh* eyes. "Erica, will explain it on the ride over."

"Thanks a lot," I muttered under my breath.

"But what about Brody?" Kenny asked. "He's still out there."

"He's secure," Rhonda answered. "I found him huddled and rocking in the shed these two were in earlier." She jerked a thumb at me and Kyle. "I handcuffed him to one of the support poles. He's not going anywhere."

"We have to get Ashley and Ronnie, though," I said jumping in. "They're by the canoes."

"Hiding?"

"Kind of. Ashley impaled her foot to the ground with her knife, and Ronnie's passed out on top of her. For warmth."

"Whoa." Rhonda blinked a few times. "I can't believe I get to meet Ronnie."

I threw her a look.

"Right. There will be time for all that later. Camera Guy, you get your producer to the boat," she said, looking at Kenny. "I'll get the women. Erica, you bring Kyle."

"Wait! My mom!" I shouted. "Her ankle's broken. She's back at the twins' in their little stone shed thingy."

"Jeez Louise," Rhonda said throwing her hand in the

air. "Okay. We'll get everyone in the boat. Then I'll go back to stay with her."

I shook my head. "No, I will. You get everyone to the mainland."

"Got it."

Kenny lifted—I guess just Kimberly?—up into his arms.

"I can walk, you know," she said, with a grimace of pain. "He hit me in the arm."

The cameraman shook his head. "There's no pretending anymore."

The producer rolled her eyes and threw her head back over his arm.

"You like me," Kenny said in a singsong voice. "You think I'm sexy."

"Just stop."

"And for the record . . ." Kenny paused dramatically as Julie's eyes snapped up to his. "I feel the same way. Well, I wouldn't say I'm all the way in love like you are, but—"

"Please," she said, closing her eyes. "Just let me bleed out."

I jerked my head at Kyle. "Let's go."

"Okay," he said, patting his jacket pockets. "But there's a big flashlight in the other room." He jerked a thumb back. "Way better than ours. I'll just grab it."

The others were already out the door.

"Kyle!" I hissed. "Leave it. We don't have time for—"

But he was already in the hallway. I moved to go after him when I heard the man on the floor suddenly wheeze.

Guess, it was hard to detect a pulse through all that neck muscle.

I froze, the hair rising up on the back of my neck.

Maybe . . . maybe that was just some kind of after-death wheeze?

"Kyle?" I hissed again, softer this time. "Let's get going. Now!" I would have gone to get him myself, but the man on the floor was blocking my path, and I didn't want to take my eyes off of him to go around. Sure, he looked dead, but that's how they always look right before they grab your ankle.

Just then his fingers twitched. I jumped back. But he wasn't reaching out for me. His hand just kind of flopped off of his chest onto the floor sending something spinning in my direction.

A phone.

My eyes stayed glued to his face as I stepped forward and crouched down to reach for it. Once I had it in my hand, I stood up and backed away again.

It was a small, cheap thing.

A burner.

I looked at the screen, eyes falling on an open text message window.

All it said was *The money is coming. I need more time.*

I had to know.

I had to be sure.

I called the number and carefully put the phone to my ear.

I held my breath as it rang and rang.

No one would answer. Brody was secure. So no one should answer.

After a few more rings, I felt my shoulders drop. Of course no one would answer . . . except . . .

Suddenly I could hear a phone buzzing.

My eyes darted around following the sound.

It was coming from the threshold that led to the back hallway . . .

. . . right from Kyle's hand.

"You little a-hole."

Chapter Fifty-four

"This sucks. It really does."

I opened my mouth to speak, but nothing was coming out.

Kyle . . . Kyle? But why? He had the money. This didn't make any sense. He . . .

Kyle's eyes darted to the ground, yanking me from my thoughts. He snatched up Brody's gun that had spun away from me, under the table, before I had even thought to move. He rose to his feet, weapon pointed at my chest.

"I had to go back for my phone," he said, waving it in the air with his other hand. "It fell out in the bathroom. That could have really messed things up for me. But, now, I can just toss it in the lake or something."

"So, this was all you?" I asked raising my hands in the air. "You hired the assassin?"

He shrugged.

"But why?" I asked. "You have the money."

"Yeah, but for how long?" he said almost sadly. "I had to go through a lot to get Rayner to change his will in the first place."

I gasped. "You poisoned yourself to get him to believe someone was trying to kill you!"

"Yeah, him too. He was having trouble believing that one of them," he said, jerking his head toward the window, "would actually try to kill him. Like it was this huge stretch or something."

"So you brought them all here to—"

"No, that was all Julie's idea for the show. Julie. Now I have to deal with that whole situation." He sighed. "She'll probably try to make a claim for the money. The old man just couldn't keep it in his pants."

I waited, too afraid to breathe.

"This get-together was the perfect opportunity for me to get him to hire a bodyguard," he said, putting air quotes around the word. "I mean, being all alone on an island with your murderous family members? It only made sense to hire somebody for protection—somebody who could also double for a bartender."

"I don't believe this."

Kyle shuffled behind the dead body of his father—the father he had killed with the help of the assassin—to walk down the far side of the room. I matched his steps on the other side, keeping the table between us. At first it was just instinctual, but my brain was beginning to fire again. The distance wouldn't make a difference if he took a shot. But maybe, just maybe, if something distracted him, I could make a dash for the hallway and get out a window before he could shoot. Maybe.

"But I still don't understand. The assassin killed your father. Why get him to come back? Did you hire him to kill your entire family?"

"No, Erica," he said, eyes suddenly flashing. "I didn't get him to come back. He came back all on his own."

I furrowed my brow.

"Why?"

Kyle shot me a pointed look. "Um, because the payment he was expecting didn't come through?"

I felt my eyes dart side to side. "Payment? Oh my . . ."

"Yeah, I totally wanted to kill you right then. But that was my bad too." He shot me a tired smile. "I wanted to pay him from Brody's phone, but it took forever to find the right opportunity, and then I blew it by showing it to you before the transaction was complete."

Heat rolled over my body. "You were going to frame Brody with all this."

"He's kind of the obvious choice," he said. His eyes dropped to the assassin on the floor. "I can't believe this guy was such a dick about the details. That's why he didn't kill you. Or your mother when I texted him to. He wanted the same amount of money upfront. If you ask me, it would have been in his best interest to knock off as many witnesses as possible, but I guess I'm not the *professional.*"

"So he didn't leave because he was going to . . . ?"

"Kill me! He thought I was trying to stiff him. I told him I would get the money, but he didn't like how any of this was playing out." Kyle's lip curled with disgust. "He almost had me outside just now, but I punched him in the nuts."

Suddenly the paid assassin let out a wet cough.

"Hey! You're still alive," Kyle said. "That's awesome. Just hang in there, dude. I'll give you a good final rating online." He looked over at me. "You'll be his last kill."

I swallowed hard. "You will never get away with this."

"I've got a pretty good shot, I think." He shrugged again. "There's the storm working on the evidence outside and—"

"Oh my God! You're going to blow this place up!"

Kyle's face twisted in confusion. "What?"

I pointed behind me. "With the propane!"

"Yeah, no," he said, squinting. "I actually don't think it's that easy to blow things up. I figured the storm would kill the power and I wanted the lights to stay out, so Brody would freak. Make him look more guilty? I got the idea when I was waiting for Rayner to arrive and set up my *shocking* entrance. It was Julie's idea for me to lay low outside. Man, that was cold. I was out there forever. I mean, I got to the island right after Brody." He shivered. "Looking back now, the generator was probably my biggest mistake, but I saw this movie last week—"

"No. Stop. I get it." I dropped my arm then raised it right back up in another vicious point. "You hit my mother!"

He shrugged. "If it makes you feel better hurting your mom was never part of the plan, but she spotted me at the generator. I panicked. I couldn't take the chance that she would ruin things. I was lucky nobody heard me. But then again, some of the others had just arrived and Ronnie never shows up anywhere quietly," Kyle said, looking me in the eye. "And just so you know, I never meant for you to die. So, sorry."

"No! No! I do not accept your apology!" I shouted, patting my chest. "I came back up here to save you. I was willing to risk my own life to save you!"

"I know, and you're so cute. Total Mama Bear. And like I said, I do feel really bad about this."

"No you don't!"

"Okay, fine," he said making his eyes go wide. "Not like really, *really* bad. But it has been an awesome night."

I shook my head in a near shudder.

"There were times I was like really, actually scared," he said with a nod. "Like when we were in that shed and your friend came with that ax? For a second there, I was like *Oh no, Erica protect me!* Because we were all"—He looked around the room like he was trying to find the right words. Suddenly he raised a fist in the air—"Kyle and Erica against the world!"

"I don't believe this." My eyes darted around the table . . . sideboard . . . floor . . . for a weapon, but I didn't see anything that would help me against a gun.

"Oh, and by the way, I was just messing with you about that whole cougar thing. I would have totally been down."

I shook my head frantically again. "Yeah, not that into braces."

"Wow. Harsh."

The still-open door banged against the wall with the wind. Kyle's eyes darted over to it, but not long enough for me to do anything. He walked in that direction, though, keeping the gun on me. Guess he didn't want me making a run for it.

"Kyle, you can't get away with this. They'll—"

"What makes you think they're going to investigate?" he asked. "I was with you the whole time. You told Rhonda someone was trying to kill me. You died trying to protect me." He snapped his fingers. "I'll make you a hero! That's awesome! I feel so much better about how this whole thing has turned out."

"I don't!"

"I get it." He shook his head. "And you're right. I need to be careful. I won't give them any answers at first. Just cry. Then when they have questions for me, well, I'll have my lawyers there to answer them. I'm thinking five hundred million dollars can buy me some good lawyers."

"Kyle . . ."

He kneeled down to the assassin's body and raised the gun toward my head. That's what he was doing. Getting the angle right.

"Stop," I said putting my hands up. "Please."

"Aw, don't make me feel bad. I said I was sorry."

I grabbed the chair again. My only hope left was to throw it at him and make a run for it. It wasn't much of a chance, but it was all I had.

I was just about to swing the chair when—

"Bye, Erica."

—someone in a bright yellow slicker tumbled through the door.

"Parkour!"

Chapter Fifty-five

"Freddie!"

A tangle of bodies hit the floor.

I dropped to my knees and grabbed the gun that the tackle had knocked from Kyle's hand. I tried to stand, but I couldn't find the strength. Instead, I collapsed against the wall, gun pointed at the squirming bodies in front of me.

I couldn't shoot. They were too close together.

"Freddie, get away from him!"

"Get away from him?" he grumbled, not sounding nearly as panicked as he should. "Why?"

"I've got the gun!"

"Yeah, no worries." I watched Freddie straighten up, seated on Kyle, hand mashing the kid's face into the floor. "Now who's wrestling marshmallows, punk?" He then looked over to the assassin. "Is he . . . ?"

I shook my head. "I think. Maybe. Yes?"

He just nodded.

"I don't . . . I can't . . . Freddie," I said blinking at him. "You saved my life."

The intensity of his gaze dropped as a thought crossed his face. "I did?"

"You did."

"Wow." He straightened up some more, making Kyle groan. A big smile spread across his face. "Well, I couldn't just let you die. You are my best friend."

Tears filled my eyes. "If you hadn't come through that door when you did . . ."

He nodded, still smiling. "You'd totally be dead!"

My face tightened. "You need to say that with a little less enthusiasm."

"Erica, you know what this means, don't you?"

"I'm alive?"

"No," Freddie said with just a tinge of disgust tainting his smile. "Well, yes, that, but this *really* means that I got one!"

"You got one?" I barely had enough energy left to breathe let alone figure out what Freddie was trying to get at.

"You got one," he said, pointing at me. "Rhonda got one." His free hand swung to the door. "Now I got one!" The same hand patted his chest.

"Got one what?"

"A murderer!"

"Oh. Yay," I said weakly. I tried to raise my hand in celebration too, but my muscles still hadn't recovered from all of the excitement. "Sorry, I'm in the process of accepting the fact that I'm not d—"

"You need to take a picture."

I blinked.

Kyle grunted something—something angry by the sound of it—but it was hard to understand him, what with his mouth pressed against the floor.

"Earth to Erica," Freddie said, reaching into his pocket. "Did you hear me? You need to take a picture."

"Now? Why?"

"For posterity's sake! The news!" Freddie shouted.

"Oh, and the website. I definitely can't forget the website."

I clutched my forehead. "Freddie, I . . . I . . ."

"Still not firing on all cylinders yet, huh?"

I dropped my hand to my lap. "I don't know if that's a good idea. It seems to make light of all that's happen—"

"What? No, it doesn't." He made a few swipes on his phone with his one free hand then passed it to me. "This is like the picture fishermen take when they catch the big one." His eyes dropped down to Kyle. "Except I think maybe I'll keep this little guy pinned to the floor."

Kyle grunted again, turning his spittle-covered chin up into the air. "You two are the biggest losers ever! Don't you even think about taking my picture! I'll have my lawyers—"

"And that's quite enough of that," Freddie said, pressing Kyle's face back down into the floor. "So, you going to take the picture or what?"

I stared at the phone in my hand, then shrugged.

"Say 'cheese.'"

Chapter Fifty-six

"You know this is the kind of day that just makes you feel like all is right with the world."

Warm sunshine broke through the clouds. "If you say so."

Freddie shot me a bright smile. "Don't worry. You'll get there."

We were on our way to the Dawg to eat *and*—with any luck—run into someone getting lunch. I was exhausted, more than a little sore, and definitely stunned, but I thought grease might help that situation.

Grease with maybe a side of beer.

"We would have gotten there sooner, but you were supposed to be at the twins'." Freddie went on flashing me what was meant to be a disappointed look, but he was too giddy to pull it off. "Next time, give me a heads up."

I nodded. After my last call with Freddie, he had decided to give up altogether on trying to get the authorities to help. Instead, he had spread the word around town that I was in trouble and convinced Ken to lend him his biggest boat to make it over to the island. Red, Matthew, and a few others came along for the ride. They had run into

Rhonda on the way up to the retreat, but, despite reas-
surances that it was over, Freddie had still come rushing
up to get me. He said his sixth sense had told him I was
still in trouble, and I wasn't about to disagree. He could
totally have that, given the outcome.

Shortly after that, the authorities finally arrived at the
island, and the EMTs found my mom and Chuck in the
shed with Caesar. She went to the hospital with Chuck
for a CAT scan and cast while Caesar spent the night on
Rhonda's desk in a cat carrier, grumbling at people. He
and my mother were now back at the retreat. Everyone
else was still at the hospital. Julie was awaiting surgery
with Kenny by her side, and Brody was in the psych ward
awaiting evaluation. Ronnie and Ashley were getting
treated for frostbite, but they were going to be okay. Kyle
had been there for a little while too—suspected cracked
ribs—but he was quickly relocated to a holding cell after
it was determined he was fine . . . and Ashley and her
mother were overheard discussing strangling him with an
IV tube. Even The Dark Web Assassin was in the hospital, but in critical care. I wasn't exactly praying for his
speedy recovery.

"Freddie," I said, hopping over a puddle. "There's one
thing I gotta ask you."

He closed his eyes and sighed. "Go ahead. Say it."

"Parkour?"

"I don't know, okay? I was scared and over-excited. It
just came out." He shook his head. "But if we're going to
armchair quarterback this whole thing, maybe we should
talk about this aversion you have to shooting people?"

I shook my head. "Or not."

I had also spent a good portion of the morning at the
sheriff's department. Unfortunately, Grady wasn't there.
After they'd found the kids in Honey Harbor—watching
movies in a friend's basement, not on the water—he had

gone to interview the family. I wasn't sure how much he knew, or if he had expected to find me there. Amos had handled my initial statement, then made me promise to come back for questioning at a later date. I kept trying to track down Grady, but when I was at the hospital, he was at the station, and then vice versa. Not that I would have been able to find him in the station anyway. Freddie may have thought the place came off as a little surreal when it had been deserted, but what it looked like afterward, well, that was straight out of a movie. People in uniforms buzzed all around. I had even caught sight of a man and woman wearing FBI jackets. I guess it made sense. I *had* spent the evening dodging a paid assassin and the psychopathic millionaire teen who had hired him. Outside the station, news reporters filled the lawn, sidewalk, and street. Otter Lake had been swarmed, and Freddie had now appeared on every major network in the country. As an additional benefit, because he was so accommodating with his interviews, the reporters were somewhat sated and leaving me alone. Which was good because I was too busy to deal with any of that.

In fact, right now I had only one goal . . .

Find Grady and tell him how I really felt. Maybe over pancakes.

Okay, fine. One goal. With three parts.

I was getting my second chance after all.

Despite everything that had happened between us, I knew in my heart that he would want to see me, and I wasn't about to waste this opportunity. As luck would have it, I heard one of the officers at the station say on the phone that Grady was taking lunch orders. Apparently, he was wrapping up his interviews at the hospital and was going to pick it up on his way back to the station.

Only one place in Otter Lake to get lunch.

I hurried Freddie along as we cut through a side street from the station toward the Dawg. The storm had done a bit of damage. A few roofs were missing some shingles. Lots of branches littered the streets. A tree had even landed on a car. But, overall, the town wasn't in bad shape. And despite all the snow that had fallen, it was melting quickly. I was willing to bet last night had been winter's last blast.

I turned my face up to the warm sun.

Spring. Perfect. The time for new beginnings.

I picked up the pace.

"So, I was thinking," Freddie said just as a bang sounded behind us. "In terms of publicity—Erica? Where did you go?"

I watched Freddie turn around, concern in his eyes.

Apparently the sound of a car door shutting was enough to throw me into a fighting stance.

I looked at my hands, flattened into boards.

Huh. That was new.

"You know," Freddie said, eyeing me sideways. "You're going to have to put some therapy on that."

I straightened up to a normal posture.

"The karate hands, though? Adorable."

We resumed our walk.

"As I was saying," he said, "before you went all twitchy on me, we have to talk about how we are going to manage the publicity of this thing. Did I tell you Amos said they don't want me using the photo?"

"I'm shocked."

"Something about it being evidence," Freddie said, waving his hands out. "That and the suspect is a *minor*. A minor! Don't get me started. Anyway, I'm going to have a lawyer look into it because this whole thing could be very big for us."

I shook my head, shoving my fighting hands into my pockets. "Kyle's not going to get the money, right?"

"What? Um, no? I think there's a law saying that you can't kill someone to get their money in the will," Freddie said. "Shouldn't you know this from work?"

"That kind of case doesn't come up too often."

"He probably won't get much time though. He's what? Fourteen? Fifteen?"

I blinked a few times. Nope, Kyle probably wouldn't get much time at all. Probably just enough to turn himself into something really scary. That might come after me. "But he killed his father!"

"I know. I know. You don't have to get all yelly. I'm on your side."

"Sorry," I mumbled, walking again. "I feel weird." I could see the Dawg just up ahead. I scanned the windows for Grady.

"Weird's good," Freddie said with a reassuring nod. "If you didn't feel weird, I'd be worried. It—where did you go now?" Freddie swirled around to find me stopped in the street. "Do we need to get you a prescription?"

"No," I said, shaking my head. My eyes weren't on Freddie, though. They were still on the windows of the Salty Dawg. Actually, they were on the person on the other side of the window . . . the person just standing there, talking to someone, with two take-out bags in his hands.

Freddie came to my side. After a moment he said, "You are really having a terrible couple of days."

I couldn't help but agree.

It was Grady standing there, of course. Grady and Candace. The same Candace I once may have accused of being a murderer.

So, she was back in town after all.

The two of them were talking. Close talking, in fact. And Candace looked pretty happy. Grady looked completely exhausted . . . but maybe a little bit happy? At least not unhappy.

Son of a—

"Maybe it's not what it looks like?" Freddie offered. "Maybe they just ran into each other and—oh, well, maybe not."

Just then Candace had reached out to touch Grady's arm. No, wait, not touch. Her hand was resting completely on Grady's arm.

And he wasn't pulling away.

"Erica?"

I shook my head slowly side to side. "Freddie. This is . . ."

"I know it's bad, but—"

"No, it's okay," I said slowly. "Maybe even good."

"I'm sorry, what now?"

I turned my head to meet Freddie's concerned gaze. "No, really. It's great."

"Okay, what are we doing here?" He cocked his head a little and gave me a sideways look. "Is this another PTSD thing?"

"No," I said, grabbing his arm and giving it a shake. "Just listen to me. It's great. Because this settles it."

Freddie looked down at my hand still gripped on his arm. "Okay, why is Grady dating Candace great?"

"Whoa. Whoa. Slow down there, Mister," I said, lifting my hand to a stop gesture. "Just because he didn't move his arm away doesn't mean they're dating. But no, not that."

"Then what?"

"I can move home!"

"You could always move home," Freddie said, still

searching my eyes . . . for the sanity, I guess. "It's just like Dorothy in *The Wizard of Oz* said—"

"No. I mean, this pain I'm feeling right now, it's just showing me once again what happens when I don't trust myself and dive into something."

"Um . . ."

"Listen. Last night. When I thought I was going to die over and over and over again," I said, rolling my finger in the air. "You know what I was thinking about?"

"What?"

"You!"

"Aww—"

"Shut up. I'm talking," I said, swatting his shoulder. "You. My mom. The twins. Although I don't want to be the one to tell them their place burned down. Grady! And everyone else in Otter Lake. Well, maybe not Jake Day. But you know what else? What's even better?"

"No. I definitely do not."

"Right now," I said pointing back to the Dawg, "I just realized I might really have lost Grady, you know, like temporarily. Which is really, really bad."

Freddie scratched his temple. "But?"

"I still want to move home!"

"Okay, not that I'm not really happy about this," Freddie said, nodding. "'Cause I am. But maybe we can talk more about this after some psychological evaluation?"

"No," I said, sticking my hands back deep into my pockets and rocking on my heels. "I'm moving home."

"Really?"

I nodded.

"Like really, really?"

"Yes!"

"Well, all right then!" Freddie stuck his hand up in the air, and I smacked it. "Yay!"

"Come on, I don't want to see any more of . . . that," I said, waving a hand back at the Dawg. "I'll talk to Grady later. There will be lots of time to talk to him now that I'm living here. Let's go to your place to eat," I said. "Oh! And we can talk salary and benefits. Does Otter Lake Security have dental yet?"

"What?" Freddie snapped, hurrying to catch up to me. "You females always be wanting my money."

I stopped dead. "Yeah, no. There will be none of that."

"Right," he said before skipping in the air. "I'm so excited. I've got to make some calls. We can take on so many more jobs n—Wait, is this one of those times where you're going to change your mind like two hours from now?"

"No, I don't think so," I said, pulling my gloves from my back pocket. "Last night changed me." It really had. All those hours I spent being afraid, thinking about my own death? They had made things super clear for me. I had known it for months, but I had just been too afraid to take the leap. Now I was more afraid of what my life would be if I didn't. "Hey, look! There's Rhonda!" I shouted suddenly, pointing down the street. It looked like she was headed for the Dawg too.

"Uh-oh," Freddie said. "She's not in uniform."

I felt some of my excitement drain away. "You don't think she really got fired, do you? For saving me?"

"Hmm, let's see. She left the sheriff's department unmanned in a massive storm. She used a police boat to get across the lake when she was given a direct order not to, and she turned over her weapon to a civilian. I would say it's not looking good. Plus, Amos told me."

"No . . . it's all my fault."

"Well, not just your fault. Let's not forget the psycho teenager, Mr. The World Revolves Around Me." Freddie spun a finger around in the air. "But in all seriousness, it really does suck. Amos said, at the very least, that Grady fought to have her turn in her resignation. They're not going to press charges."

"I can't believe this," I said, feeling the weight of it all drop over me. "Rhonda loves being a cop."

"I know it is pretty sad—Hey! Why are you hitting me again?"

I was hitting him. In fact, I was frantically slapping his arm with the back of my hand. "Freddie, are you thinking what I'm thinking?"

He swatted my hand away. "That maybe the worst damage you suffered might be the kind that can't be seen?"

"No!" I shouted, now grabbing his arm and shaking it. "Rhonda! Otter Lake Security!"

"What? Oh . . . you're not thinking," Freddie began, "that we should . . . hmm, I don't know."

"What are you talking about? This is perfect." I then gasped so hard I hurt my lungs. "She can be a private investigator. She qualifies for the license!"

I felt Freddie go still. "You're right. I'll have to rework my business model, but—whoa!"

"Let's go talk to her!" I said yanking him across the street. Just then a man standing near Rhonda dropped the lid to his garbage can, making her spin around and reach for her phantom gun. "Hey!" I chuckled. "She's got it too!"

"Oh yeah," Freddie said. "I'm just loving how my employee roster is shaping up."

I pulled him hard. "Oh, stop it you. Let's just—"

"Erica!" a voice called out from behind me. "Wait!"

I froze in my tracks.

"You dropped something!"

Both Freddie and I turned.

Grady.

"You . . ." his voice trailed off as his eyes tracked over a piece of paper. A piece of paper that I had dropped. What could that b—

The freaking good-bye letter! Where I said I love you!

"Grady! No!" I pivoted hard and shot back across the street nearly getting clipped by a car—which in Otter Lake meant it was still a hundred yards away and moving at about ten miles per hour, but the horn was honked, so it would be talked about as a near miss all around town. "Don't read that!"

He looked up at me quizzically. Probably because it had his name scrawled across the front fold.

"I mean it, Grady! Don't you—"

He flipped it open.

As I watched his eyes track over the page, it felt like a chipmunk had somehow managed to find a way into my chest to cutely pick and gnaw at my heart.

For just the briefest moment I thought, this might be good. Grady would finally see how I really felt, and maybe . . .

He carefully re-folded the paper and held it out for me to take.

I walked forward, reaching for it, scanning his face for . . . anything.

What I saw was him clench his jaw. Actually his whole face tightened.

Wait. Was he mad?

"Sorry. I shouldn't have read it when you asked me not to." He turned and walked back into the restaurant.

For a good moment, I couldn't breathe.

"Erica?" Freddie asked, coming to my side. "What was that all about?" He reached out his hand to take the letter from mine, but I snatched it away.

Suddenly Rhonda was at my other side. "Oh man,

Candace? See, Erica? I tried to tell you, you should've put a ri—"

"No," I said sharply. "No."

"Come with us, Rhonda," Freddie said, leading me away by the shoulders. "Erica and I want to invite you to lunch. We have a proposition for you."

"You do?"

"How would you feel about becoming the newest member of Freddie's Angels?"

"You say that again," I murmured lowly, "and I will kill you."

"And so it begins."

Chapter Fifty-seven

"Hey," I said with a half-hearted point. "There's a crocus."

"Very pretty," my mother mumbled back, barely glancing at the purple flower poking its head up through a thin patch of snow. "I think maybe they have some yellow ones around the side of the cottage." I felt her tense. "Or where the side of the cottage used to be."

A red squirrel chittered at us from a tree.

"Yeah. Yeah. I think I remember seeing them there. With the little uh . . ." I tried to snap my fingers to jog my memory, but they just couldn't seem to muster up the enthusiasm to make a sound.

"Stone turtle," my mother said with a pained nod. "The twins, they love their animals."

We both looked back to the charcoal cairn covering the general area of where the turtle now rested. Most likely *eternally*.

A cold breeze rushed through the trees making me shiver. The sun was warm today, almost hot, but it was still cold in the shade of the forest.

Another silent moment passed, before I finally said what we were both thinking, "They are going to freak out, aren't they?"

My mother sighed again. "Probably."

"How much do they know?"

"Nothing. Everybody was too afraid to tell them." She adjusted her crutches. It was amazing how well she was managing on them after only a week.

"They asked me to keep an eye on the place."

My mother nodded. "Hopefully, we can explain before they kill you."

I nodded back.

"Besides, we all need to look on the bright side. They have insurance. They can rebuild, and in the meantime, they can stay with me at the lodge. It will be fun." The sigh she let out told me she wasn't convinced. "There's plenty of room. Your bedroom will be empty of course."

"Oh," I said, scratching my temple. "Well . . ."

"What?" she asked, eyes snapping over to me.

"I was kind of hoping that . . ." I met her eyes, same shade of blue as mine.

Was I really going to do this? Once I said the words out loud to her, there was no turning back.

I took one last steadying breath. "I was hoping I could stay in my room until I found a place of my own."

My mother didn't make a sound, but her eyes began blinking at an alarming rate.

"Here," I said, pointing to the ground. "In Otter Lake."

Silent. But still blinking.

"Mom?"

"I'm so happy!" Her crutches hit the ground as her arms flew around me.

"Whoa. Careful," I said, trying to keep us both on our feet.

"I've waited so long for this day!"

"I know," I choked out. Her shoulder was dug deep into my windpipe. "But let's just maybe—"

"I always knew it would happen, but . . ."

I lost the trail of her words as the sound of a boat engine tore my attention to the lake.

Uh-oh.

Yup, that looked like Kit Kat and Tweety. I couldn't tell which one was driving and which one was holding . . . actually, I couldn't tell what she was holding either.

"Mom."

She couldn't hear me, what with all the laughing and crying she was doing.

"Mom," I tried again, whapping her lightly on the back. "Incoming."

We both turned to the water, just as Kit Kat cut the engine, allowing the boat to drift toward the dock. Her jaw was at her chest. Tweety's was too. Her hands empty. She had dropped the thing she had been holding into the water.

My mother hopped a little to adjust her stance before leaning toward my ear. "Was that a . . . did Tweety just drop some poor alligator's head in the water?"

"I think so."

"But she didn't shoot it?"

"No, it's a souvenir. From her cousin's sh—" I cut myself off with a sigh. "Never mind. It's a long story."

She squeezed my waist in an excited hug. "And now we have all the time in the world for you to tell it!"

"Yup," I said, returning the squeeze. "Goddess help me, I guess we do."

Catch up on the Otter Lake series!

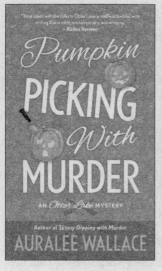

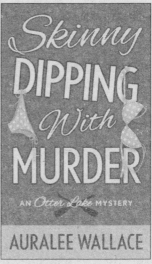

Available from St. Martin's Paperbacks